Carla —
Happy reading!
Kathy

READY FOR WHATEVER

The UnBRCAble Women Series, #1

By

KATHRYN R. BIEL

KATHRYN R. BIEL

READY FOR WHATEVER, The UnBRCAble Women Series, #1

Copyright © 2019 by Kathryn R. Biel

Ebook ISBN-13: 978-1-949424-04-1
Paperback ISBN-13: 978-1-949424-05-8

This book is a work of fiction. Names, characters, places, and incidents are either products of the author's imagination or are used fictitiously and any resemblance to actual persons, living or dead, business establishments, events or locales is purely coincidental.

All rights reserved.

No part of this book may be reproduced, scanned, or distributed in any printed or electronic form or by any electronic or mechanical means including information storage and retrieval systems, without permission in writing from the author. The only exception is by a reviewer, who may quote short excepts in a review. Please do not participate in or encourage piracy of copyrighted materials in violation of the author's rights. Purchase only authorized editions.

Cover design by Becky Monson.

DEDICATION

To Erin:

Ironically, words will undoubtedly fail me in expressing my love and gratitude to you, partially for all the help with this book, but mostly for our friendship. You make previving look good.

And to all the Previvors and Survivors fighting the good fight: Hang in there

CHAPTER 1

Holy crap on a cracker.

"You're no longer my friend," I say, limping past my former BFF.

"You've got to trust me, Millie. I swear, before you know it, you'll be addicted," Lisa reassures, falling in step beside me. It's almost like her crotch isn't on fire and screaming.

"If I ever become addicted to someone pouring hot wax on my nether regions, please get my head examined," I murmur. "I can't believe you talked me into this."

"I only wish I'd timed it better. If I'd known you were going to the gynie last week, I would have convinced you to do this weeks ago."

The esthetician leads us into the next room where our faces are prepped and slathered with mud. Or something that feels like it.

Now this kind of beauty treatment, I can get behind. Things that make my skin feel soft and smooth. Without ripping the hair out of the follicles. Hair that, by the way, was really attached to my body.

"See? I told you this would be worth it," Lisa offers.

The jury's still out on that one. At least until we move onto the paraffin hand treatments and pedicures. I may have to concede that the pain of waxing is a small price to pay for Heaven.

Pure Heaven. That's where I am, and if I had it my way I'd stay here forever. Preferably without the Brazilian first.

"Uuuuhhhh ... aaahhhh."

The sounds emanating from the next chair could be construed as either those of great pain ... or great pleasure, and generally not the kind you have in public.

"Lis, ssshh. You're making weird noises again." I laugh, knowing it will do no good to hush her.

"I don't care. Ooooh, this is the best thing ever. RIGHT THERE!" she exclaims and the poor technician working on her hot stone foot massage turns about four shades of red in response to her fifty shades of—well, you know—sounds.

I lean forward. "I will apologize yet again for my friend who makes sex noises during her pedicure. If you think this is bad, you should hear her during a full body massage."

Her technician looks down quickly, but not before I see a smile dance across his face. I'm trying not to smile, but I can't seem to hide my amusement.

Lisa sighs deeply. "You know, I think this is better than the last time I even had sex. From what I remember about it. It was so long ago."

"It hasn't been that long," I say, trying to keep my own voice from moaning. I totally agree with her. This might very well be the best thing I've ever felt.

"Too long," Lisa says on a deep exhale. I glance over to see her eyes closed, her face in complete relaxation under the charcoal mask. "This was a great idea, this girls' weekend. Why didn't we think of it sooner?"

"Because—and rightly so—I've been afraid of you making me get things waxed that should have stayed attached to my body. On the other hand, if I could make a living getting pampered like this, I would give up teaching in a heartbeat."

"Aaaahhh … don't be ridiculous. You'd never give up teaching. You're one of those weird people who are oddly enthusiastic about your job. You'll probably never even want to retire. I swear, they'll have to bring you from your classroom right to the funeral home."

"Make sure I'm laid out in my first-day-of-school dress. It's my favorite." The dress has so many perfect qualities that I've considered buying it in multiple sizes in case my weight fluctuates. Any woman knows how hard it is to find the Holy Grail of a dress that fits, flatters, and is comfortable. Then, I drop the caveat.

"It has pockets."

Lisa may be the lawyer here, but I rest my case.

"You're right. Pockets for the win," Lisa acquiesces. "Leave it in your will. Your kids and grandkids will have to follow your dying wish."

I look down at my hands, which are starting to sweat, thanks to the layers of paraffin and warm towels that are ensconcing them. I shift a little and wonder if it would be unreasonable to ask for a bag of ice to stick on my crotch.

We're really going all out this weekend. "We should totally do this again before your cruise. NOT the waxing. Everything else though. Get you all buffed and polished in case you meet someone on the ship. If you want to strip your bits, go ahead. "

Lisa waves her towel clad hand toward me in what I imagine is a fist bump. "Yes, that's a great idea! I still think you should come with me. Be my plus one. Travis won't care. He's like your brother anyway. It'll be great!"

"Lisa, you know I can't. I was invited to the wedding, but the boat leaves the last day of school. I can't miss the end of the year."

"I know. You and your stupid dedication. Someday I'll break you of that bad habit." She laughs.

"You're one to talk. When you're preparing a case and in the middle of a trial, I don't even hear from you. It's what, the first week in March, and I haven't actually been in the same room with you since the beginning of January!"

And not that a cruise to a bunch of tropical islands doesn't sound wonderful, but I'd never be able to miss the last few days of the school year. Not even taking into account packing up my room and all, but I couldn't not say goodbye to my kids and parents.

"Oh, you're right. I don't know why Travis and Melina picked that week to get married."

"Right? They should have checked with me first. Obviously," I kid.

"I wish I wasn't going alone. It'd be so much more fun with you there."

"Lis, you'll be fine without me. Ten bucks says you meet someone. I'd just end up being a third-wheel."

"Maybe you could meet someone too and—"

"I don't need to meet anyone. I've got Johnny," I cut her off.

"Right, right. My mistake. Let me clarify. Maybe you could meet someone *worthy* of you."

I sigh, not thrilled to have this conversation yet again. Lisa's looking out for me, which I appreciate. I don't appreciate the nagging to dump him. "Johnny's fine."

"You hate fine. You think fine is a cop out."

Dammit. Why does my best friend have to be so smart? So insightful? Bad guys don't stand a chance when she puts them on the stand.

"Millie, look at me."

Crap. This is getting serious. She wants eye contact. I don't need to meet her eyes to know what's coming. It's nothing I haven't heard—or thought about—before.

"Yes, Lisa?" I cock my eyebrow as a last line of defense.

"Millie, you are wonderful. You're loving and kind and compassionate and funny. You light up a room simply by walking in. You are everyone's favorite teacher. You are my parents' favorite child, and they have three of their own that they gave birth to. You can do better than Johnny. You're right—he's fine. But you're not. You're so much more than fine. You can do better than that."

I feel my cheeks flushing under the charcoal mask. Isn't it about time to take these off? I'm getting a little warm.

Although truth be told, that's somewhat welcome, since I'm almost always cold.

Lisa continues. "I wish you'd think about breaking it off with him. Find someone who deserves you. There has to be someone better out there for you."

"Like who? Johnny's the only unattached male in my building. He's cute. He does a good job at work. He has a job."

"Setting the bar real high there, Millie. What about the dads? Surely there's bound to be some single dads. What about that guy with the car?"

"Myla's dad? The one who drives the Lamborghini?"

"Are there other dads at school who drive Lambos?"

"If you ever say 'Lambo' again, I will permanently disown you and no thank you. He's too on-again, off-again with Myla's mom."

"Okay, what about the kid who was the baseball player for Halloween? His dad seemed cute from the pictures."

It's somewhat annoying to have a friend with such memory for detail. "Owen? Which one of his dads?"

I smile a little smugly, feeling the mask begin to crack around the corners of my mouth.

"I KNOW!" Lisa practically jumps out of her chair, knocking over a bottle of lotion and nearly kicking the esthetician in the process. "The British dude."

"Sterling Kane?"

"I don't know his name. You told me, and I quote, 'Piper's dad has the most adorable accent. He's so cute with her.' End quote. Hot British Dad."

Stupid photographic memory.

I'm saved from this particular torture—the second most painful thing I've been through today—because it's time to de-robe our hands, finish our facials, and have a lovely lunch that involves tiny sandwiches and cucumber water.

Lisa may have a fantastic memory for details, but she's also sometimes easy to distract, if you know the right keywords. While our tea is steeping in the most delicate and feminine little teapot, I take charge and swing the conversation back my way.

"So how are the wedding preparations coming? What's Melina driving you crazy about this week?"

Mentally, I pat myself on the back. Lisa will be off and running, and all talk of setting me up with the dads from my class will be forgotten. Though if I had to date one of my available dads, Sterling Kane would be on the list. Partially because of the accent and partially because he seems like a really good dad. But mostly because of the accent.

Frankly, he'd probably be the only one on the list.

"My dress is in. I have to go for a fitting next Friday. There's a good chance the stupid thing isn't even going to fit. Oh, I know! You should call in and come with me." Lisa starts clapping her hands together, like a little kid about to get a puppy. Sometimes I have trouble reconciling this friend with the competent, hard-hitting prosecutor. If I hadn't seen her in action with my own eyes, I don't know that I could believe it.

At least with me, what you see is what you get. Seven-year-olds are my jam.

I pull out my phone and look at my calendar. "Nope sorry. Taking a half-day on Thursday for my doctor's appointment. Can't be out two days in a row."

Lisa frowns. "You were just there. Is something up?"

I shrug. I've been doing my best *not* to think about it. "I don't know. I don't think so. They ran a bunch of tests, but I don't think they'd let it wait weeks if there was a problem."

"You're right. They call you the next day if there's something really wrong. Do you want me to come with you?"

I shake my head. "Nah, I'm not concerned. I've never had any abnormal tests ever before, so it shouldn't be that. He probably wants to talk to me about my blood pressure or something. You know doctors make me nervous. Or maybe they didn't do the test right and have to get more cells."

Yes, that's got to be it.

"Did you start the pill yet?"

I shake my head. "Not for two more weeks."

"Then you know you have to go through the full pack before it starts fully working. And if you take an antibiotic for any reason, it's not effective."

"Yes, mother."

"Don't patronize me, young lady. The last thing you want is to be saddled with a kid with some random dude who you don't even refer to as your boyfriend. Not to mention, you've neglected your health for long enough. Before the last visit, when was the last time you went to the doctor?"

Lisa's words cut right to the quick. No, I cannot have a kid with Johnny. Plus, I'm almost positive Lisa will blow a gasket if I tell her the last time I was checked out was senior year of college when I had mono, so I shrug rather than respond. I'm healthy. Why waste my time in the doctor's office?

Time is too precious to spend it leafing through dated magazines and sitting in paper gowns.

"It's about time you started taking your health more seriously." Lisa picks up her tea cup. "Here's to good friends, good health, and good men. May we be them, may we have them, and may we find them without having date all the losers first."

I clink my cup against hers.

"From your lips to God's ears."

CHAPTER 2

"Look on the bright side, Millicent; at least you don't have cancer."

This is not a bright side. It is not good news. Well, technically it is because having cancer is bad news. Terrible news. The worst news. So yes, at least it's not that.

Dr. Tremarchi's hand pushes a stack of papers across his polished desk. "Here's some information for you to read through and digest. I know this is a lot to handle, so please refer to the handout if you don't remember what we've discussed."

I stare at the packet. "Understanding BRCA-1 Mutation." That's a horrible title. Seriously, people, you need to do better. Suddenly, I feel like an alien, dropped onto a planet where I don't speak the language. I don't need to be called a mutant too. Dr. Tremarchi keeps talking but none of his words seem to be penetrating my understanding.

Is this what my students feel like when I'm explaining a math lesson? Some of them sit there, smiling and nodding, but when it comes time to practice, it's like they've never heard of numbers before. This is an absolutely terrible feeling, and immediately I feel badly for not being more patient with my students when this happens.

He's still talking. Dang, I need to try and pay attention. "Cheryl at the scheduling desk will go through it with you. After you talk to her, read through the literature I provided and think about what's the best fit for you. Let me know which procedure you choose. There are merits to both, so do your research and let me know. My PA, Dana, will see you for your pre-op visits, and I'll see you in the operating room."

Dr. Tremarchi's words cut through some of the fog and haze that descended upon me as soon as he called me into his office. Being called into the office is never a good sign. I even said that to him—that it was like having to go see the principal. And even though I'm a second-grade teacher, reporting to the principal is still a scary thing. I should have realized reporting to the doctor's office, with his polished desk and fancy framed diplomas, is so much worse. Good news is never shared in here. It's the room of bad. On the door, instead of Dr. Tremarchi's name, the sign should read, "Enter at Ye Own Risk."

Slowly his words start to sink in. "Wait, what? Operating room? I don't understand."

"Millicent, you need to read through the paperwork and make a decision. If you choose to go the surgical route, which is what I recommend, due to the family history and your age, we should get that ball rolling. Generally, we do the salpingo-oophorectomy and hysterectomy first, and then the mastectomy and reconstruction are at a later time. You'll need to find your own surgeons for that, although I can recommend general and plastic surgeons for the mastectomy, if you're interested. I'm happy to do the oophorectomy, and if you choose, the hysterectomy." This is a lot of information—important information—and I should probably be paying closer attention. But I know the deal. It's bad news.

News I don't want to hear.

News I feared was coming.

Yet somehow, perhaps in a last-ditch effort of self-preservation, my brain revolts and refuses to cooperate and focus on what Dr. Tremarchi is saying. All that registers is he keeps calling me Millicent. I hate that name. I mean, Millie's bad enough. It should automatically come with a housecoat and glasses on a chain, but Millicent? I mean dreadful. Simply dreadful.

"Millie. Call me Millie."

"Okay, Millie, do you have any questions?"

I should have questions. Lots of questions. Instead my mind continues chugging along at a snail's pace, refusing to pick up speed for any reason.

Despite my mind's best efforts not to listen, his words are slowly starting to shift into place, one by one clicking into order so they make sense. My brain feels like it's swimming underwater and desperately needs to pop up for a breath of air.

I know he gave more details, but it was like he was speaking a different language. I glom onto the only easily pronounceable words. "Surgery? Hysterectomy? But I don't have cancer. And I don't have kids!" At this point, hysteria *may* start to bubble to the surface a bit. I'm not sure who this crazy lady is that has possessed me, but I feel powerless to stop her. Suddenly, all the energy I've spent over the years squashing down the fear of developing breast cancer has been redirected into a raving lunatic who looks a lot like me.

For the record, I'm terrible under pressure and this, right here, right now, is stress like I've never imagined. Stress and I are not a good mix.

I jump to my feet and point at Dr. Tremarchi. "You should know that. You're my lady bits doctor. Have you seen any babies down there?"

At his blank stare I add, "Nope. Didn't think so. Now, I haven't gone to fancy-dancy medical school, and I don't have all the diplomas that you have, but even *I know* that you need a uterus to have a baby. They don't just grow in there on their own. How am I supposed to have a baby if you take out my uterus?"

Now my arms are flailing, my hair has escaped its containment system, and I know I've unlocked a new level of off-her-rocker.

"Millice—Millie, calm down." Dr. Tremarchi stands and makes a motion with his hands. It looks like he's trying to dribble two imaginary basketballs at the same time. His hands are huge. I don't know if I want him sticking those massive mitts up my hoo-ha to pull a baby out anyway. "Do you have any questions?"

Suddenly my mind which was whirring at light speed a minute ago has ground to a halt and everything has gone blank. I couldn't come up with a question if you paid me to, though I know I should have many. I shake my head.

"Cheryl is available for questions if you think of something. You can also talk to the PA, Dana, if you think of anything else. You have options and a little bit of time left to make the final decision."

Somewhere, in a deep part of my brain, I know what he's saying. I know what he means. There's a reason I'd avoided coming to the Ob/Gyn since I was sixteen. If things with Johnny hadn't progressed to the point where I'd needed birth control, I'd still be living happily in denial. But he really hates using condoms, so we both agreed to get tested, and well, here we are.

Damn, I wish I was still happily ensconced in the land of denial.

Really, anywhere would be better than here.

"But I'm only twenty-nine. I'm not married. I don't have kids yet."

Dr. Tremarchi offers a sympathetic smile as he says again. "I'm sorry, Millie. I know it's a lot to deal with. But look on the bright side—at least you don't have cancer."

~~~***~~~

I'm a dumbass. I should have requested the whole day off work. I didn't see this coming. Even though I should have. The doctor's office never calls you to come in for an appointment to discuss test results if it's good news. Now I'm faced with entertaining twenty-four seven-year-olds. At least the kids will go to gym for forty minutes this afternoon, which will give me a few seconds to sit and collect myself.

Or vomit.

The latter is a more distinct possibility.

I'd worked through a small portion of my hysterics by the time Cheryl finished reviewing my options. She suggested I go home and review everything she went over, as well as the handout, before making any decisions.

She also probably deserves a raise for dealing with the likes of me.

For the past twenty years, I've worked very hard on convincing myself this wouldn't happen to me. Lightening couldn't—wouldn't—strike twice. Well, three times, if you count my grandmother too. Yet here it is, the trifecta of crap. I suppose I should be grateful—happy even—that genetic testing has come this far. It's not too late for me, like it was for my mom. As Dr. Tremarchi so kindly pointed out—I don't have cancer.

What he meant was: I don't have cancer *yet*.

I will. It's coming. Cheryl went through the statistics with me. Thanks to the gift of the BRCA-1 gene mutation from my mom, I have almost an eighty percent chance of developing breast cancer and up to a seventy percent chance of developing ovarian cancer. Even though I am only fluent in math facts up until about the third grade level, I know enough to see that this is bad.

Real bad.

Superbad.

I am a ticking cancer time bomb. *Tick. Tick. Tick.*

Right here, right now, my cells could be mutating. Dividing. Forming an army hell-bent on taking over and killing me. I can practically feel the coup inside my bra right now. I picture the bad cells with little tiny megaphones screaming at the other cells to rise up and multiply.

Ironic, huh? They get to reproduce, and I don't.

This sucks balls.

Nasty balls. Sweaty balls. Ugly hairy balls. All the balls.

That's probably too many balls, but that's how much this sucks.

Okay, I need to focus.

I have to walk into school now with my happy face on. I need time to absorb this before I can even consider rationally talking about it.

"Hey, Mil. How'd it go?" Johnny asks as he casually strolls by. With the exception of how he cares for the school grounds, Johnny does everything casually. The way he walks. The way he drives. The way he dates me. Nothing's ever serious or important or imperative. He's the epitome of laid-back. He balances out my sometimes over-the-top exuberance. Normally, it doesn't bother me. However, today is not normal.

Nothing will ever be normal again.

I unexpectedly burst into tears, right in the middle of the hallway. Johnny stares at me like I have three heads.

"I have the braca gene," I tell him. I say it as a word, rather than the abbreviation of B.R.C.A., because:

A. I can't remember what the letters stand for even though Cheryl told me and

B. I don't know if most men would understand what I'm talking about.

"I'm sure the jeans will fit fine, Mil. Do you even have a casual day coming up?"

"Not jeans, the Braaaacaaaa gene mutation," I lengthen the words in an attempt to help him understand them more. He stares blankly. "The gene that causes breast cancer!" I finally say, throwing my hands in the air. I know it doesn't actually cause it, but I'm not splitting hairs here. My voice *may* be a smidge loud for the hallway, and Dianna pokes her head out of her fourth-grade classroom.

"Everything okay out here?"

"No, everything is not okay," I say at the same time Johnny says, "Yeah, it's cool."

I look at him. "Cool? This is not cool. This is the furthest thing from cool. It's ..." I draw a blank. All I can think is the word 'tepid' and I'm pretty sure any argument that contains the word tepid is already lost.

Dianna looks from me to Johnny and then back, clearly picking up on the massive tension in the air. "Okay, well, we're about to start a math test, so do you mind keeping it down a bit?"

I know how annoying it can be when you're trying to get your class to work to have someone causing a commotion in the hall. I look at Johnny and shake my head. "This is a big deal. I have the gene that means I'll probably develop breast and ovarian cancer."

Now I know we're keeping our relationship on the down low at work. We're so incognito I'm not sure *anyone* realizes we're together. I know what it's like to work with co-workers whose relationship implodes. Never a good thing. In an effort to squelch any of that potential disaster, we decided not to make our relationship public knowledge. Johnny doesn't seem to mind that our relationship is basically of the "Netflix and chill" variety. But even though I've put all these limits, I'd think he'd at least hug me. This is hugging news. The type of news where anyone would say, "Man, this girl needs a hug."

Anyone except Johnny, of course.

He starts to walk away. I catch up with him, heading down the hall toward my class. At least he offers, "So what does that mean?"

"I have really high chance of getting breast and ovarian cancer. My mom died of it."

"So you have cancer?"

I stop. "Did I say I had cancer? I said I'm likely to get cancer."

"But you don't have cancer right now?"

"No, not yet. But it's pretty much inevitable."

Johnny shrugs before turning into the kitchen. "Look on the bright side, Mil. At least you don't have cancer."

Big, fat, hairy balls.

CHAPTER 3

3 months later

"I know, babe, but this is too intense." Johnny's looking down at his feet, which haven't stopped shuffling since he entered the room approximately four minutes ago.

Too intense? Too intense? If I wasn't in a narcotics-induced stupor with tubes sticking out of various places, I'd probably get up and punch Johnny.

"You've been a total downer lately. No fun at all."

I look at him, unable to form a coherent thought that's not a long string of expletives or that doesn't include massive physical injury to his nether region.

"You've been a drag the last few months, and well, I ..." He looks at all the tubing and lines. "I'm not ready for serious. And this shit's serious."

"I'm not asking for a lifelong commitment here, Johnny. I just got out of major surgery. I thought you were going to help me for a few days." *You know, water my plans, bring me some Jell-O, keep me from throwing myself out the nearest window.*

Now who's going to keep my plants alive? For the first time, I finally have a shot of outliving my Christmas cactus, and it's going to wilt and die because Johnny's a wimp.

I hope I can remember to ask Dad to add that to his to-do list.

"Yeah, but I don't think I can. It's gross." He points at the chest tube, draining a reddish fluid from under my armpit.

The expletives fly through my brain and maybe a few out of my mouth as well.

"So, I'll see you around. Get well soon, Mil. Hang in there." Johnny turns to walk out, dispensing greeting card slogans as if he were a kitten with a balloon. If I could lift my arm to throw something at him, I would. As it turns out, there's an IV in one arm and an oxygen monitor and blood pressure cuff on the other, and I feel like my chest was run over by a Mack Truck driven by a gorilla.

He came to dump me right after I had life-altering, major surgery.

What a douche.

I can picture my back-to-school essay: What I did on my summer vacation by Millie Dwyer. I had my breasts amputated and got dumped all in the same day.

I've cried so much in the past three months I didn't think it was possible to cry anymore. I was wrong. Except it hurts to cry so I try to stuff those feelings down. Johnny was not a long-haul guy. I knew that going in. I always date guys like Johnny—the okay for now guy.

Life is too short for that crap.

Funny that it's taken this drastic move to make me realize that. When I probably didn't have time, I was squandering it foolishly on men who didn't deserve me.

I deserve more.

My mom would want me to have more than okay.

She certainly wouldn't want me to be with a douche.

I'm saved from another round of pity by the sudden entrance of my Aunt Polly. "How are you doing, baby doll? Do you need anything? Does it hurt? Do you have nipples?"

In any other world, this would seem like an odd string of questions. However, with the parallel universe I've seemingly been dropped into—I cannot think of any other reasonable explanation for this current hell— my nipples are a frequent topic of discussion. I mean, not in everyday casual conversation, but with Aunt Polly and Lisa. My dad's sister has been the closest thing I've had to a mom since before my own died.

I hate to admit it, but I don't remember tons about my mom. It would kill my dad if he knew. She got sick when I was in first grade and died when I was in fourth. Many of those in between years were spent with her in treatment or in bed, and I was encouraged to carry on as normal as possible. Aunt Polly swooped in, taking care of me so Mom and Dad wouldn't have to worry about it. She was like my very own Mary Poppins.

But even though I don't remember a lot, I miss my mom. I miss having that person when I was sad. Or happy. Or scared. I miss having that constant, unconditional love.

"For now they're there, but you know that doesn't mean anything."

"Okay, but it's one hurdle. How do you feel?" Deep lines stretch over Aunt Polly's forehead, and dark circles frame her eyes.

Physically I feel terribly, and emotionally I'm even worse. "Like I got hit by a truck."

A really big truck.

A convoy of big trucks.

And then they backed up and ran over me again.

Which is what I deserve for not believing what I read on the internet. People said this was bad, but I thought they were being wimps. I know a few women who had breast augmentation and were up and going within a day or so.

There's no way in hell I could move, even if I was on fire or Chris Hemsworth wanted to make out with me.

Even if Chris Hemsworth *and* Tom Hiddleston wanted to make out with me.

This is so not the same as a regular boob job.

Aunt Polly pats my hand comfortingly. "That's to be expected, with how invasive the surgery is. They have to be sure they take out all the breast tissue so it doesn't turn cancerous." She should know. She watched my mom, her sister-in-law, go through it. Apparently, they didn't get it all. "Was your dad here?"

I turn my head to look out the window. She's not going to handle this well, and I'm too tired for a Polly freak out right now. "He sent a balloon arrangement."

The silence hangs heavy. I can practically hear the expletives raging through her brain. Explosion coming in five ... four ... three ... two ...

"THAT IDIOT! When I get a hold of him, I'm going to pound the crap out of him!" It doesn't matter that my Dad and Aunt Polly are in their fifties. They still fight like kids. I saw her bite him not that long ago during a game of dominoes that went awry.

"Aunt Polly, it's fine. Really. I ... I don't want him here. It's too much. Plus, Lisa was here before she had to go to the airport, and I knew you'd be stopping by. Look at me. I'm not much for entertaining right now."

And let's face it, Lisa would be better at taking care of me than Dad would anyway. She already delayed her flight a day to stay with me last night and drive me in this morning.

She must have stayed until they brought me into recovery. There's a note hanging in my line of sight.

I waited until they wheeled you out. You are funny on drugs. I have video. We will discuss the blackmail terms later.

Lisa's note made me smile. The stupid balloons from Dad ... sigh.

"But he should be here for you. He was there every minute for Erica. He should be there for you."

I look at the balloons again, bright shiny colors that seem to mock me with their cheerfulness. The only thing worse than knowing that Dad's not coming is having to defend him. I've tried my whole life to understand his choices. I wish it didn't bother me, but it does. Tears threaten my already tired eyes. Aunt Polly's always been disappointed in how my dad handles things with me.

She's not the only one.

I doubt my dad's set foot in a hospital since my mom died, and I doubt he ever will. I'd hoped one day, a grandchild would be a good reason to overcome that aversion, but thanks to my hysterectomy, that's not something I'm going to make happen.

Not now anyway.

My dad didn't come when I had my first round of surgery six weeks ago. Today is no different. He said if I needed a ride home, he'd come and pick me up. Gee, thanks.

Wonder why I have issues with dating losers.

I try to tell myself he's not uncaring, just super sensitive about cancer trying to kill the women he loves.

He's traumatized.

His balloons dance in the air conditioning, and I hate them. Why couldn't he send flowers like a normal father?

A normal father ... ha.

Par for the course with me. Nothing's normal. It's never been normal. Even my normal was only temporary.

What now? My mind is a fog with black dancing at the edges of my jumbled thoughts.

The past three months have been a swirling black vortex of doctor's appointments and WebMD. Dreams of what might have been and hopes dashed under the wheels of my runaway train of a diagnosis.

Along with the realization that my biggest fear in life has come to fruition.

I've seen more naked breasts online than a porn addict.

By day, I kept up the sunny, happy Miss Dwyer persona, leading her second graders through their math tables and spelling words. By night, I was an insomniac with a compulsion to Google all things prophylactic. Not *that* kind of prophylactic because, as you can imagine, Johnny didn't come around much since the test results came back, and certainly not since the shop closed up with the first surgery. I guess it's hard to get hot and heavy with someone who cries all the time and is depressed, especially every time he got to second base.

Speaking of which ...

Ever so gingerly I reach my right index finger up and oh so cautiously poke my left boob. Rather, what was my left boob. What is now my new left boob. The boob formerly known as my left boob. The fake boob.

The foob.

The foob feels weird. Hard and stiff under my finger, but I don't feel the poke itself. I'd read about this, but wasn't prepared for it. Where the girls used to be full of vibrancy and life, now it's like there's a rock or a massive gummy bear sitting in my chest.

I'll never eat gummy bears again.

A heat rushes over me, starting in my head and spreading throughout my body. My legs are tired and clumsy in their attempt to kick off the sheets and blankets that cover them. Foobs and a hot flash. Awesome.

Aunt Polly springs into action, gently pulling the covers down and fanning my face with a piece of paper. "Relax, Millie. It will be fine."

Fine is a terrible word. Fine is settling. Fine is code for, "Sure this sucks, but there's someone, somewhere who has it worse than you so quit your bitching."

I hate fine.

Aunt Polly sits down. "My brother should be here."

I shrug a little and then stop because it hurts.

I hurt. I'm hurt. Aunt Polly's hurt. All because of me. "Nah. He can't give me advice about my hot flashes. He's not going through menopause with me like you are. Hell, you were the one who got me through periods to begin with."

Aunt Polly laughs. "And I never thought we'd be menopausal together. Any errant chin hairs yet?"

I rub a hand over my chin, trying to feel for those wiry whiskers that are sure to sprout any minute. "Not yet. And no offense, but I'm not exactly thrilled to be sharing this experience with you."

Aunt Polly sits down, now fanning herself a bit. "I know, baby doll. I wish you weren't either. I'll try to give

Peter a break on this, if you're okay with him not being here."

"I'm okay, Aunt Polly," I lie. I'm the furthest thing from okay. But she wouldn't understand. Dad wouldn't understand. Lord knows Johnny didn't understand. I'm twenty-nine years old and have lost every iota of my womanhood. I'm barren and single. I'm never going to be able to date again. I'm never going to be able to have kids.

Chris Hemsworth will never want to make out with me now.

But it's all supposed to be hunky-dory because as least I don't have cancer.

CHAPTER 4

I can do this. I can stand up and walk. It's no big deal. I've been doing it for at least twenty-eight years now.

Oh my God, I cannot do this.

The ground waves under my feet. Or maybe my feet are waving over the ground. Either way you put it, the gray-blue scratchy hospital socks with the grippers on the bottom aren't making me feel as safe as they're supposed to.

Instead of rubber dots, they need claws.

The nurse holds my elbow, clearing my IV line. "Take your time, honey. You'll be okay."

I nod because if I try to talk, I'm going to cry.

I am not okay.

I think I might die.

Or vomit.

I take a deep breath in through my nose, letting it out slowly through my mouth. Mentally, I'm trying to find my happy place. The place where tremendous amounts of pain and nausea are not allowed in.

The place where I still have my own boobs and uterus.

Apparently, my guardians—I picture two men bearing strong resemblance to the Hemsworth brothers—are slacking as waves of pain crash through my imaginary oasis.

"It's good to get you moving," the nurse says. I try to remember what her name is, but I can't. I'm not sure what my own name is. "Relax your grip, honey. You're going to pop your IV out."

My knuckles are whiter than the top of the Alps. I try to unclench them, but the pain is too much. My left hand clutches a pillow across my chest. If I was able to retreat to a fantasy world in my head, I'd imagine this pillow like Wonder Woman's shield, protecting my vulnerable new assets from the enemy.

In this case, enemies include movement, gravity, and air flow. Molecules of any kind.

Cold air is the arch-nemesis to reconstructed breasts.

I don't know how I'll ever handle winter. I may need to move to some place tropical. Do they need second-grade teachers at the equator?

Oh God, the feeling of fabric hurts me chest. And all I'm wearing is a stupid hospital gown. Two actually, if you consider the one they put on backwards so my keister isn't hanging out.

Add the sexy socks and the explosion of hair, and I probably look—well I can't imagine how bad I look.

Nothing like Wonder Woman.

At least I don't have to put on a brave face and pretend everything's okay. With Lisa sailing somewhere on a clear aqua sea and frolicking on white sandy beaches, only Aunt Polly's been in to visit. I don't have to hide my pain from her.

I wonder if this is what my mom went through. I vaguely remember lots of surgeries. Are they better than they were twenty years ago? Did Mom hurt like this too? Was it this hard for her to get around?

At least my suffering will be worthwhile. The surgeries maybe prolonged Mom's life. They'll save mine. I asked the doctor to guarantee it. He laughed. I may or may not have imagined punching him in the nads at that moment.

At least without my dad here, I don't have to worry about fixing my face, censoring the curse words, or controlling my body language.

I hurt like a mo-fo, and I don't care who knows it.

"Miss Dwyer!"

Son of a—

"It is you, Miss Dwyer!" And then my student—former student—lunges to hug me. Oh no.

"Piper, no!" In the nick of time, her father reaches out and grabs her shoulder, pulling her back. "Sorry."

"It's okay. Piper, I'm sorry but I can't give you a hug right now. Mentally I'm hugging you."

Mentally, I'm dying. Maybe physically too.

Sterling—Hot British Dad is here!—opens his mouth to say something when a loud voice rings out. "There you are! Sterling Kane, you are one of the most useless men I've ever met. Look at her hair! How could you let her go out looking like that?"

I see him close his eyes and take a deep breath.

"Piper looks fine." He glances down at his daughter, who's still smiling up at me. "She did it herself and didn't want me to fix it. I respected her autonomy."

I give Piper a thumbs up. I don't want her feeling badly. She smiles back and proudly flips her ponytail. She really is the sweetest kid. I miss her, and the rest of my class.

My gaze shifts back to her father. I wish Lisa was here to see how hot Hot British Dad is.

"She looks like a homeless child!" Piper's mom wails, drawing the curious eyes of the other patients in the hall. "What will my mother think?" I remember this woman from the school year and shudder.

I was fortunate Piper didn't take after her mother. At least she didn't in the classroom.

Sterling grits his teeth and perhaps mumbles something.

At least I think he does. Things are foggy and if I didn't know better, I'd swear I was drunk.

A growling British accent is even hotter than a regular British accent. I swear I can feel the ghost of hormones surging through my body in response.

Or at least meandering a little.

I must be drunk. Or at least high.

Why do people say drugs are bad again?

All I know is there is too much going on, and I need to rest. The nurse must sense it as she steers me toward a blue barcalounger that's outside the nurses' station.

I can't make out what Piper and her parents are saying until the mom—her name escapes me right now—and Piper walk by me.

"Come on. Grandma was asking why you weren't here sooner."

Sterling nods at me. "It was nice to see you again, Miss Dwyer."

I'm so tired that I don't know if I even respond.

I wonder how far I've walked. Ten, twelve miles?

At least it feels like it.

Everything hurts. I can't even identify the source of pain. I'm just one big radiating ball of ouch.

I've never hurt like this before. I'd rather get a thousand Brazilian waxes. That would tickle in comparison.

Too soon, my nurse comes back. "Time to get up and head back to your room."

"How far is it?"

Marathon distance, easily.

She looks ahead and I see her mouth moving. "Probably about another hundred, hundred and fifty feet."

I think she said feet, but she must mean miles.

As I round the last corner, I can finally see my door. Sweet relief. I'm going to sit down and never get up again.

Or maybe I'll just die to insure no one tries to make me get up and walk again.

I must say this out loud because my nurse escort laughs. "Oh no, you don't. You'll be getting up at least once more today. More likely once a shift, if you're looking at being discharged in the next day or two."

Initially, all I'd wanted was to go home and sleep in my own bed. That was before reality sunk in. I don't know how I'll move around at home. Food won't magically appear. There won't be a call bell.

Aunt Polly's going to have to stay with me.

She'd offered, and I'd placated her by saying yes. I didn't think I'd actually need her.

I need her.

I need the entire staff of Buckingham Palace.

I don't know how I'm going to manage.

I'll think about that after I take more painkillers and sleep for about twelve hours.

Two more doors to go then—

"Hi, Miss Dwyer again! Dad!" Piper calls out, scanning the halls for her father. She's popped out of a room to the left.

"You're done?" He addresses his daughter and then shifts his gaze to me. "Hi again. Did you have a nice walk, Miss Dwyer? Are you felling any better after your walk?"

So. Much. Pain.

The correct answer is one-hundred out of ten pain. Instead I say, "Millie. We're not in school now."

Then the mother comes walking down the hall and addresses her ex. "My mother isn't up for company right now. Take her home."

Sterling doesn't hide his exasperated eye roll. "Already? I thought we'd be here for a bit."

"Well, she's tired and needs to rest."

Aren't we all? I wish they would move so I can get back to my room. They're blocking the path to my doorway. All I can think about is going back to sleep for a year or two. I try to keep shuffling forward, but now Piper's mom is blocking my way. I look at my nurse and she jerks her head to the side. I guess we're going to try going around.

"Right. Why is she in again?" Sterling's asking. I see him reach over and pull his ex toward him, out of my way. Thank goodness for small favors. That's about ten less steps I have to take to get around them.

"She had a vaginal rejuvenation."

At these words, Sterling drops her arm like it's made of fire.

Eeewww.

Words I never want to hear, especially in relation to a woman who must be in at least her upper fifties.

And, why would anyone choose to have elective surgery? This is terrible. I can't imagine what it feels like to recover in the downstairs, lady cake department.

Piper's mother storms off. I must have missed something. Apparently she's mad. I don't know why. Not my problem. I keep shuffling. If I go any slower, I'll be going backward. My only problem is trying to make it the last ten feet back into my room so I can pass out.

"Millie," Sterling says. "Sorry to hold you up. Are you okay?"

No. Nope. Not at all.

I'm almost to the door. Piper and Sterling fall in step beside me. At least they're not holding up my progress. I try to put a smile on my face. I probably look constipated. "I will be eventually."

I notice Piper has a very concerned look on her face. Maybe she's worried about me. Maybe it's my hair. I have a feeling it's doing a great impression of Cher, circa 1988. If only I could turn back time and not run into them. I muster enough strength to ask, "How's your summer going, Piper? Doing anything fun?"

"I'm going to have a water balloon fight at camp this afternoon!"

Water balloons. Ha. I've got some stored in my chest. But Piper's simple joy at such a fun activity makes me smile. Oh, to be a child again. "That does sound fun. I'd love to do that."

"Do you want to come, Miss Dwyer? Connor is at camp too. You could probably hit him with a balloon, and no one would care. You know, pay him back for all the times he didn't listen in class."

While I'd never admit this publically, Connor was, simply put, hard to love sometimes. I hope he never knew that I felt that way, but the idea of pelting him with a water balloon does hold some appeal.

Not that I could pelt anyone in my current state.

We reach my door, and they pause while I go in and my sainted nurse gets me settled in bed and restarts my IV. I'm hoping it contains enough drugs to tranquilize a horse. I see Sterling hovering in the doorway, unsure of where to look or what to do. I nod for them to come in once I'm in bed and the blankets are pulled up to my armpits.

"Where were we?" I ask. I have no idea what we were talking about.

"My water balloon fight. Wanna come?" Piper smiles hopefully.

"Oh, that does sound like fun, Piper, but I'm afraid I can't. I have to stay here for another day or two, and then I'll be hanging out at home for several weeks. I'm afraid I don't have a very fun summer planned. You'll have to have the fun for me."

"Piper, I need to talk to Miss Dwyer for a minute. Can you go sit down over there?" Sterling gently rubs a hand over his daughter's head.

I miss my dad.

We watch as she scampers over to a couch over by the window, her crooked ponytail swinging down her back.

"Miss Dwyer—"

"Millie," I correct. I shift in the bed a bit, trying to find a position that's more comfortable.

That position doesn't exist.

That position doesn't exist.

"Millie, I—are you—is there anything I can do? Do you need anything?" Sterling stutters a bit.

Though the narcotics are making it difficult, I think about all the times Sterling was there to help me out in the classroom. He's a staple volunteer at the school barbeque, manning the grill. If memory serves me correctly—and I cannot believe I can even remember this right now—he was mystery reader three times, filling in when people would cancel last minute. He could

40

always be counted on to be there for his daughter and her friends.

I shake my head.

"Are you coming back to school in the fall?"

Suddenly, tears well in my eyes. "That's the plan. I should be back to school in September, good as new."

"And you'll be right as rain?" His eyes narrow.

I nod. Or at least I think I do. "I'm getting tired. This is the longest I've been ..." I trail off. I don't even know what day it is. It's getting harder to put words together. "I'm supposed to go home tomorrow."

He waves for Piper to come over and they start heading toward the door. "If there's anything I can do, please let me know."

"Piper, hit Connor with a water balloon for me. He really was a pain in my behind." My hand flies to my mouth. "Oh my, I can't believe I said that out loud. I'm on a lot of heavy-duty pain meds right now. Don't do that. I'm so sorry. That was unprofessional."

Sterling laughs. "I've heard Piper's stories about that Connor kid. If I were you, I'd keep a Nerf gun in my desk to shoot the kids."

"I believe shooting your students, even if it is with foam bullets, is frowned upon."

"Yes, well, you know what I mean. And it's why I'm a numbers bloke instead of a teacher." Then, he winks. WINKS at me! "Do you need anything else?"

"I'm okay. Thank you anyway. Have a nice summer. Piper, have a wonderful time. You will have to stop in my room in September and tell me all the fun things you did. I want a great list."

"Really?"

"Yes. I'm not going to have much fun, so I need you to have it for me. Promise?"

She nods solemnly.

"Pinky swear?" I hold up my hand and she sneaks over to it. We take our sacred oath and then I give her my best smile. "I can't wait to see your list."

I can no longer fight the fatigue that's pulling me under. Thoughts swirl and mash together.

That was so weird, running into a student. Surreal.

My brain is foggy, and I try to remember what we talked about.

I have no idea.

CHAPTER 5

This is the pits.

Really, truly, the pits.

Meet Gertrude, my new recliner. Originally, I'd planned on convalescing on my couch, but I had so much trouble getting comfortable that my dad went out and ordered me one of those electric gizmos that lifts me right up. It doesn't fit with my style or decor at all, so I have a love-hate relationship with the monstrosity. On the one hand, I feel like I'm ninety when I use it. On the other hand, the freedom the chair gives me is the only reason why I'm flying solo right now. On the other hand—wait, how many hands do I have?— I could totally film one of those infomercials right now.

Gertrude is an eyesore. Gertrude is expensive.

It was really nice of Dad to pick up Gertrude for me. I guess I won't write him off this week. He came through big time.

Gertrude for the win.

Dad's been here almost every day, taking care of tasks like garbage and the lawn. He took my car for an oil change and got it inspected.

Safe things. Tangible things.

Things that don't involve much conversation or emotions.

Better than nothing.

Better than I expected.

Today, eight days post-op, is my first time alone. Aunt Polly had a doctor's appointment, something she'd scheduled months ago. I certainly can't begrudge her that. While we'd tried to plan ahead for her absence, I'm worried I'll have to use the bathroom before she gets back. I look longingly at the cup of water on the end table next to me. I'd better not.

Yes, I'm that helpless. At least I had the foresight to install a bidet attachment to my toilet. I will never take wiping or pulling up my own pants for granted again. Lifting restrictions for at least the next week have me barely able to lift my drink and certainly nothing more.

The house is quiet. Too quiet. I haven't been alone in days. Over a week at this point. I don't even have Cornelius here to keep me company. Though Dad claims not to be a cat guy, he and Cornelius will have a chance to work on their budding bromance while I convalesce. We couldn't risk him walking on my chest, and I can't lift his fluffy frame off of me. I can see me explaining it to the doctor. "Why yes, the cat walked on my chest and killed my nipple."

I don't need the cat for that. I'm pretty sure the left one is dying. It's darker than the one on the right. I may have to take Aunt Polly up on her offer to have my nipple mentioned in the prayer of the faithful during Sunday's mass.

Words I never thought I'd even think, let alone say. "Pray for my nipples."

Just as another crying jag threatens to bust through, my doorbell rings. I swear, if it's someone selling something or someone trying to convert me, I will not be held liable for what I do to them. I'll ignore it.

Ding dong.

I have a will of steel. I can outlast this intruder.

Ding dong.

Ding dong.

Ding dong.

I'd bash that mo fo ding dong over the head with a pot if I had the strength. Or was allowed to lift. Or could get my arms up that high. Gertrude lifts me almost vertically, and then I gingerly stand up and make my way to the front door. This had better be good.

Publisher's Clearinghouse good.

Naked *Ragnarok* Chris Hemsworth carrying a piping hot pizza good.

I delicately pull open my front door, using both hands—when did it get so heavy?—and am shocked to see Tom and Roberta standing there. I was expecting someone asking to re-seal my driveway or to save my soul. I did not expect to see my principal and his wife.

"Hello" I quickly pull my sweater together, closing off the view of my dad's faded flannel shirt, as well as the drains hiding in the ever-so-sexy fanny pack type thing around my waist. I don't want anyone looking at my chest. My foobs. My dying nipple.

45

Roberta lifts a covered dish. "We signed up for today. I hope you like bacon mac and cheese! I used the recipe from Paula Dean's cookbook." I step aside to allow them to come in. I mean, it would be rude not to, right? I mentally reschedule my impending nipple death and crying jag for a later date and time. "Please, come in. Roberta, if you don't mind putting that on the counter? Thanks."

I'll probably want a taste the minute they leave, and I can't lift something that heavy yet. I can barely lift a spoon. Okay, I'm really not having that much trouble getting food to my mouth.

Tom sits down on the loveseat across from my chair and moments later, Roberta joins him. Gertrude springs into action, lowering me to sitting. Silence hangs awkwardly.

Hell, everything about everything is awkward right now.

"Thank you so much for bringing dinner. I'm not able to cook much right now, so I really appreciate it."

Would it be out of line to ask for a foot rub while they're here?

"If you tell me where the lawn mower is," Tom says, "I'll get started." It's then that I notice he's in basketball shorts and sneakers. I never knew my boss had such pale, knobby knees. The things you learn.

"I ... I don't know what you're talking about." Maybe I should think about cutting back on the narcotics. I might be hallucinating. "Did you say you were going to mow my lawn?'"

"Yes. We're going out of town for a few days, so we signed up to take some of the first slots. Other people will be by. You can access the Helping Wagon site to see who's doing what."

Helping Wagon?

Other people?

I'm not accepting people right now. Aunt Polly, Dad, and Lisa don't count as people. They're more like staff. Poor them.

So what is he talking about?

I know Tom's speaking English and technically I can understand all the words, but I don't understand what he's saying. My confusion must be evident.

"The site? Helping Wagon?" I shake my head. He might as well be speaking Russian.

"The teachers wanted to do something. You were supposed to let us know when you were having your second surgery. You didn't. We had to find out through the grapevine. Lots of people are upset. They wanted to be there for you."

While I don't want anyone to see me in such a bad state, this whole thing is nice. Super nice.

Now I feel badly that people are going to all this trouble for me. It's not like I'm going to be sick or need ongoing treatment. Just a few nips here and tucks there.

And foobs.

It's embarrassing to be caught off guard like this. I didn't know people would want to do this for me. I look down at my lap, unsure of what to say.

Tom says, "It's okay, Millie. You have people who care about you who want to help. You know you'd be the first in line to do this for one of your co-workers. Let us help you."

I don't like needing help, but I certainly don't mind giving it.

A card on my side table catches my eye. It says, "Gratitude helps us to see what is there instead of what isn't." Lisa and her inspirational messages.

"Thank you for your help. I am grateful for it," I murmur quietly. According to Pinterest, practicing gratitude is supposed to help boost your immune system and aid with healing.

"Are you really okay, Millie? You're not your usual peppy self right now. I definitely don't see Dynamo-Dwyer here."

That stupid nickname. It's what I get for being short and energetic at the same time. I look down at my chest. "I suppose not. Hopefully I'll be back to my old self soon."

He stands up. "I take it the lawnmower is in the shed out back? Anything I need to know?"

I shake my head. "I don't think so. Pretty straight forward. Backyard is the size of a postage stamp, so it shouldn't take long." I hesitate for a minute. "Thank you, Tom."

As he leaves, Roberta looks at me for a minute. I know her casually, but I wouldn't consider her a friend. "Tom said you had surgery?"

Her tone is obviously fishing, and since she brought a casserole, I suppose it would be rude to deny her answers. "I had a double mastectomy and reconstruction."

Her hand flies to her mouth. "Oh, dear. So young to have cancer. I'm so sorry. What stage?"

This is one of the many reasons I hate to answer these questions. I feel like an idiot. "I don't have cancer."

The wrinkle across Roberta's face indicates that she has no understanding and will need more details.

"I tested positive for the breast cancer gene mutation."

"Oh, well that's a relief. At least you don't have cancer."

Big, fat, hairy balls.

"No, and hopefully I won't have it after all this."

"Look at the bright side. You get a free boob job out of all of this!" She looks down at her own ample chest. "I'd love to have the girls lifted. You even get it paid for by insurance. It's like a win-win."

I don't feel like a winner. In fact, I feel like the world's biggest loser right about now. I've lost so ... much. But in this moment, all I can think is that I've lost the privacy to wallow because Roberta is sitting there, staring at me. I should focus on feeling grateful, but it seems like an insurmountable distance away. Still, I try to stay present.

"What is this site you were talking about? Some wagon?"

"It's called Helping Wagon. People can sign up to bring you food and do chores, like the lawn and take out the garbage. You can go on there and customize it, if there's something the creator hadn't thought of. And this way, you don't end up with seven pans of ziti in three days."

Honestly, if I wasn't the recipient, I'd be all over it. It sounds great. I bet Amy or Shelly set it up. The other second grade teachers were supportive when I told them what I'd have to have done. Plus, they helped my sub the last month of school when I was out for my first surgery. They'd already done enough for me that I didn't want to ask any more of them. It's why I didn't tell them when the surgery was to begin with. I wonder if one of them reached out to Lisa?

I know Lisa would do anything to assuage her guilt at not being here for me the week following my surgery. Only Travis and Melina would book a ten-day destination wedding cruise. I bet Lisa stops here on her way home from the airport tomorrow. The feeling of missing fills me, and I take a deep breath, willing the tears to stay in my eyes.

Roberta continues, "You should go on and put the things you need or want. It's really very fun."

"Okay, I can try to log in and see. I can't set the computer up, so when my aunt gets back, I'll ask her for help."

"Oh, your aunt? I thought your mom would be here to help you."

Roberta doesn't mean to be insensitive, I know. I'm sure she has no idea that her words are cutting. Maybe I'm just oversensitive right now. Like to make up for the lack of sensation on my chest. And if that's the case, well, someone up there has a perverse sense of humor.

"My mother died twenty years ago. My grandmother died of ovarian cancer and my mom of breast. The odds weren't in my favor, which is why I had the surgery."

"Oh, honey, that's terrible. I'm so sorry. Still, you should consider yourself lucky."

Yup. Lucky. I should go out and walk under a ladder or buy a lottery ticket. Buy thirteen black cats and break some mirrors while I'm at it.

Thankfully, Aunt Polly comes breezing in like a hurricane. "There's a strange car in the driveway!"

I feign tiredness. Not feign really, because I am tired, but I could stay up. I simply don't want to visit with Roberta anymore. A quick glance out the window tells me Tom's almost done. I apologize quickly for not being more social and ask Aunt Polly to thank Tom for me when he finishes.

F.Y.I., sleeping on an incline sucks, especially when you're a lifelong stomach sleeper.

But so much of this sucks right now, I can't even make a list.

If I could, though, I'd call it my Suck-et List.

No, I will show gratitude.

I am grateful for Gertrude so I can stand up and go take a nap.

I am thankful for naps.

CHAPTER 6

It's the next day before I remember about the website. It comes flooding back as I'm measuring the drainage from my chest tubes. It's nasty, this sanguine-like fluid that is dripping out of my chest. I use the mirror to see if there is any sign of infection around the drain sight. The right tube is barely draining any more, which is a good sign. I hope they take it out today. I want them all gone.

The fog of anesthesia and pain meds has left me with disjointed thoughts running through my head at the most inopportune times. As I struggle to put the drains back in the fanny pack, my mind meanders, strolling alongside a stream of consciousness. My appointment ... Aunt Polly's appointment ... her test results ... I don't know, why didn't she tell me? ... Tom and Roberta were here ... the website.

Oh right. I need to go check that out. I should do that before we leave. At my request, Aunt Polly helps me to the couch and sets up my laptop on an old TV tray that used to be at my dad's house. He must have brought it over while I was in the hospital. She puts another pillow behind my back so I can sit up better and reach the keyboard without stretching too far. I'm supposed to be moving my arms around throughout the day, but well, it hurts if I have to hold them out too far.

I find the site and put my name in for the search.

Help Miss Dwyer! Our beloved second grade teacher, Millie "The Dynamo" Dwyer is currently down for the count. Recovering from a hospitalization and surgery, Miss Dwyer could use a hand. Please sign up for a slot and keep Miss Dwyer in your thoughts and prayers for a speedy recovery.

Well, I don't love that my personal business is out there for everyone to see, but at least whoever created the site didn't tell details. Gratitude, gratitude, gratitude. It could be worse—it could say, *"She had every last bit of her womanhood removed! She's sterile and barren and no longer has any gender whatsoever!*

No mention of my gummy boobs. Thank God for small favors.

I scroll down to the bottom of the site, and site owner surprises me. No, surprise is not the right word. Stunned. Shocked. Flabbergasted. A blow to the head would be no less surprising in this moment.

Site hosted by Helping Wagon. This train was created by Sterling Kane.

My hand flies to my heart, and the touch instantly reminds me of how everything is different now.

Instinctively, I pick up my phone to call Lisa, but remember she's mid-flight right about now. I wonder how the cruise was. I wish I had gone. Not now, obviously. Pre-boobectomy when I still looked and felt like myself.

My mind heads back down that meandering path as I think about how a cruise or vacation won't work for me now. They're the first on a long list. Bathing suits. Dating. Marriage. Children.

I may not have actually had cancer, but it's robbed me of my life just the same.

This is so not fair.

And I should thank Sterling. Did I see him at the hospital? It's all very foggy. I can't tell what's real, what I dreamed, and what's a drug-induced hallucination. Was he there? Did I talk to him? Did we talk about ... vaginas?

Oh, dear heavens. Please let me not have gone into detail about my lady business.

Part of my brain thinks seeing Sterling and talking about vajayjays was a hallucination, but if I made it up, why would he have known enough to set this site up?

I'm not thrilled about the attention. Mostly because, like when Roberta was here, I'll feel I owe the volunteers an explanation. It's the least I can do for all the trouble they're going to. And, because, like Roberta, they'll say the wrong things.

But I have no right to complain. I'm not going through chemo and radiation. I'm not going to lose my hair. I don't have cancer. I'm not a survivor. I should feel lucky.

To stop my negative spiral, I close my eyes and focus on gratitude. The most basic form of giving thanks is a thank you note. Like most of my fellow teachers, I find shopping for good paper products to be slightly arousing. Perhaps titillating even. I click on Amazon and after some deliberation, order a package from Krafster with various designs in black, white, pink, blue. The variety of stripes and polka dots make me happy. Plus, they come with stickers to seal the envelope. I figure a package of thirty-five will be more than enough. They're generic, so I'll be able to use them in the future.

I might as well order some new pens too. All my favorites are at school, not like I need an excuse to order a new pack. My current pen of choice is the FRIXION. Let me tell you why I love it. Not only is it a smooth, non-smudgy gel pen but—wait for it—it's *erasable*. And it really erases! No more messy mistakes. Okay, yes, I'm a geek about stationary and whatnot. Lisa makes fun of me whenever I go to Staples. She says containers and school supplies are like a fetish for me. She calls me "50 Shades of Organized."

Whatever. Could be worse. At least I'm a teacher so I have an excuse to geek out about said things. There is part of me that thinks I'm a teacher just so I can buy this stuff every year.

Since my hormone factory has gone out of business, stationary shopping may have to take the place of sex in my life.

~~~***~~~

Following my appointment later that afternoon (yes, the drains are out!), a fancy fruit arrangement appears. The pineapples are cut to look like flowers and there are the most divine chocolate dipped strawberries. I have the fruit for dinner, making a note to send a thank you card to Dianna.

My list is growing by the day, but a simple card doesn't seem like enough for Piper's dad. He went far above and beyond what could be expected, especially since I'm not even his daughter's teacher anymore.

Why would he do so much?

In my Valium-induced-haze (I'm off the big guns, but still need something for the muscle spasms in my back), I try to remember our brief interactions from the year.

I wish I could remember our conversation from the hospital.

Please don't let it be as embarrassing as I think it might have been.

What exactly did I talk about with him? Please tell me I didn't call him 'Hot British Dad' to his face. I still can't believe he set the site up. He seemed so nice and caring throughout the year, but this takes the cake.

Piper's mom on the other hand—she's a piece of work. Try as I might, I can't remember what her last name is. We all had a good chuckle playing the 'what if' game when we saw that Piper Kane's mother's name was Candice. It would be unfortunate, unless she was in the adult entertainment business, and then it would be fortuitous.

As a rule, I ask for separate conferences for children with split households. I don't want to be in the middle of what might be a contentious relationship. If I sit with the parents on their own, I can be sure the meeting stays about their child. Piper's dad had no problem with this, but the mother was annoyed. If I didn't know better, I'd say she looks forward to annoying her ex every chance she gets.

How you can want to annoy anyone with that accent is beyond me.

A little British never hurt anyone.

Sometimes it helps. A lot.

Especially when combined with piercing hazel eyes.

Hot British Dad indeed.

But then I try to move a bit and feel the twenty pound (or so it seems) deformed coconuts on my chest and remember that it doesn't matter if he seems like a nice guy or he has a sexy English thing going on.

I'm closed for business.

Regardless, I still need to thank him.

After another power nap, I turn on my computer and login to my school account. I skim past the dozens of well-wishes from my co-workers and pull up my address book from the past year.

Dear Mr. Kane,

Dear Sterling,

Hello Piper's dad,

Dear Hot British Dad I would have thrown myself at if my parts were still working,

Hi!

Thank you for arranging the Helping Wagon. I ~~was really surprised to have people show up on my door out of the blue.~~ It was a pleasant surprise. ~~While I had been hoping to keep my surgery and recovery private, I guess it's nice to know people care. Do you want to shag? I wouldn't mind it but all I can do is knit you a pair of slippers as an act of intimacy.~~ I'm overwhelmed at the show of support.

I stare at the email. I don't think I can express my thoughts and feelings in writing at the moment. There are the ones I have and then the ones I think I'm supposed to have.

Despite chanting my gratitude mantra, feelings of irritation sneak in, winding their way through my mind. Who does he think he is, telling my private information to the world like this? Isn't this a HIPPA violation or something? This is not something I would ever have shared so publically. If I had wanted people to know I'd had my surgeries, *I would have told them myself, dammit.*

If I wanted help, I would have asked for it.

That last statement is a lie. I mean, Aunt Polly has been helping. I don't know what I would do without her. Lisa will help me too, when she gets back. My dad, in addition to keeping my cat, has been doing the household stuff, so this is more of a help to him than to me. I mean, his back is a bit tricky at times, so this is a big help to him. I hate to see him all twisted up and in pain. It's not like he goes to the doctor when his back goes out. It wouldn't surprise me if he never goes to the doctor again. But I digress.

Still, Sterling Kane had no right to do this. This is none of his business. He should stay in his lane. Fueled by lack of quality sleep and relaxed inhibitions (thanks Valium!), I channel my righteous indignation.

Right into my cell phone.

CHAPTER 7

"Hello?"

I will not let the accent distract me. I mean business.

"Mr. Sterling. I mean, Kane. Sterling Kane."

Smooth.

"This is he."

He must think I'm the worst telemarketer in history. I must stay calm. "Who do you think you are?"

A silence hangs on the line. He's going to hang up on me. I know it.

"How can I be of assistance?" There's an edge to his voice that I can't attribute to the accent. He's pissed.

"You had no right."

"With whom am I speaking?"

"Oh. Yes. It's Millie Dwyer."

Duh.

I'm an idiot.

"Millie Dwyer, as in Piper's teacher, Millie Dwyer?"

"Do you know other Millies who aren't nine-hundred years old?"

"How do I know you're not nine-hundred years old? It's not as if I can see you. I can only hear you right now."

"Do I sound nine-hundred? Sheesh."

"Well, I don't know rightly. I've never spoken on the phone to someone nine-hundred years old. I don't suppose someone of that age would even know what to do with a cellular phone."

This phone call has certainly taken a turn.

"How do you know I'm on a cellular phone? I could be on a regular phone."

"Are you?"

His question makes me actually pull the phone away from my ear to look at it. "Well ... no."

"So this *is* the Millie Dwyer who was my daughter's second grade teacher."

I have no response to that.

"I will take your silence as affirmation. How are you feeling?"

"Eh, okay. I got my drains out today."

"Sorry? Drains? Are you having plumbing issues? Do you need that added to the website? I'm sure someone has some plumbing skills."

"No, but that reminds me. Thank you, but seriously, what gave you the right to do that?"

"Do what?"

I sigh, unable to conceal my exasperation. "The site. Telling everyone about me."

"Oh, well, I thought you could use some help. You said you were by yourself."

Dammit. He's got me.

"Did I get that wrong? Had you had help lined up? Is the site redundant? We can always change your needs so you get the help when it works best for you."

"I've got some help. My aunt and my friend. My dad is around, but he's got a bad back. This is actually good for him."

"Has the food been sufficient?"

"Oh, yes. More than that. Lots of it, and quite delicious. Don't tell anyone, but most of the people can cook better than Aunt Polly."

"Miss Dwyer?"

"Millie, please. We're not in school now."

"Right. So, Millie, tell me, who makes the best dish? I've always wondered about what people bring on these sorts of things."

"Can't you see the list yourself?"

"I suppose, although I haven't looked recently. But what do you like?"

This conversation is unexpected. I try to think about the various foods people have stopped by with. I can't think of a blasted thing. Then, I see the large sculpture of fruit. "Um ... it was all so good. There was a fruit arrangement that was nice."

It's Sterling's turn to be silent for a minute. "Um, you mentioned something about drains. Is it something simple, like a clog, or are you in need of an actual plumber?"

I hear a rustling of paper on his end. I wonder what he's doing.

Oh, right. He's waiting for me to tell him what the heck I'm talking about.

"No, not those kinds of drains. I had drains in my ... well, my ribs, I guess, to drain fluid off after the surgery. They're both out so that's a relief. No more fanny pack for me."

There's another long silence on the line.

"I may not know much about medical things, but you've got me thoroughly confused. What do the ribs have to do with your ... your ... fanny?"

"The fluid from the surgery in my chest region had to drip out. I know," I sigh, "totally gross. So I had to wear this fanny-pack type thing around my waist to hold the bags that the stuff drained into. But I'm all done with that now, thankfully."

"Yes, thankfully. I thought you were talking about ... something else."

"What else could I possibly be talking about?" A Brazilian butt lift? I don't know about this guy. He's a bit of an odd duck.

"Most Americans don't know that to a Brit, fanny does not mean arse. If they did, they probably wouldn't use it as a first name."

Wait, what?

"What does it mean?"

There's another sigh. "I can't believe I'm talking about this with my daughter's teacher—"

"Former teacher," I interject.

"It doesn't matter," he continues. "Fanny is how we refer to the, um, vagina."

Oh. My. God.

Then something strikes me. A memory. Or hallucination.

Please let it have been a hallucination.

"Did we talk about vaginas in the hospital?"

I'm not going to lie, this may be the first time I've ever said the *v-word* to a member of the opposite sex. I prefer grown-up terms like hoo-ha and spam purse.

"Can we change the subject? We need to before I tell you that we did, in fact, talk about vaginas, as my ex-wife's mother was in for a vaginal rejuvenation."

Gack.

"That may be more than I needed to know. So, anyhoo, I had a bag around my waist to hold my drains which is nowhere as gross as the thing you just said."

I need to pour bleach into my brain to erase the thoughts of that kind of surgery. I was much happier when I thought it was a figment of my imagination.

"Right. Do you have a nurse to help you with those drains and such?"

"No, I did it on my own. I mean, my aunt's here because I'm basically an invalid. But now they're out so it's fine."

"Oh, you seem so well-versed with the medical. I'm not very good at it, I'm afraid."

I didn't used to be either.

"I've sort of had to become immersed in the lingo since all this started."

"We all do what we have to, I suppose. I never pictured myself raising a daughter on my own either. Like I said, not the same, but I felt like a stranger in a strange land when it all went down."

"Becoming a father or becoming a single father?"

I don't know why it matters.

"Both, actually. I didn't even know if I wanted kids, and I'm not sure I was ready at twenty-five, and needless to say, Piper's mum was probably not a good choice, but I loved her and thought that would be enough."

What do you say to that?

"We didn't plan on kids, and then she didn't plan on staying with me. And then we split, which I didn't want at the time. Hindsight, it's for the best. But still, nothing how I thought it would be."

"We all make mistakes, I guess. I was dating someone who at least waited until I was awake from the anesthesia to break up with me."

Did I really just say that?

My Valium should come with a warning label not to talk while taking them.

"You're joking, right?"

"I wish I could say I was. In truth, it's for the best. He's not ... let's just say he's not a knight in shining armor. He's more like a jester in a tin can. But still, his timing leaves a lot to be desired."

Silence fills the line again, but this time, it doesn't seem awkward.

"Millie?"

"Yes." My voice is suddenly hesitant and quiet.

"We got quite off the beaten path, but I seem to remember you being upset with me when you called. Did I do something to offend you?"

Well, crap. How do I complain about that? "No. Not anymore. I'm good."

"But if you don't tell me, I'll never know, and I'm liable to make the same mistakes over and over, never learning my valuable lesson. You're a teacher, correct? Please help me learn."

I don't know if I can even find my voice. "No, Sterling, I'm the one who needs a lesson. You are one of the nicest people I've ever met."

CHAPTER 8

Three weeks out from surgery, and I'm almost starting to feel human again. Well, sort of human. Partly human.

As human as I can be with alien boulders on my chest. The PA, Dana, said I should be massaging them to help soften things up because I'm still in the rock-hard stage. I think my idea of a massage and the PA's idea of a massage are totally different. A good massage should include soft music, a dark room, scented essential oils, and total relaxation.

I wish I was back at the spa with Lisa.

What this massage actually involves is like kneading the hardest, most immobile dough you could ever imagine, while trying not to vomit at the thought of what is really inside my body.

Trust me, you do *not* want to know.

On the bright side, the nipple prayers have been successful thus far, and they're still alive and kicking. So I guess I shouldn't complain that they're always ... pert.

I thought one of the benefits of having the reconstruction would be not having to wear a bra anymore. Well, unless I want people permanently staring at my girls, that's not a great idea. It's a moot point, as the surgical bra looks like it'll be a wardrobe necessity for weeks to come.

Logging into Helping Wagon, I write an update for all the generous people who have signed up and helped out the past few weeks. Windows were washed, shopping was done. The house was vacuumed and Sterling Kane even took out my trash.

Today, I start physical therapy in the quest to get up and at 'em. Or to at least be able to reach the top of my head again. I'm not super tall so not even being able to reach the top of my head severely limits what I can do. Wouldn't it be funny if my homework from P.T. would be to have to write on the chalkboard?

My notifications ding, indicating a message from Sterling, inquiring if I need a ride to P.T. Aunt Polly's driving me, of course, but I file away his offer in case I'm ever in a bind. Lisa's my backup driver, but daytime appointments are hard because of her work schedule. She's swamped from all the time she took off. I know she wants to be here for me. If I wasn't an invalid, this would be another stretch of time where we go months without seeing each other.

Truth be told, I want to drive myself. I'm not used to being an invalid. But even getting in the car, I can barely pull the seatbelt across my body and buckle it without assistance, so driving might not be the best thing for me. Not to mention the seat belt hurts my chest so I have to put a stuffed animal in between to cushion things. I can't really carry my purse, so I use a light canvas bag for my stuffed penguin and my phone.

I absolutely cannot wait to get my old life back.

Except it's a new life. It shouldn't be that different, I keep telling myself. If I repeat it enough, maybe I'll actually start to believe it.

Picking up the phone, I call Lisa. She's at work, which means she can't always take my calls. I don't think she's in court this week, but I know she's preparing for a trial in the near future, hence the long work days.

"Millie, what's up? You okay? Do you need anything?"

I miss the days when she wasn't so concerned about my everything. When the drama was about her, instead of me. "I'm good. Nothing new to report."

It's my shorthand for the update on the status of my implants and nipples. It's not always kosher to be discussing cadaver pockets and silicone implants and nipple covers, especially while she's at work.

"Okay, if nothing's wrong, then I can't really talk. I've a client meeting in five."

I disconnect, wishing I had someone to keep me company. I could probably call one of my teacher friends, but I didn't really socialize with them outside of school activities before all this, so it wouldn't be right to lean on them now.

I could call Dad, but he's not a small talk kind of guy. If I need him for something tangible, he's there. The story of my life really—physical doing but not emotional supporting.

I try some mindfulness meditation to fill the void. I'd read that it has health benefits. I can use all the added benefits I can get.

In reality, I only have about five minutes before Aunt Polly bustles in, here to help me get ready to go to P.T. Even though I insisted the regular P.T. clinic would be fine, Aunt Polly insisted on getting me in at the Genevieve T. Wunderlich Women's Health Clinic. I shouldn't be going there. That's for women who are sick. You know, cancer survivors.

I'm not a survivor.

I don't know what I am. I don't identify with the pink ribbon, save the tatas people. There was nothing wrong with my tatas per se. I simply wanted to avoid the stress of constant diagnostic testing and worrying. It was more for my potential anxiety than anything else.

Maybe I made the wrong decision.

Maybe I leaped before I looked.

Speaking of looking, I glance down at my chest. The foobs are certainly bigger than my natural girls were, not to mention sitting just under my chin and much further apart than they should be. If they were any more east-west, they'd be under my armpits. I miss my itty bitty titties. The new ones might as well have a flashing neon sign saying, "Square silicone boobs here!"

If not that then one that says, "Available for lap dances!"

Since I'm leaving the house, real pants are needed, but I can only manage these pajama bottoms on my own. Peeing by myself trumps regular pants any day. I have to wear a soft camisole under my surgical bra because the seams in the bra irritate everything. Slowly, I inch into a light hoodie. Once I slip into my Birkenstocks, I look like I should be the cover model for *Hobo Life Magazine.*

My hair is beyond help, at least any help I can provide without being able to lift my arms up. Aunt Polly's always worn her hair short and chic, which turns out to be unfortunate for my unruly hair. With appropriate product and styling, my hair can fall in soft waves. Currently, I have the real possibility of dreadlocks forming.

I'm not sure which is worse—not being able to pull my own pants up and down or not being able to fix the monstrosity on my head.

I know I have much to be grateful for. I won't be facing the death sentence my mother and grandmother had. But still, this sort of blows.

~~~***~~~

In case you were wondering, P.T. doesn't stand for Physical Therapy, like you might have previously thought. It's short for Pain and Torture. Or Physical Terrorist. I want to officially file a complaint with every book and movie that portrayed people happily going through P.T. without crying.

No such thing exists.

Yes, I was that person sobbing through the session.

The tears started as soon as I gave my history. Isn't this all in my file? Why do I have to tell Kristina, my ever-so-patient therapist, things she should already know? It's stupid that I have to go through the whole diagnosis and hysterectomy and mastectomy and reconstruction. At least we can skip to the alphabet soup that is now my life.

She looks at the pink form, ignoring the tear splotches on the paper. "NSPBM, DTI?"

I nod. "Yes." It's nice not to have to explain *nipple sparing prophylactic bilateral mastectomy, direct to implant*. "UTM," I add. *Under the muscle.*

Kristina jots that down. "Okay, so how's everything going? Are you massaging the pockets like you're supposed to? I know I don't need to tell you how important it is to make the tissue soft and supple so the implants can settle and fluff. I promise, they won't be this high forever."

"I didn't think it would be this bad. I mean." I lean in and whisper, glancing and seeing the other women with their head wraps and arm compression sleeves, "It's not like I have cancer."

"Direct to implant has a tougher recovery initially. In the long run, it means less surgeries, so that's the benefit, but it's definitely a rougher go for the first few weeks."

I nod. I think I read that somewhere online. "I thought I'd handle it better. That I was tougher."

Cue waterworks.

I feel sorry for Kristina, having to deal with this blubbering mess. She hands me a box of tissues and brings a wastebasket over, though she has to stop and lift it for me, since throwing my wadded up snot rags is too much for my arms.

Kristina moves and stretches my arms, using a weird ruler-protractor thingy to take measurements, making notes on a Post-it as she goes. I look at her pen. It's a standard Bic. Blah. I should bring her one of the FRIXIONs. If she gets me through this nightmare, I'll send her a case as a thank you.

She asks me to move my arms and records what I'm capable of.

For the record, it's not much.

Then comes the dough work. Have you ever stood outside a pizza joint—a real old-fashioned Italian one—and watched the guys beat and knead and toss the dough so that it goes from a solid lump to a thin crust delight? Yeah, like that but without the actual pizza.

"You know what? I'm going to beg my aunt to take me to get pizza after this. The thought of it is making my mouth water, and I haven't had much of an appetite since the surgery."

I don't need the food—thanks to the Helping Wagon my fridge and freezer are stocked—but I'm having one of those *need* moments. Kristina looks at me, obviously trying to talk about anything but my condition. "Have you considered a support group? You're not the only one going through this, you know."

I think about what she's suggested. Aunt Polly, and even Lisa, have mentioned it as well. I tell Kristina what I told them. "I would feel like an idiot. I don't have cancer. How can I walk in there and complain about this? I'm the lucky one."

"Not a breast cancer support group. A previvor support group."

"Say what now? What did you call it?"

"Previvor. You're officially a cancer previvor. It means you have the genetic disposition to have cancer, but haven't yet had it. There are lots of groups out there for women like you. Going through a double mastectomy and reconstruction isn't a walk in the park. It's not a simple augmentation. There's a lot more to it than that. You don't have to do it alone."

CHAPTER 9

"Are you sure about this?" Aunt Polly asks as she parks the car. The lot's crowded, which means this might take a while.

Even though I want to sleep, my need for pizza is greater.

"Just drop me off and come back when you're done running errands. I can rest while I sit and wait. No big deal."

"Okay. Remember, you'll be on your own tonight. It's my book club night."

I look at my aunt. I know as well as she does that book club is code for 'let's get together and drink copious amounts of wine.'

I could use a book club right about now.

Aunt Polly gets out of the car and comes around to open my door. "Call me when you're ready."

I walk the twenty or so feet to the door. Aunt Polly pulls out of the lot like the flag has just gone down at the Indy 500. Book club my foot, she's on her way to the liquor store.

It's all fun and games until I get to the pizzeria door.

The heavy, glass door.

The heavy, glass door with the shoulder-height handle that I have to pull open.

Big, hairy balls.

I did not think this through. If I can't open my own car doors, why did I think I'd be able to open building doors? The women's health center had those nice buttons that automatically open the doors.

Why don't all places have them?

Everyone, regardless of disability, should have access to pizza.

Okay, well, I don't have much of a choice. If I can reach the handle, which is so high because the door is not street level, maybe I can keep my elbow at my side and step backwards to pull. The bottom of the door is about six inches higher than the cement pad where I'm standing.

I'm not sure this is going to work.

I try to lift my arm.

It doesn't get quite high enough. I angle my body and try again. Just as my hand *almost* makes contact with the bottom of the handle, the door swings open, nearly knocking me flat over.

"Millie?"

I don't even have to see who's talking to know that voice.

"Oh, hey, Sterling." I step back and he pushes the door fully open, holding it for me. He nods.

The perfect manners. So very British of him. I can also see him tipping his cap to me, if he were wearing one.

"Thank you. My aunt dropped me off while she runs some errands, but I forgot I can't open the door yet. Stupid, stupid, stupid." I mutter the last part under my breath, looking down at my feet. I see my baggy pants and want to crawl in a hole. While I'm sure I look better than the day I saw him at the hospital, I'm definitely not back to my old self. I know my hair's a fright, and I probably look frumpy in my pants and hoodie. Make that a hippie hobo, because I'm carrying a macramé bag over my forearm. Total fashion icon in the making here.

"Well, come inside. I'd say where it's cooler, but I think the temperature is only a degree or two below the inside of the pizza oven." Sterling smiles as I pass by.

Reflexively, my arms cross over my chest, trying to hide the freak show underneath. "I got a hankering for this pizza while I was in P.T. I probably should have called an order in." I shrug slightly, then wince. I'll be so happy when I can move again. "At least Aunt Polly will have plenty of time to get her errands done."

"Do you mean to sit here and wait for it to be ready? It's taking at least an hour."

My remaining energy drains immediately, and I want to crumple. "Drat. I really wanted this too. This is the longest I've been out since my surgery, but I don't think I can make it another hour."

Sterling's brows crease and then rise. I can practically see the light bulb above his head. "Do you like bacon?"

"Of course I like bacon. What sort of sociopaths are you dealing with that *don't* like bacon? I don't want to know those people."

A wide grin spreads across his face. "Thank goodness. I was being evaluated for sociopathy, but adding bacon to my pizza may have just saved me."

I don't bother trying to conceal my smile. This man is delightful. "I mean, it's not the only criteria, but I have a feeling you know the difference from right and wrong. So I take it you're suggesting I order bacon on mine?"

"No, I'm suggesting you share mine. It should be out"—he looks at his watch—"twenty minutes ago, so why don't we enjoy it together?"

My face feels hot. You could probably cook a pizza on it. "Oh, that's so nice of you to offer, but I can't. It's too warm in here, and I'm getting a hot flash. I'm not sure I'll be able to stay in here much longer without asking to sit in their cooler."

"We can go to my place," he answers quickly. "Or yours," he adds. "Wherever you'd be most comfortable."

I start fanning myself with one of the paper menus on the table. I have to keep my arm close to my body and basically use my wrist. My left arm is still wrapped across my abdomen. I'm in the exact terrible posture Kristina told me to avoid. I sit down, but I'm not sure it improves anything.

In this moment, I am thankful for not having to wait and for this man, who is kind and compassionate.

My gratitude training is working.

"That's very nice of you, Sterling." My voice is coming out all breathy. Not in the sexy way but in the "I just ran a marathon and I might die" kind of way. "Let me text my ride to let her know."

"KANE!"

We both jump at his name being bellowed.

Sterling heads to the counter and retrieves his steaming hot pie. He turns to me. "Come on. My food is ready to go. Let's get you out to the air conditioning."

I stand up, and it requires more effort than it should. "Are you sure? Would you mind going back to my place? Things are set up better for me there."

"Not at all. Ladies first." He nods, gesturing toward the door with his head.

That damn door. It's a push from this direction, but still ...

Maybe if I use my butt. Then I see the sign cautioning about the step down. Knowing me, I'd fall ass over teakettle. I need to ask for help.

"Hang on, love. I've got it." He moves so smoothly, balancing the pizza box on one hand while he pushes the door open and steps down. All one fluid movement, like a dancer. I don't even have to ask him to do it. I follow him to his car and try not to think about the fact that he called me 'love.' It's probably one of those cultural differences.

He opens the passenger side door for me as soon as we get to his car. God, he probably thinks I'm a helpless feck.

I smile to myself at my own use of a British-ism. I should ask him what feck means though ...

"I think I can get this one. Sometimes building doors are too heavy. I'm not supposed to lift more than four pounds yet."

"Well, I am opening the door for you regardless, because that's what a proper gentleman does. There you go." He steps aside, letting me slide in.

Huh. I don't know that I've ever had a man open a car door for me just because.

While Sterling opens the back door and slides the pizza in, I'm confronted by my next car-related, post-mastectomy obstacle.

The seat belt.

I know what you're thinking—I can't reach for it and buckle it.

While it's true that that's a bit challenging and takes some twisting and turning that I don't love, it's not the real issue. The biggest problem is the actual seat belt *hurts* going across the foobs.

In my limited car rides since the surgery, I've addressed this issue in one of two ways: don't wear the seatbelt or use Pepé.

I'm going to go for option A.

As Sterling turns the. key, the indicator bings, alerting him the passenger seat belt is not engaged. Traitor.

"Buckle up, love. We're going."

He's giving me no choice. Pepé it is. I stare straight ahead and pretend that this is totally normal.

Then I pretend I don't see Sterling's double-take when he glances in my direction.

I should explain, but for some reason, I don't. The idea of having to justify all these new things I can and can't do is exhausting. I just want to be. Me and my stuffed penguin.

You know, because a real penguin might make this weird.

I'm not even sure if Sterling knows what I'm going through. He's never asked. Until he does, I'm not going to say anything.

I give Sterling direction. "Turn here. At the next stop light, go straight, then take a right."

It's only after we're pulling up in front of my house that it occurs to me that he's been here before. Seriously, the drugs are addling my brain.

Just say no, kids.

"I forgot you were here last week to take out the trash. Why didn't you stop in and say 'hi?'" If I hadn't been looking out the window, I wouldn't have even seen him pull up, wheel the can out to the curb, and drive away.

"I didn't know if you'd be sleeping, and I didn't want to disturb you. Plus, I was running late to pick up Piper."

He rushes around to open the door for me, first the car and then my aqua-colored front door.

In theory, the blue of the door shouldn't work with the red steps and yellow siding, but it does. Perfectly.

I take a minute to stare at my beautiful bungalow.

Being cooped up inside for the past few weeks, I've missed the bright, cheerful colors of the exterior of my house. I could use some cheering up.

I notice Sterling looking too. "Your spirea and rhododendrons need to be trimmed back a bit. I'll add those to the Helping Wagon site, if that's all right with you. I don't know how I missed them when I was here last."

I nod and head in. Sterling sets about surveying my yard for more tasks to add to the Helping Wagon site. I need to sit down and relax. I'm tired and sore and need some more Advil and Valium. I'd rather not take pain pills while Sterling's here, but the soreness after P.T. is creeping up, and I was strictly advised to stay on top of the pain. I pop the pills into my mouth and take a swig of water from the large cup still on my end table. I let the recliner power me down into a comfortable position. I forgot to put Pepé away, so he rests next to me on the seat.

I am wiped out, my eyes too heavy to stay open.

"Do you want me to put this in the kitchen or would you like it out here?"

Without opening my eyes I say, "The kitchen please. There are paper plates and napkins on the counter, if you don't mind."

There's a good chance I doze off while waiting. It could be ten seconds, it could be ten minutes. I'm fairly confident it wasn't ten hours.

Either way, I wake to the melodious sound of Sterling's voice. "Here it is. The best pizza in the world."

I push the button on my recliner to bring me to a more upright position. I don't have to say anything, and Sterling pulls a TV tray in front of me. The pizza looks—and smells—delicious. "I sometimes get to be a creature of habit. I usually order the margherita. I could eat fresh mozzarella every day."

"Okay, if this doesn't win you over, next time you get to pick."

Next time?

Oh my God. Am I going to have a date?

I'm going to spend hours reliving this moment. You know I am.

CHAPTER 10

"Okay, wait. Tell me again what he said about next time," Lisa says.

I rehash my conversation with Sterling. Again.

"This is fantastic. I'm looking him up right now." Silence on the line. "OMG. Those eyes. That smile."

I shift a bit to my side, barely noticing the pain, and sigh. "They're nothing compared to his voice."

"Hot British Dad."

"Yes, and he's so nice and thoughtful. And he introduced me to bacon pizza."

Lisa's squeal forces me to pull the phone away from my ear for a bit. "And you're going out with him!"

"Lis, let's not get too excited. It's not a big deal. It's just pizza."

"It's not just pizza. He set up the site and now he wants to make plans for pizza again!"

I squirm, trying to take the pressure off my left foob. It doesn't work, so I have to sit up again. At least getting to sitting and standing is getting easier. I'm definitely feeling a difference this week. I don't know if it's the P.T. helping or not. I don't feel like I'm doing much when I'm there, pushing a washcloth over a table and up a wall like in The Karate Kid. Wax on, wax off. But the next day, I'm always sore like I lifted kettle bells or tossed tires. At least today, I can touch the top of my head. Not enough to wash it or brush it well, but it's an improvement.

"He doesn't want to make plans. It was one of those casual remarks you make." This is what I've been telling myself all week. Who in their right mind would want to date this mess?

"But he's done so much for you!" Lisa's using her litigator voice, trying to convince me that this could be something.

She's a good litigator.

"Well, he did come back this morning for a quick minute to trim my bush."

Lisa's laughter bursts through the phone. "Yeah, I'll bet he did."

Four weeks of inactivity, not to mention four months of incredibly high stress, have dulled my wit. I miss the innuendo totally. "He wanted to make the front look good."

"Did he go for a clean trim, or did he do something fancy like give you a heart?"

I lean slightly, looking out the window at the freshly-groomed spirea. "No, just a regular trim."

"So this is your alternative to the Brazilian. Are you going to have Sterling Kane trim your bush again?"

It's then that her double entendre hits me, and I feel my face flush. I'm glad she's not here to see it; otherwise, I know she'd make fun of me. At least this time, the rising color in my cheeks is not from a hot flash.

"Lis, stop. You know that's not going to happen. And sheesh, now I'm going to have to ask him to do a different chore, just so you can't make fun of me."

"Like snaking your drain?"

I feel a rogue hormone stir at the thought.

"I'm closed for business. You know that."

"All I know is your fun bags are under construction. As soon as the yellow caution tape is lifted, you should be good to go, new and improved. Even better than before. He'll probably love the new and improved girls."

Lisa's been my rock since we were eleven. She's been through it all with me and has demonstrated more patience than a saint. She means well. But she doesn't understand.

Aunt Polly doesn't understand.

No one understands.

I don't feel like explaining it, yet again. Lisa was there with me, doing all the research months ago. We earned our Google M.D.'s together. Maybe it's because she didn't see me right after, when my breast tissue had been scraped out like the inside of a honeydew.

In a related story, I'll never eat a melon again.

That doesn't factor in to how it feels to have my chest cavity re-stuffed fuller than a Thanksgiving turkey until it's the consistency of rock. Not to mention the nerve damage and permanent scarring.

And I know I can't tell Lisa about something like using Pepé under the seat belt. She'd just laugh and make fun of me. Maybe someday I'll laugh about it, but today is not that day.

Like I want to be doing it. I can't even imagine what Sterling thought about it.

For the first time, there are all these things she doesn't understand. That she doesn't get.

And I resent her for it.

So understandably, my patience at having to explain all of this to Lisa is wearing as thin as the skin left covering my fake boobs.

She's functioning like she always has in our relationship, which would be okay except I'm not the same. I swear, the surgeries not only altered my body but my brain too.

Kristina's words drift through my mind. "You know, my P.T. thinks I should join a support group."

"You totally should, but quit changing the subject."

Grrr. Why is she fighting me on every little thing?

"Don't tell me what to do. You don't know what I'm going through."

"Fine." Lisa's clipped tone matches my own. "I'll talk to you later," and she ends the call.

I don't know how to tell her why what she's saying is bothering me. More like hurting me. Even though I know she doesn't mean to.

Am I ever going to feel like me again?

~~~***~~~

I expect the UnBRCAble support group to look like something out of a sad movie where everyone sits in a circle on uncomfortable chairs in the basement of a church, reeking of desperation and despair.

I don't know why I have this expectation. It's not in a church. It's at the Genevieve T. Wunderlich Women's Health Center, right where my P.T. is. As I walk through the doors, I'm stunned that this support group could not be further from my expectations. The room is warm and comfy, with lots of plush (but not too deep) couches, and plenty of pillows to prop or brace or whatever we need to do.

There's a fancy coffee machine, a fruit bowl, and pastries. I should probably have some fruit.

Cheese Danish it is.

What this place really needs is an open bar.

I take my seat, preferring an upholstered armchair, like in the doctor's office. I still can't use my arms to push up but it looks like it'll be easier to stand from than the couches.

I'll just sit here and listen and observe. Maybe in a few weeks I'll get up the nerve to participate.

"What're you in for?"

I look up to see a woman wearing a white T-shirt that says, "Does this mastectomy make my butt look big?"

I need that shirt.

"Oh, um, I'm new here."

"I know that. I'm not. What's your story?"

Her frank demeanor makes me stumble over my words again. I take a quick breath and then spit out my letters, like I'm giving rank and serial number. "Millie. NSPBM, DTI, UTM."

"How many weeks post-op?"

"Four."

"You're through the tough part. Should get easier from here on out."

"I can wipe again, but I still love the bidet, so I might keep on using it." These are not words I could say to anyone else.

"BRCA?"

"Type One," I say, confirming my mutation. Every person carries the BRCA gene. It's the mutations (type one or type two) that make the genes not work to suppress tumors and cancer like they're supposed to. That's why we mutants have such a high chance of developing the Big C.

"Mom?" I notice her eyes soften, the wrinkles around them deepening.

"Breast and grandmother ovarian."

She gingerly puts her hand on my shoulder. "I'm Claudia, PBM with DIEP flap. My mom and three aunts. All four girls. But it won't be me. Oh, and relax. You're with your people now."

I want to ask what she means by that and what a DIEP flap is, but I feel like I should know both. I make a mental note to look up the latter when I get home.

As if some silent signal goes out, the women take their seats. It's less formal than the circle of chairs I'd envisioned but the same effect. Claudia is apparently the group leader.

"Hey ladies. We've a new member with us today." She turns toward me. "I have a quick spiel for new members."

"Don't feel the need to spiel for me."

She smiles sympathetically. "This is a safe space. There are no dumb questions, only dumb people, and they're not the people in this group. Feel free to ask whatever you need to. Trust us," she looks around to the group, "if you have the question, someone here's been through it. We're all at varying stages of healing and recovery, but everyone here is a previvor, just like you. Welcome, Sister Millie."

I lift my hand in a tentative wave as the members of the group say their welcomes and hellos. When the room grows quiet again, I manage to squeak out, "I'll just listen for right now, if that's okay."

Heads bob up and down in agreement. A woman across the room breaks the tension. "Well, I'm losing the nip."

Everyone's attention turns to her, alleviating some of the pressure on me. In spite of all the horrible things we've already endured, the thought of losing your nipple after going through a nipple-sparing procedure is absolutely devastating. I don't know why. I mean, the rest of the breast is gone. There's nothing inside the chest. The nipple is a small thing, and it doesn't even have the sensation it used to. I can't even feel mine.

But Claudia was right. As I sit here for the hour, which flies by faster than a massage, I laugh and I cry. But for the first time since Dr. Tremarchi gave me the news, I don't feel alone in this battle.

Hope, a tiny little light, begins to swell in my chest.

"Anyone have anything else?" Claudia asks.

Before I know it, my hand is creeping up, as fast and as high as it will go. I wince a bit, but straighten my back.

"Sister Millie?"

"I'm sure this has been covered before, but can I ask something?"

Claudia nods. "Feel free. You have the conch."

I take a deep breath, steeling my nerves before starting. "Okay, so I know this sounds stupid, but whenever my best friend—who's been totally awesome and supportive throughout all this—makes a comment about getting new and better boobs, I want to punch her. It's probably a good thing I can't lift my arms."

Instead of hearing that I'm overreacting or that I'm a terrible person—which is what I've been telling myself—the responses go something like this:

"Preach it, sister."

"I went off on my sister-in-law who complained that I got a free boob job."

"Ugh, I hate that."

"If I had a nickel for every time ..."

Claudia finishes with, "Girl, you are speaking our language. At least one person every week brings it up. It bothers us all. If only it were so easy as a boob job. Is this easy?"

I shake my head. Claudia continues. "Then you need to tell your friend why it bothers you. Educate her. She doesn't know. Before this, did you know?"

Again with the head shake.

"There's your answer."

The ladies stand up to leave. I should linger and thank Claudia for the warm reception but suddenly I need to get out of there. I need air and room to breathe and to wake up from this horrible dream.

I still cannot believe that this is my life. My reality.

The feeling that everything might be okay evaporates into thin air. Some of these women had their procedures years ago, but they're still in the group. I don't want to be like that. I want to get better and move on and go back to my old self, complete with all my reproductive organs and mammary glands intact.

Claudia's T-shirt flashes into my mind. If I can't remember that I'm lucky, then maybe plastering it across my new body will remind me.

Time to go T-shirt shopping.

CHAPTER 11

This is not good. Completely and totally not good. Drink plenty of water, they say. You need to stay hydrated, they say. There's a reason why teachers are chronically dehydrated. Because when you drink a lot, you have to go to the bathroom a lot.

And this is my current predicament.

I have to pee.

Not really an earth-shattering need except for one thing. In the six weeks or so since I had my surgery, I became quite addicted to my bidet. (I wonder if there's a support group for that?) Based on things I read online, it was a necessity to maintain some dignity while staying clean *down there*. Plus, when I couldn't shower regularly, it was a godsend for helping me feel not so icky.

So now I have to go—badly—but on the wall, *right above my toilet*, is a stink bug.

Bugs are bugs.

Except for these monstrosities.

You only kill one once.

The memory of the smell *still* makes me want to vomit.

So crushing the sucker is not an option on the table. My bladder tells me to come up with a solution and quick.

There's no way I can sit down and take a chance that it will fly into my hair.

Staring at the intruder, I'm interrupted by my doorbell ringing. Dad and Aunt Polly come right in, so I can't image who's here. Lisa is working through the weekend on her case. I don't have anyone from Helping Wagon scheduled for today.

Well, what do you know? It might be the answer to my problem.

"Sterling, I didn't realize you were stopping by, but I'm so happy you're here! There's a very—oh, you're going to laugh."

Not only is he a man, and therefore adept at all things bugs, but he can reach up. He'll trap the thing and I can go and get clean and things will be wonderful again.

He bends over in a mock bow. "Promise I won't, miss. How may I assist thee?"

The lilt of his voice. His slightly tousled hair. Swoonsville.

I feel like something out of an Austen novel. I put my hand over my heart, sliding it up quickly until I get to the part where I can feel my skin again. "Oh, please keep talking like that. I could listen to your voice forever. Even if it's reading tax code."

"Section three-a, subsequent to the previous predicate..." Sterling smiles, talking absolute gibberish, as I step aside to let him in.

I can't help but laugh. But then the laughing reminds me of the issue that will not go away. I may have to suck it up and use my other bathroom, but it won't solve the issue of the stink bug. "You can continue but there's a more pressing issue. I have to go to the bathroom."

His eyebrow arches in interest. "I see. Well, not really. How exactly may I be of service in the bathroom?"

"There's a stink bug on the wall above the toilet. I can't get it, and I'm afraid it will jump into my hair or something. Can you please get it for me?"

Sterling freezes and his face pales. "I'm not sure— stink bugs may be outside my wheelhouse."

Crap. "Oh, well, okay then. No worries. Did you need something from me?" I shift uncomfortably. I'm going to need to use my other bathroom.

"Do you have another toilet you can use? You look like you really have to piddle."

"Yes, I suppose. It's just ..." I trail off.

Sterling squares his shoulders and takes a deep breath. "Point me to this insect. I'm sure I can handle it."

I lead him down the hall and point. On the wall, about six feet from the ground, sits the potentially offensive insect, its tan exoskeleton like a wardrobe of prehistoric armor.

I hand him a disposable cup and a piece of paper. "Normally I'd get it, but it's too high for me right now."

Sterling glances at me and then back at the bug.

Approaching slowly but then moving as fast as lightning, he traps the bug by placing the cup over it and against the wall. Once the paper slides in between the cup and the wall, he gingerly pulls the cup back. The angered bug flits up against the paper and his hand.

Ewww.

If that were me, there's a decent chance—okay a one-hundred percent chance—that the bug's flitting would have made me drop the cup. And bug. And probably wet myself in the process.

I step aside so he can dispose of the offensive creature outside. I wonder if it'd be imposing to ask Sterling to take the bug a few blocks away. Like maybe over a river and across a highway or something.

While he takes care of that, I take care of nature calling.

So ... much ... relief.

I'm not sure why Sterling arrived when he did, but he's got to think I have a few screws loose. First the penguin, then the refusal to kill the bug. Thank goodness I didn't pee my pants in front of him.

I don't think it needs explaining, but I'm not really myself these days.

Sterling walks back in, phone to his ear.

"Alright, mate. I'm going to put you on speaker."

Confused, I look at him. He sits on the couch, so I sit next to him. A tap or two on his phone and then I hear a voice. It's similar to Sterling's, but the accent is heavier.

"Yeah, am I on?"

"Stu, you're on."

"Who's there?" the voice says.

"Stu, Millie. Millie, my brother Stu."

"Okay. Um, hi Stu." I don't know what else to say.

"I slayed a dragon, brother, and this pretty lady here won't get the significance of it, so I need you to tell her what a big deal it is." Sterling grins at me. My face matches his.

"Can't resist the urge to jump in and fix things, can you? What did you do this time? Let me guess ... hmm ... well, it could be ... that thing that we are forbaten to mention." I never knew you could hear someone being cheeky, but that's exactly how I would describe Sterling's brother's voice.

"No, and is forbaten even a word? Don't you mean forbidden or verboten?" Sterling interjects quickly. He looks at me. I shrug my shoulders and shake my head. I don't think so, but then again, there are a lot of words I don't know. "Next guess."

"Shut it, brother. Now Millie, it is Millie isn't it?"

"It still is Millie." I like how Sterling and Stu talk to each other. I wonder how many other kids there are in his family. It'd been my dream to have brothers and sisters growing up.

"Millie, can you provide some information for me about my younger, much uglier brother's moment of triumph? In what location did it occur?"

If Sterling is the less attractive brother, I need to see a picture of Stu.

"Um, well, my bathroom."

"Does it involve a bidet?"

What a random thing to ask. Especially considering bidets are not hugely common in America. How did he know?

"Sort of," I answer. Sterling looks at me quizzically.

He interjects. "No."

I hold up my hand to pause Sterling, not that Stu can see me. "Wait. Stu, why did you ask if it involved a bidet?"

Stu laughs. "You see, our aunt's house in the south of France had one."

It's Sterling's turn to interrupt. "Yes, and you see, Millie, I got into heap loads of trouble playing with it. I bet Samantha is still miffed about that. I was banned from using it."

At first, I thought they sounded the same, but after even these few moments, I can tell the difference. Stu drops the '-er' sound at the end of words. Younga brotha. I really do need to see what Stu looks like.

"Who's Samantha?"

"Our sister," Stu answers.

"So what happened?" I'm not sure I want to know, but I can't not know at this point.

"Let's just say there was a bit of a kerfuffle with my brother and my sister, and I took the fall," Sterling answers.

"A *bit* of a kerfuffle?" Stu laughs.

"Alright, it was totally my fault, but I didn't think I'd go down alone. Stu was totally in on it as well."

"No brother, that was all you."

Sterling clears his throat. "But that's not the point of this call, Stu. Guess again."

"Before I do, Millie, why did you say it sort of related to a bidet?"

"I have one in the bathroom. That's why I needed Sterling to—" He waves and shakes his head to prevent me from spoiling the surprise. "I went to use it and was unable. And then Sterling saved the day, even though he said he couldn't. He came to my rescue."

Stu starts laughing. "Oh my God, brother. Did you actually kill a bug?"

Sterling covers his face. "Worse. I had to capture and release."

"A STINK BUG!" Stu's laughing so hard there's barely a sound coming from the phone.

Sterling hangs up without saying another word. Huh. Interesting behavior. Someone hanging up on me, short of being disconnected due to a natural disaster, is a deal breaker in my book.

Sterling's laughing too, so obviously I've missed the inside joke.

"Are you going to tell me what this is all about?"

Sterling wipes his eyes. "I shouldn't, because it's not very manly, but I don't like bugs."

"That's okay. My dad is scared of snakes. Just like Indiana Jones."

"Yes, but I doubt your father has a brother with a proclivity for putting insects of all sorts in various places where they didn't belong. Like my pants. Underpants that is ... while I was wearing them."

Maybe it's a good thing I never had a brother.

I join Sterling in his laughter. "Well, then I really need to thank you for going out on a limb for me. As it is, I will forever be in your debt."

His face reddens a bit. "We're square."

Why? This makes no sense. So I ask him that.

"Piper told me about the Teddy Grahams."

Now it's my turn to blush. "What can I say? I need a sweet snack sometimes during the day." I look down at my hands and try not to notice that we're only inches apart on the couch.

"But how you went about it ... making it a special treat to 'share' them with you when you knew very well she had no snack packed." He looks down. "I'm still livid that Candice would send her without a snack."

I search my memory. "It was only a few times. And she's not the only one." I shrug. "I don't think anyone realized."

"My ma didn't always make sure we had proper food. It galls me to think my own child could be experiencing that. And for no reason, really. Candice can afford food. She doesn't put forth the effort."

I look into his eyes, and can see the agony on behalf of his child. The pain of his own childhood. "Sterling, it's okay, really. Even the most diligent of families have a bad day and forget a snack now and again. Plus, it gives me an excuse to buy them. The chocolate chip ones are my favorite."

"It's not fine with me, but I never got the chance to thank you."

"Um, the Helping Wagon? Not only setting it up, but all the help you've personally provided. Not to mention conquering your fear of bugs to rescue me. I'll never be able to repay you."

"Anything for you, love."

My heart skips a beat. I need to rein this in before someone—namely me—gets their heart broken. He's only trying to repay a kindness. I need to stay in a safe zone.

"Where are you in relation to your siblings? Are you the youngest?" Family. A nice safe subject.

"Stuart is eleven months older than me, then Samantha is two years younger, and Sarah two years after that."

"Wow. Irish twins. You mom must have had her hands full." I can't imagine how noisy and chaotic the house must have been. And how wonderful.

"No, I'm English. I grew up in Ipswich. England, not Massachusetts."

His response confuses me for a minute, then I realize he didn't get my reference to Irish twins.

"No, the fact that you and your brother are less than a year apart. We call those Irish twins. I didn't mean Irish-Irish. I know you're English." Then, for some reason unbeknownst to my brain, I keep talking. "Wouldn't it have been funny if you lived in Ipswich, Mass too? Ipswich." More words continue to spill from my mouth. It's like watching a train wreck in slow motion. I'm powerless to control the verbal diarrhea. "Ipswich, Ipswich, Ipswich. I just like to say it. I may have to move there someday, if only to be able to have an excuse to say Ipswich."

"Well, now you can say, 'I have a friend from Ipswich.'"

"I will work that in at every chance I get. Sterling, my friend from Ipswich."

Sterling glances at me, and I can't read the look on his face. Pleasure? Horror? I can't tell.

Leave it to me to scare him off just when we were getting to know each other. Before he runs for the hills, maybe he can add a spot to the Helping Wagon to give me lessons in how to talk to other people.

Probably can't hurt, right?

CHAPTER 12

I'm a moron. A totally idiot. Okay, partial idiot.

You can't just announce someone is your friend, especially not when you barely know him. Especially not when he feels sorry for you.

Especially not when he has those piercing hazel eyes.

But most especially when you can't date again. Ever. Because I can never, ever imagine a time when I will be comfortable enough with my body to let someone else see it. Touch it. I don't want to see it or touch it. There's no way anyone—even Sterling—is saint enough to get past the scars and disfigurement.

But Sterling's still sitting there. Smiling even. "Indeed. Please do that." He reaches out and puts his hand on mine.

"Tell everyone you're from Ipswich?" Saying that word really does make me smile.

"Tell everyone I'm your friend." He looks at his feet and clears his throat. "If that's okay with you, I mean."

"Sure. I guess. Yeah. Okay." Coherent thought much?

"So, friend, I've something important to ask you." He gives my hand a squeeze and stands up. He walks over and looks out my window for a moment.

Well, crap. Here it comes. Sterling's been one of the few Helping Wagon volunteers who hasn't asked direct, pointed, and honestly rude questions about my health and medical status. I can't not answer them, so many more people in the community know about my bits and pieces. Well, where my bits and pieces used to be.

Not super comfortable on my end.

I steel myself for Sterling's inevitable questions. Even if he were considering me more than a friend—which I totally know he's not—the knowledge of my empty pelvis and foobs would end that right quick.

He turns to look at me, playing nervously with his phone. "Can you show me your bidet?"

This is not what I was expecting.

He never says what I expect.

I like that.

"Um, sure. It's not a full extra toilet thing you know." I'm making motions with my hands as I'm walking, partially because I'm flustered, but mostly because I don't know what to call it when you have a separate toilet bidet.

"Right. I saw that. I didn't know they made extra attachments. Quite interesting."

It takes me a minute to remember that my hiney hose, as I'd dubbed it, is what started this conversation with Stu, which meandered into bugs in underwear, siblings, Irish twins, my potential faux pas, and Ipswich.

I've had rounds of Mad Libs that were more mundane than this conversation.

He says nothing as he follows me down the hall to the bathroom. I step out while he looks, and pray that the toilet is clean.

Now that the excitement of my bidet is done, Sterling looks at me. "I've got to go get a new air filter for my car. I was going to run to Master Auto Man. Want to come?"

"To the auto parts store?" It's not like I have tons of other plans. UnBRCAble doesn't meet until tomorrow, and I'm down to going to P.T. twice a week. Getting out of the house wouldn't be the worst thing. I look down at my loose-fitting yoga pants and shirt. Shirts, really, because I'm still layering a camisole over my surgical bra, and then a T-shirt or button up over that. At least I don't have to wear the camisole under my bra anymore. I've graduated to wearing it over the bra.

Baby steps.

Kristina keeps telling me I'm clear to stop wearing the surgical bra, and frankly, wearing a pull-over shirt was a moment of victory. Sure it was three sizes larger than I normally wear, but the idea of a regular T-shirt was a relief.

"Yes. And then maybe we can grab a bite to eat, if you're feeling up for it."

OMG, is this a date? I'm guessing anything that involves auto parts should not be considered a date, but beggars can't be choosers.

It must be a pity invite. I mean, he clearly stated we were *friends*.

And even if Sterling wanted more, it's not like I'm dating material. I'm in the damaged goods bin.

"Oh, do you have other plans?" Sterling asks. "I'm not trying to pry. I didn't mean to be rude."

"No, it's fine. I was, uh ... it's nothing. Can you give me a minute to change?" .

"I like you just the way you are, Millie Dwyer."

Swoon.

"My clothes. These are lounging clothes, not out-in-public clothes."

"Right. Take your time. I'll be here waiting for you."

As I walk to my bedroom, I can't help but think maybe he means more than the time it'll take to get dressed.

Now crap, what am I supposed to wear? Master Auto Man would normally call for housework clothes, but food after ...? I haven't worn real clothes in the six-plus weeks since my surgery.

Then I see it. That great maxi dress Lisa bought for me. Since my previous cup size was the equivalent of a sippy cup, strapless wasn't in my repertoire. Lisa found this—in a petite size no less—and convinced me that my new foobs needed it. She asks me every day if I've worn the dress yet. I can't wait to tell her tonight that I finally wore it. To go out with Sterling, no less.

It's not a date because I don't date anymore, but if I did, this could be. Except it can't.

At least the dress will be great. Considering that it's over ninety degrees outside, the dress, with its airy fabric, will be perfect. Except for the ugly, white surgical bra.

I can do this. I can go without and let the girls stand up for themselves for once. My sutures are healed and the scars are even starting to fade, thanks to daily use of cocoa butter and vitamin E. My nips appear to be here to stay.

It's time.

The cream top is decorated with a salmon and gray embroidery which matches the pattern in the skirt. It's weird as I pull up the dress, sans bra. What's the term for going braless? Upstairs commando? Tits on the loose?

I adjust the top, pulling it up a little more. I'm looking at it in the mirror, but I don't feel it against my breasts. Where my breasts used to be. I put my hands over them. My hands feel my foobs, but my foobs don't feel my hands. I don't know that I'll ever get used to this lack of sensation. The doctor says it might come back. Someday.

Might.

My hands smooth down the front of the dress, the fabric sliding between my fingers. Despite the numbness, for the first time since my hysterectomy, and definitely since the mastectomy, I sort of feel like a girl.

Not a real girl, because I'm not that anymore. Not a girl who goes on dates and falls in love and gets married and has babies.

But this dress makes me feel feminine in a way I didn't know I still could feel. Almost as if feeling feminine has nothing to do with my ovaries or breasts.

The humidity outside means my curls are threatening a coup, so they are pulled up into a clip.

Silver hoops and flip flops complete my easy summer look.

As I come down the stairs, Sterling jumps to his feet, a smile stretching across his face from ear to ear. I feel like I'm having that movie moment where the main character appears all beautified, ready for the prom. I'm Rachael Leigh Cook, Julia Stiles, and Julia Roberts all rolled into one.

I'm so ready for the air filter department.

~~~***~~~

The gods are finally smiling on me. Here I am, finally starting to feel good again. I haven't had a hot flash at all today, and I'm walking next to a hot British guy who also happens to be a caring father and a genuine soul.

To quote Oliver, "Please sir, can I have some more?"

Let's face it, it's not like I was a rock star with romance before all this either. I've got a knack for picking the wrong guy. Exhibit A. Johnny the Weasel who dumped me post-op. So really, it's not a bad thing. Before Johnny there were Tommy and Billy.

Perhaps I need to stop going for men whose names sound like ten-year-olds boys.

If I were still dating, I would make that a rule.

But I'm not.

What I am doing is trying to tell the butterflies in my stomach to simmer down. It's not a date. It's not a date.

Then why is Sterling looking at me like it's a date?

"Am I too dressed up? Did I go overboard?" I look down. This dress is stupid. We're getting car parts, not going somewhere fancy. He must think I'm an idiot.

"You look smashing."

Smashing.

It's all I can do not to do a little skip as we head out to his car. Once again, Sterling opens my door.

He's an honest-to-God gentleman. And if I weren't me right now, I'd be giving a little squee.

What the hell. *Squee.*

Internally, I'm telling myself to play it cool.

"Where should we go after?"

"I don't care. I'm easy. Well not *easy*, easy. I mean, I'm not a prude either. I put out. I mean not now because I'm still recovering. Plus it's daylight and I—"

So much for playing it cool.

I clear my throat and try to recover. "I could go for a burger."

Do you think he'd notice if I started banging my head against the dashboard?

Sterling glances at me and smiles. "You are a breath of fresh air, Millie Dwyer. Absolutely delightful."

The butterflies are back, and this time, they've brought friends.

We hit Master Auto Man, and I'm practically walking on air. This is so a date.

Maybe I've been too hard on myself about not being able to date. Maybe a date here and there would be okay. A relationship—that's another story.

But if someone finds me *smashing* and wants to take me for a burger, I should be able to handle that.

Mission: Air Filter is complete, and we're heading toward the front of the store. There's only one person ahead of us as we get in line.

"Oh, crap." Sterling stops abruptly. His eyes dart from side to side, obviously searching for something.

"The bathroom's in the back of the store. Do you think you can make it?" I try not to grimace at my stupid response. I have absolutely no idea why I said that. It's like I have the sense of humor of a ten-year-old boy, always making a bathroom joke.

Sterling smiles. "Clever. No, I need to get new wiper blades."

"That's not a big deal. You stay in line and I'll run and get them. What year is your car?"

"Brilliant. You're so much more than a pretty face. You're the best." He tells me the make and model, and I hurry off to the back of the store.

I think I float to aisle six. My feet can't possibly be on the ground.

Sterling Kane called me pretty.

I find the replacement wiper blades. A quick glance at the chart, and I've got the right ones, I hope. I'm glad he sent me for these and not a car battery that would probably be too heavy for me to life. I head up toward the front of the store.

I see one man, an elderly one, watching me. I'm sure they don't get many women in dresses here. I hold my head high and keep walking. The look on his face makes me uncomfortable, though I can't tell why. Maybe he thinks I'm smashing too.

Next I pass a tired looking woman who glares at me. Okay, I'm not seeing things. That was definitely a dirty look. Maybe she's bitter that I'm young. God, if she only walked a day in my shoes, she'd be a little more kind.

I'm approaching the register when I get the distinct impression that people are really watching me. I thought I looked good, and the compliment from Sterling really boosted me. My confidence radiates from me in waves.

I, Millie Dwyer, am having a kick ass day in Master Auto Man.

I see Sterling and give him a little wave with my right hand. He starts to wave, approaching me. As he gets nearer, his speed accelerates.

God, he can't wait to be near me again.

Sterling is practically running to me. He pulls up just short of barreling into me. Before I know it, his hands are reaching up.

He's going to grab my face and kiss me, just like in the movies! I never thought this would ...

Wait.

What's he doing?

What is he reaching for?

Oh, God, I want to die.

CHAPTER 13

Thank the Lord for my support group.

But seriously, they really need to serve adult beverages here.

"Oh my God, what did you do?" Claudia's covering her mouth.

I swallow, reliving the horrible embarrassment of the moment. My face flames at the memory, and I still want to puke. "Well, first off, I leaned in and puckered my lips, getting ready for our first kiss. Then I felt his hand on the underside of my arm, right by my armpit. And then I looked down."

There it was, for the entire world to see.

My left foob.

Hanging out where the top of my dress had slid down.

Erin uncrosses her long legs and hunches forward, almost to a fetal position. She starts rocking back and forth. "What did you do?"

I take a deep breath. "What every single one of you would have done. I shoved the wipers at him and ran out of the store, hands clutching the top of my dress. Of course he drove, so it was even more awful. I had to stand by his car, sobbing like a baby, and wait for him to come out to drive me home." I don't mention how my sad crying turned into a hysterical mixture of laughter and tears. I walked around Master Auto Man with my breast exposed and had no idea.

I will never, ever, as long as I live, get over this.

In a related news, I will never be able to go in an auto part store again. I may give up driving.

I take a deep breath and look around the room. There's nodding and worry and empathy but no pity.

These ladies get it.

Tracey offers. "I once texted about thirty pictures of my breasts—pre and post surgical—to my accountant instead of my plastic surgeon."

"Your accountant?"

Tracey grimaces. "They have the same last name. I actually think they're brothers. So close, yet so different. I've got to be the laughing stock of their family dinners. I must have typed the wrong thing in. And the worst part is I always thought the accountant was hot."

"What'd he say the next time you had to get your taxes done?" Claudia asks.

"Don't know," Tracey shrugs. "Never went back. I've been filing my taxes by myself. If I ever get arrested for tax evasion, it's all because of my boobs."

One by one, women speak up, sharing their stories. Terrible stories. Mortifying events that most people would never recover from. But we're all laughing. Laughing and crying and laughing some more.

I look around the room, warmth spreading through me. I don't know how to explain it, but even though I've only been here a few times, I feel so close to these women. My sisters in survival. People I didn't know existed and certainly didn't know I needed. The siblings I've always wanted.

I wipe my eyes, certain my mascara is running down my face. And I don't even care. It's not like Sterling will be back again, certainly not after the hysterics in the car.

Not after I walked around Master Auto Man like I was auditioning for a nudist colony.

Did I mention the hysterics?

"What did he say?" Somehow the conversation has returned to me and my indecent exposure.

"In all honesty, I don't know. I was too upset." This is true. I've been trying to recall what his mortification looked like, but I can only remember my own horrifying display.

I didn't even tell Lisa. She wouldn't get it. I'm afraid that she'd laugh at me. She'd try to tell me it wasn't that bad or I should have played it off or I should have asked him if he was interested in what he saw. Plus, I'm mad at her for buying me that dress. Really this whole blessed thing is her fault. I know she thought she was being helpful. Trying to make me see the bright side, all the new clothes I can wear. To show off my "new and improved tatas."

Which of course, is exactly what I did.

Just not in the way that was intended.

Today my foobs are safely harnessed back in the surgical bra. I'm wearing a T-shirt that says, "Yes, they are fake. My real ones tried to kill me." Since I've flashed the whole world, I might as well own my foobs. Claudia has the same shirt.

"I think part of what makes it so awful is that I should have explained to him why it happened and why I look so disfigured." Maybe I can wear this T-shirt every day until he sees it. Which means I should probably buy a few more. Piper still has three more years until she goes to middle school, which means I'm bound to see him sooner or later.

I suppose I could look for another job.

It might be easier than having to speak to him again.

I can always move.

"He doesn't know?" Claudia looks concerned. "How can he not know? Didn't he trim your bush?"

"My actual bush, not my bush-bush." I look at my hands, tightly wound in my lap once again. "I don't know what he knows. Whatever he does know, none of it came from me."

Erin shakes her head in confusion. "What?"

"One of the things I've liked about hanging out with him is he doesn't ask me what's going on. I don't have to listen to his platitudes or tell him embarrassing things, though I seem to be doing a good job embarrassing myself all on my own. For all I know, someone at school filled him in on the goings on with my lady parts."

"But you don't know that for sure?" Erin clarifies.

"I've never said anything to him, and he's never asked. He knows I had surgery, but that's about it."

"Do you think if you told him, it would make things better?"

I don't know how to answer that. I've told the billions of people who've asked me.

I like that Sterling never asked.

It was like he didn't care. He didn't pity my poor barren womb. Make that the area where my womb used to be. Maybe things started with him feeling sorry for me, but I don't think that's the reason he keeps coming by. I think he genuinely likes me.

For the time I was with him, I was normal Millie.

Old Millie, normal Millie is gone forever.

Just like my chances of anything with Sterling Kane.

It's time to get Cornelius back from my dad, and, I should probably look into getting a few—dozen—more cats. I might as well embrace the crazy cat lady thing too.

Oh, and I'll take up knitting. I'll be the stereotypical spinster. I'll probably even start giving out pencils and dental floss on Halloween. As soon as I get home, I'm going to look for an eyeglass chain.

And I don't even wear glasses.

CHAPTER 14

He has to think I'm a lunatic.

I don't blame him. I keep acting like one. I was all sorts of a mess after ... the incident ... yesterday. Who wouldn't be?

Even the girls of UnBRCAble couldn't make this one better. It wasn't for lack of trying, either. They all have their stories. We all have our stories. I mean, it's nice to know that I'm not alone in the abject humiliation. Seems there's always room for one more at that party.

When I see his car pull up, I shouldn't be surprised. But I am.

Of course Sterling's the type of guy to dump me in person rather than through a text or by ghosting.

He even has flowers. They're yellows and greens, which does not indicate romance.

No duh. Who'd want to romance this?

Best to face the music.

I open the door as he approaches. Of course, his eyes go right to my chest. *Yes, they're covered.*

Sterling freezes, staring right at my chest. His mouth opens and closes. I have to look down to see what he's looking at. Heck, for all I know, I could be hanging out again.

Oh, right. The shirt.

Yes, these are fake. My real ones tried to kill me.

Well, I guess the cat's out of the bag now.

Sterling's arm drifts up, presenting the flowers. They're at a weird angle, like his arm doesn't have the strength to hold the bouquet. Then he starts talking.

Rambling is more like it.

"I moved here when I was sixteen. School in America was different than back home. There were all these tests. And answer sheets."

Once again, I have no idea where he's going with this. That doesn't stop the words from tumbling out of his mouth.

"The answer sheets that you had to fill in the little circles with a pencil, but only a certain type of pencil. And the circle had to be exactly filled in, and you couldn't have any extra marks or it would be wrong. Since I transferred schools right in the middle of secondary, I was already paranoid about my chances at going onto a decent uni. I didn't even know if I'd be able to in America. But the last thing I wanted was extra marks on my answer sheet to be the cause."

I briefly wonder if I'm high. I have no idea what he's talking about or what this has to do with anything.

He continues. "So there I am, brand new kid in school. It wasn't the easiest transition and lots of people thought I was odd. I didn't dress like anyone else, and I had acne. Plus, my hands and feet had grown, but my limbs had yet to catch up, so to sum up, I was funny looking."

I look at the gorgeous specimen in front of me. "I find that hard to believe."

He gives me a tight smile. "Plus, I hadn't yet had the benefit of American dental and orthodontic care."

That makes me laugh. He returns my smile, showing a row of straight white teeth. I guess he got that taken care of.

"So it's the first time I'm taking one of these tests. The only pencil I could find that was the right kind was this little nub. Like a golf pencil, I suppose. I'm about two-thirds of the way through the test when I realize I skipped a question, and I've been coloring all the wrong circles. My pencil is woefully unprepared to handle this task."

I still can't see what this has to do with my public nudity. It's an odd way to break up. Can you break up if you aren't even dating? "Sterling, I don't know what you're doing here, but can you please wrap it up? I'm not feeling up to company right now."

"Right. So I need to correct what I've done. I lean over to the girl next to me—Stacey Mulligan—and ask her if she ..." Color rises in his cheeks.

As a teacher, I don't like where this is going. Dread fills my stomach. Why would you talk to someone during a test? "Did you get in trouble for cheating?"

"No, but I wish it had been that simple. You see, there are many words that are not the same in America as they are in England."

"Obviously." I remember the whole fanny, vajayjay debacle.

"So, I asked Stacey, who was the most popular girl in my class by the way, if she had a rubber I could borrow."

"A rubber?" *Why would he ask for a condom during the middle of a test?*

"An eraser, of course. But we call them rubbers. Stacey didn't know that, so she said just what you did. 'A rubber?' to which I replied, 'Yes, a rubber.' I didn't know what she didn't understand about it."

"Oh my God, what she did say?"

"She gave me a look that would kill a cat and said, 'what do you want to do with it?'"

"What did you tell her?"

His face is full-on scarlet now. "I told her, 'To rub one out, naturally.'"

My hands fly to my mouth, unable to control my laughter. Oh. My. God.

"You see, Millie, we all have moments of mortification. I asked the most popular girl in all of high school for a condom to masturbate during the middle of a math test. One does not live that down."

The words come tumbling out. "I had a mastectomy and reconstruction, and I can't feel my chest. I had no idea I was hanging out."

He nods toward my shirt. "So I gathered."

I step aside. "Please come in. I'm sorry for yesterday."

"I'm sorry too. I ..."

I get it. No one knows what to say to me.

Might as well get on with it. Time to lighten the mood. "So did you ever recover from your faux-pas?"

"Certainly. Almost no one calls me 'Pink Pearl' anymore."

"Oh, God. I put those on the school supply list every year. They are the bomb in the eraser world. And trust me, I know my stationary."

"Nothing but the best to rub one out."

I laugh and sit down gingerly in my recliner. Now that the cat's out of the bag, I should probably explain Pepé.

"Are you okay now?" He's still clutching the flowers. Finally, he remembers they're in his hand and lays them gently on the coffee table.

"I think I won't be going to Master Auto Man ever again. Or wearing that dress."

"Don't be rash. It looked nice. Very nice."

I look doubtfully at him. I don't need his patronage.

"Right. I meant nice when we left the house. Not nice after it fell down. Although come to think of it, that looked pretty nice, too." He takes a moment to catch his breath and try to back up the diarrhea-mouth bus. "I don't know much about any of it, I'm afraid. I think I'll apologize in advance if I ask stupid questions, and, you know, other stupid things I might say. Like the thing I just said." His face is progressively turning pinker by the moment.

"You would not believe what people feel free to ask. Especially the people who stopped by with the

Helping Wagon." The list of invasive questions is long and horrifying.

"Really?"

"Yes, well, most people wanted to know what happened to me. Probably to see if I was worth the effort of their tuna casserole."

"Probably because they're nosey arses."

"Or that." I laugh.

"I'll ask my one question. Are you going to be okay?" He seems genuinely concerned, as opposed to simply being nosy.

"Yes. I'm good to go. I may have to have one more procedure, but the doctor is thinking maybe not. It'd be minor, especially compared to all this." I wave my hand in front of the foobs.

"What about chemo and radiation and all that?"

"Oh, I don't have breast cancer."

That's the stumper. Sometimes it's nice to see people process that. I'm fairly confident they all think I'm certifiable. But I don't want Sterling thinking that so I continue. "I tested positive for the BRCA gene mutation, which means I had an eighty-percent chance of developing breast cancer. My mom died of it when I was ten, and her mom died of ovarian cancer. So I decided not to take that chance."

"Oh." He seems stymied. "Well, that sucks, doesn't it?"

I love that answer. I could practically kiss him for not telling me to look on the bright side.

"On good days, I consider myself lucky. I grew up thinking that I would die young. I've now got the best odds in at least three generations. I'm more likely to be hit by a bus than to die of cancer, which is the first time in my life I can actually say that."

"So, that's it, and you're fine and good as new."

I look down at my shirt. "I don't know that I'd call it good as new, but new nonetheless."

"When I ran into you in the hospital?"

"I'd just had this done." Please don't ask more. Don't ask the personal questions. Don't ask me if I'd wanted kids before.

He holds up his hand. "I don't need to know, unless you want me to. Tell me what you want to. What you need to. Tell me if I'm not saying or doing the right thing."

"Sterling, you need to tell me one thing."

"Certainly."

"Why are you here?" I can't believe I came right out and said that.

"Because, Millie Dwyer, I cannot seem to stay away."

Swoon.

CHAPTER 15

"I thought last night he was going to kiss me, but he didn't."

"Where did you go?" Lisa's voice is distant, like I'm on speaker. I hate when she does that.

"We got ice cream from Lickety Splits and then took a walk. It was nice."

"Yeah, so what do you have to complain about?"

"It's like he thinks I'm in a bubble and he's afraid to pop me." I'm trying not to notice that he hasn't held my hand since he found out.

"And he's okay with it all?"

I wish Lisa's tone didn't hold so much surprise. She's been telling me my dating life was just beginning all along.

Obviously, she was placating me.

"He seems to be. He's been great really." I want to add that he's been better than she has recently. I know she's trying, but ...

"Only you could go in for surgery and pick up a guy. Maybe I should try cruising the surgical ward."

See what I mean?

"Yes, well, I guess all the pain and body mutilation was worth it. I mean, it was that or certain death. Next thing I know, you'll tell me I took the easy way out."

There's silence on the line for a bit.

"You don't have to get nasty about it."

"Lis, I know you're trying to be helpful, but some of the things you say, well, they're hurtful."

Lisa mutters something that I can't make out.

"What was that?"

"Nothing. I'll talk to you later." She disconnects before I can interject anything else.

Well this just sucks.

Now who am I going to dissect every little thing Sterling says and does with?

I mean, I'm not even sure what's going on. He comes over most nights when he doesn't have Piper. Sometimes Piper's mom is unpredictable with her schedule, which means Sterling cancels at the last minute. At least it's for a worthy cause, and not because he wants to grab a beer at the bar with his guy friends.

That was a frequent Johnny excuse.

And Tommy.

And Billy.

Funny. Most of them would cancel for a date but somehow still found their way to my place late at night.

Sterling's the polar opposite. We've done dinner, and tonight we're heading to the movies. It would appear as if we're dating. Except for the fact that he hasn't kissed me yet. Hasn't even tried.

Does he remember that I thought he was leaning in for a kiss during the Master Auto Man debacle? We've never discussed it.

Maybe he's repulsed by the foobs and knowing that I'm not au natural anymore. Hard to tell at this point. But he keeps texting and calling and taking me places. Everything with the exception of physical contact tells me he's interested.

I keep hoping that things will happen. Our hands will brush, our gazes will lock. We'll be overcome by the urge to dirty salsa dance at the same time. Or you know, some fabulous Rom Com set up where I trip and land on his lap, and we accidentally have sex.

All of that works.

Although truthfully, I'm not sure how any of it is supposed to work for me anymore.

There's also the fact that I didn't tell Sterling about the hysterectomy. It's not the easiest thing to work into conversation. I'm not sure if we're even dating, so talking about my uterus seems premature.

I think most guys would be super-stoked. No pregnancy scares here!

Even though I try and make light of it, the gravity of the situation brings on tears again. I can't even blame my hormone-replacement therapy (HRT for those of you who like abbreviations) this time. This is pure sadness.

I never knew my grandmother. I barely remember my mother, and the cherry on this crap sundae is that now I'll never be one.

I hate this disease.

I also hate that I don't feel comfortable in new clothes yet. My old clothes don't work either, which makes the prospect of dressing for a maybe date with Sterling even harder.

This is when Lisa would normally come through for me. Maybe I should call her back and apologize for ... what? Being human? Being sensitive to the suck-fest that has become my life?

If I can't figure out what I'm supposed to say sorry for, then I don't need to say it.

I stare at my closet and hope something jumps out. Inexplicably, my clothes remain stationary. I wonder if I can rent the forest animals from Cinderella to help me dress?

Clothing is going to be problematic when school starts in a few weeks. I can't really afford a new wardrobe, yet I can't seem to fit into my old stuff. I'm not cleared for exercise, and I have a feeling my changing body shape is due more to the hormones than anything else.

Great. Sterile and chubby. Always a winning combination.

At least my first-day-of-school dress still fits.

Maybe I should focus on growing taller. It might be the only real solution at this point.

I finally settle on capri leggings and a flowy top. It's comfortable for the August heat, but doesn't look like it came from the tent department. I hope.

I've graduated from a surgical bra to utility bra in a sexy nude color. Real progress, right?

The humidity is giving my hair a volume in the next stratosphere, so I tame it in a thick braid. It's the first time since the surgery that I've been able to reach up to braid the whole thing.

Oh, the things I used to take for granted.

At least this whole mess has given me a new perspective. Seems immature and childish to complain about the things I used to be able to do. I've been given the gift of time, and I intend to use it to the fullest.

Starting with Sterling.

I don't need to wait for him to make a move.

His lips are mine.

With a braid trailing down my back like a warrior princess—back off, Elsa—I rush to answer the door as soon as I hear him in the driveway. Cornelius lets out a low growl even before I can hear the footsteps on my front steps. He only came back today, and he's still in a pissy mood at being shipped out while I was recovering.

You'd think he'd have been more sympathetic, having been neutered himself.

Stupid cat.

Except it's not Sterling at the door.

"Johnny, what are you doing here?"

"Yo, Mil. How are you? How's things?" He's staring at my chest. It doesn't take a rocket scientist to figure out that he thinks maybe I have a porn-star chest and wants a chance to play. "You all healed up?"

"I'm fine."

"Are you still crying?"

128

I guess I shouldn't blame him. I was a bit of a mess the last few months. *But he dumped me before I was even out of anesthesia!*

"Johnny, you need to go."

"Aww, come on, Mil. You look good." He has yet to look at my face.

Why did I date him again?

Movement behind Johnny gets my attention. Well, this should be nice and awkward.

"Hey," I look right past my ex, hoping he'll get the hint.

Johnny turns around. "Who's this? What are you doing here?"

Sterling looks at me, and I hope he can read the plea in my eyes.

"Darling, I'm so sorry I'm late." Sterling brushes past Johnny, forcing him to step aside. As he reaches me, Sterling's arm snakes around my waist, pulling me into him. I look up at him and smile, hoping he can interpret my thoughts. His eyebrow cocks slightly, and he leans in. His lips brush mine, first gently and then with a bit more intensity.

Johnny coughs uncomfortably.

"Oh, are you still here? Shouldn't you piss off?" Sterling's hand never leaves my waist, instead pulling me in even closer. He leans in and kisses me again.

This time with tongue.

Score.

CHAPTER 16

Holy snikeys.

He's finally kissing me.

Okay, maybe it's because he could tell from my panicked look that I was trying to get rid of Johnny, and he took pity on me.

Maybe Sterling could smell the loser-vibe wafting off my ex.

Man I sure could pick 'em.

And man, Sterling sure can kiss.

"Thank you," I finally manage, still breathless. Truth be told, I'm a bit weak in the knees. "I'd told him to go, but I don't think he was listening to me. He's the one who dumped me right after surgery."

"I should have clobbered him."

Not the reaction I pictured from Sterling. He didn't seem like the caveman type to me.

"While I would have loved to see that, it's probably best you didn't."

My hand is still on his arm, and his hand is still around my waist.

I do not mind this one bit.

"Although, I'm sorry for kissing you like that."

I don't even have time to hide my reaction. My face falls faster than a soufflé in a draft. My hand goes limp.

"What I mean," he quickly corrects, "is that I wish our first kiss hadn't been in front of that eejit. I've been thinking about kissing you for a long time, and it was never like that."

What?

Yessssss.

"So you've been thinking about kissing me?" I'm going for coy. I'm probably failing.

"Yes of course. Have you been thinking about kissing me?" Sterling leans in, whispering in my ear. His breath is hot on my neck.

I glance around. Don't need any pesky neighbors getting an eye—or ear—full. "Let's take this discussion inside. It's bad enough that we had an audience for our first kiss."

"Right. At least it'll be a great story to tell the kids." Sterling takes my hand as we go through the door.

Crap on a cracker. How do I respond to that? Should I tell him? Was he joking? He can't be serious, can he? What if he is? What if this is his deal breaker? My mind is whirling too fast for me to form a coherent sentence. "I ... Sterling ... ah ..."

"Millie, relax. I'm kidding. Let's not put the cart before the horse."

So he was kidding. Thank goodness. Right? Yes, of course right. I inhale sharply and step away. I need a little distance from his touch.

His smell.

His taste.

"Of course. Let me grab my purse, and then we can get going to the movies."

I dash back into the house to get my sweater and purse. He didn't mean anything by that comment. But he needs to know.

I need to tell him.

It's too early to tell him. Like Sterling said, let's not put the cart before the horse.

We need to go, otherwise I'm liable to say something stupid. Or do something stupider. If we're sitting in a movie, it might buy me a whole two hours without embarrassing myself.

I dash back out to the porch. "Ready to go?"

"A sweater? It's about ninety degrees."

"I'm always cold. At least I used to be. I'm cold until I have a hot flash." It's probably too early to tell him that my breasts are now like weather barometers. If it gets cold—air conditioning or temperature drop—the foobs know and tell me through pain signals.

Another awesome perk of livin' the mastectomy life.

I head out and get in the car. I'm at a loss of what to say to Sterling. The guys I've dated in the past didn't make a lot of conversation. Not about real things. Like jobs and families.

God forbid we discuss families. It might have encouraged me to ask to meet theirs.

Sterling's different. He wouldn't have called his brother with me, if he were just like all the others.

Suddenly, I want to know more. I *need* to know all about him.

"Why did you come here?"

He jumps and I realize we've been quiet for a long time. "Um, because we agreed that I'd drive to the movies tonight."

"No, to America. You said you moved in the middle of high school. Did you move around here? Pennsylvania seems like a random choice. Why did you move here?"

Sterling lets out a deep sigh. "Ended up near Philly first. Ma came here for a man. He was a real winner, like most of the other men she chased after."

"Oh, I'm sorry. What about your father? And why do you say, 'Ma?' I always thought British people used Mum instead."

"Where I was raised—"

"Ipswich?" I jump in. I really do like the way that word sounds.

He chuckles. "Yes, Ipswich. It's the Suffolk dialect, which is a bit different than most of England. I've worked hard to get a lot of the odd words out of my vocab, but Ma's one that stuck around."

Now that I'm listening closely, I do hear some of the differences in his speech from the likes of Downton Abbey. He says 'hard' like someone from Boston. Haad. "It makes me think of Little House on the Prairie. You know, Ma and Pa."

"Let's put it this way, my ma is nothing like the Ma on the show. And Da? He's included in the category of losers that was Ma's special type. It's hard to believe he stuck around to father us." His grip on the steering wheel tightens as I see his jaw clench.

"At least you have your brother and sisters." Look at me, trying to find the bright side.

"Sort of. Stu—Stuart and I are still very close. He didn't move here with us. He stayed with a friend until he went to Uni. I speak to Samantha a few times a year. She's up in Boston. Sarah is a bit harder to pin down, and Stu and Samantha have cut her off."

"Sarah's the youngest?"

He nods, glancing at me quickly. Once his eye are back on the road he says, "Yes. We found out after Da left that he wasn't her father. It never mattered to us, but it mattered to Sarah." He pauses and the look on his face indicates that he's far away. "She's a bit of a lost soul."

Oh, that makes me sad. He's obviously concerned and emotional about her. "She's lucky to have you. Siblings are a gift."

"What about you? Do you have any siblings?" His shoulders relax as his grip loosens. I see he likes talking about this stuff as much as I do.

Ah, crap. Now we're going to go down the sad road of my life. Someday, I want to live on happy street. "No. My mom got sick when I was six. I'm not sure if they tried to have any before that or what."

"How old were you when she passed?"

"Ten."

"Oy, that's rough. What about your dad? Didn't he remarry? Have more kids?" He pulls into a parking spot and turn off the ignition. I feel his full attention as he unbuckles his seatbelt and turns toward me. I stare at my hands, knotted in my lap.

I've thought about this a lot. My whole life really. I'm sure my mom didn't know for certain she would die, but she must have felt it, just as I did. And she was selfish.

She loved my dad and made him love her. And he never got over it.

Or her.

And she left me too.

She should have known better. What it would do to him.

I knew better.

I don't know anything anymore.

"No. My mom was his soul mate. She completed him. He was never the same after she died. I think part of him died then too." I don't think part of him died. I know it did.

"Did he date even?"

"Never. I used to try to set him up but he wasn't interested. He used to say"—my voice drifts, soft and distant— "He used to say that she was irreplaceable, and he wouldn't even try." While I knew no one would ever replace my mom, how I wished for that female presence in my life. Aunt Polly tried, but it wasn't like she was there every day or anything.

Sterling doesn't say anything for a moment. Finally, he clears his throat. "It's quite endearing. My ma is incapable of being without a man. If she thinks one is even considering leaving, she's got the next one lined up. It's pitiful really. She rides my tail about finding a new ma for Piper all the time. I don't know how to tell her that I'd rather be alone than be like her."

"That's got to be rough too." I can't imagine what that'd be like.

"How was your da after your ma died?"

Awful. Vacant. Empty. Broken.

"Distant. I mean, he was there all the time. For whatever I needed. School plays and soccer games and dance recitals. Graduations. That sort of thing. But he was physically there. Still is. I mean, he can't handle the emotional part of my health, but he was willing to take care of the house. That's about it. His sister, my aunt Polly, stepped in, but she ... well she wasn't my mom."

"Millie, that's ... I'm ..." Sterling stutters, not knowing what to say. Most people don't know.

"The hard part of having your mom die is that the only person you want to talk to about it is your mom. But she was sick for so long. She suffered for years. And then she left us."

"Does your father realize how hard losing her was on you?" Concern and sadness dominate his face.

I shake my head, tears silently rolling down my cheeks. He reaches over and ever so delicately wipes them with the pad of his thumb.

My wounds—the ones etched in my soul since I was little—pull open. My voice is barely above a whisper. "And I always sort of knew that the same fate awaited me."

I hold my breath, waiting for the platitudes. The empty promises. The "you'll be fines." The "don't worry's."

"But not anymore. Now you can have the life your ma never got to have."

My eyes close tightly, squeezing fat tears out. "Now I will have the quantity but not the quality."

He pulls me into him, practically crawling over the center console to my seat. Why'd they stop making cars with bench seats?

It's his turn to whisper. I close my eyes as his words soothe me. "Millie, you'll feel better one day. I promise. And things are different but different isn't always bad."

I pull back. "Promise?"

He nods. "I promise. You were given the chance that your ma never had. And you're going to make the most of it. You have a long, healthy life ahead of you."

I look at him, not sure if I can believe it yet. "I needed to hear that. I try to be positive, but ... well, I've had a lot of loss."

"Yes, and now it's time to cut your losses and move on to something new and wonderful."

"Does that include you?"

"I hope so."

~~~***~~~

Walking into the movie theater, I feel lighter than I have in years. I haven't told many people that I thought I was going to die young. They tend to look at you like you belong in the nuthouse when you say that.

On a side note, this movie is totally stupid, but it's what I need.

To be able to laugh.

And to not have to think too much when Sterling's hand sneaks over and threads through mine.

I feel like I'm sixteen. At least until the hot flash hits. Then I feel sixty.

I pull my hand out of Sterling's, hoping he didn't notice the sudden moisture.

Let's be honest, it's at least the second, maybe even third, least embarrassing thing that's happened in front of him.

As the credits roll, I stand up. I hope Sterling doesn't think I'm childish and immature for laughing so much.

I also hope he didn't notice me snort laughing during that scene with the epic fall.

"What did you think?" I finally ask. We're almost to the back of the theater, and he still hasn't said anything.

"It was ..." he seems to be searching for words. "A bold initiative exploring the juxtaposition of good and evil," he declares.

Huh?

I stop dead, and Sterling runs right into me. His hand slides around my waist, stopping me from pitching forward and landing on my face. "What?"

I don't even know what he said, but I know it didn't make any sense.

"What?"

"Were we in the same movie? What did you say? A bold ..." I trail off. His hand is still around my waist. I don't want him to let go, but I also feel like I might start freaking out any second.

"A bold initiative exploring the juxtaposition of good and evil." His voice is less confident this time.

I step forward and then turn around to look at him. Luckily, the theater is mostly empty, and we're the only ones there, save an usher sweeping up scattered popcorn and Milk Dud boxes.

"How did you get that in a movie about time travel back to a seventies keg party?"

He grins sheepishly. "I didn't pay attention to the movie at all. I couldn't even remember which one we'd decided upon."

"Was it that bad? Why did you agree to see it, if you had no interest in it?" Oh God, now he's going to think that I'm some kind of sophomoric imbecile who can't follow a deep plot.

"I don't know if the movie was bad or not." He looks sheepishly at his feet, and then back up at me.

How could he not know this? "Didn't you watch it?"

"I couldn't."

Oh no. What if he's sick? Does he feel feverish? Is this like in *Twilight* when Jacob turns into a wolf? Is that's what's happening to Sterling? "Why not? Are you okay? Sterling, you should have said something."

He steps toward me. He doesn't feel hot. "Millie, I can't concentrate on anything when you're around. All I can think about is you."

He has probably spent the last two hours trying to figure out how to get away from me and the disaster that my life is. "You mean all you can think about is what a mess I am."

"All I can think about is kissing you again and hoping that you feel the same."

I hope my ear-to-ear grin tells him all he needs to know.

CHAPTER 17

"I'm not ready to have sex with you." So much for subtlety. At least I put it out there.

FYI, I have no chill. It up and left, along with my ovaries and breasts.

"Duly noted," Sterling says dryly, his eyes never leaving the road.

I can't tell if he's being sarcastic or just British.

My head's still spinning from the kiss he planted on me right outside the movies. We were totally making out up against his car. For a woman with only laboratory-made hormones pumping through my veins, I felt *something*.

Praise Jesus.

But everything is different now, and I've got to slow it down a bit.

The whole way home in the car I've been trying not to gawk at him and to tell my body that WE ARE NOT READY.

Luckily, I get a reprieve as we pull into my driveway. Once in the house though, for some reason, I keep talking.

Seriously, I need a mute button. "It's not you. Really. It's not. If I'd met you before ... everything, dude I'd be jumping your bones right about now." I flop down on my couch. It's nice to be able to flop again.

Sterling does that eyebrow cock thing, making me reconsider my stance on not wanting to have sex yet. I think *technically* speaking I could. Despite the drought, Dr. Tremarchi cleared me for launch down there. It's more the upstairs that I'm concerned about.

Not to mention, I feel about as sexy as a bag of old potatoes.

"Did you say something about old potatoes, love?" Sterling slides next to me on the couch where I am apparently unaware that I'm speaking out loud.

"If I don't mention that you didn't know what movie we went to see, can you forget that you heard me talking to myself?"

"Deal. Now let's discuss the other elephant in the room. You don't find me shag-worthy?" As he says this, he slowly drags his finger up and down my bare arm. Up and down. Up and down. I'm having a hard time putting words together.

"I'm the one who's not shag-worthy. Not yet. You've found me at a tough time. I've fallen off the horse, and I'm not quite ready to be back in the saddle yet."

"Millie, I hope you know that I'm not here for the shag, though I will admit that perhaps I was thinking about that rather than watching the movie." His finger is still tracing up and down my arm. Since when did my arm become an erogenous zone?

"Really?" That doesn't seem likely, though I don't know why he'd have any reason to make that up. I just can't see how he sees me as sexual when there's nothing sexy about me.

Not that I was hot-to-trot before, but I could certainly hold my own.

Would it be unreasonable—and unfair—to ask him to wait?

I need to ask the UnBRCAble women how long it took for them to get their grooves back.

I know Lisa would tell me just to go for it. Rip the Band-Aid off.

Sterling's hand slides in mine again. I hope I don't have another hot flash like I did during the movie. I swear, when I have one, it's like molten lava exploding inside my body.

And not in the good, romance novel kind of way. Not even in the chocolate lava cake kind of way.

At some point, I might have to explain to him what's going on with that. Hopefully I can play it off as a reaction to the weather for the next ten years. You know like, "My God, it's thirty-six degrees out. Damn global warming!"

Yeah, I don't buy it either.

"I don't know why you find it so hard to believe I find you sexy, Millie."

Another topic I'd like to avoid for the upcoming decade.

"It's just that, well ... um ... okay," I hope his attraction to me isn't based on my ability to be articulate. I need to up my game. "I can't believe school starts in three weeks. I really need to get my act in gear and start prepping for the year."

I am the queen of lame.

"Will you be able to go back?"

Maybe he didn't notice how uncool I am.

"I go to the doctor's again in a few days, but I think I'm good. Nine weeks now, and I finally feel human again. I think I'll probably head into my room on Monday. Wanna help?"

"Oh, I'd love to, love, but Piper and I are away. We're leaving on Saturday."

That's three days from now.

"Where are you going?"

"The beach. Cape May."

"Nice. How long of a drive is that?"

"About six hours, depending on how many times we have to stop. Candice is notorious for her small bladder."

I swear I actually hear the sound of a record scratching through my brain.

"Excuse me?"

"Candice can't hold it, and we usually have to stop at least twice."

I've never dated someone with an ex-wife and kid before. Are there rules about this? Is it normal to go on vacation together?

I need to play this super cool so he can't tell that I'm freaking out.

"Yeah. Cool. Sounds fun. Do you all stay in the same hotel room?"

Super subtle.

Hastily, I add, "Never mind. Don't answer that. It's none of my business." Right. Cool. I'm practically an ice cube. He's going on vacation with a woman he used to sleep with. And I won't sleep with him.

"Blimey no. I can't be in that close quarters with that woman. You've met her. She's bonkers."

Phew. See? Nothing to worry about.

"We rent a small house. Actually this year, it's a few rooms in a house. Other people will be in the other rooms. Like a B&B." He shrugs, I think in an attempt to be casual. It doesn't look casual to me. He looks tense.

That answer is really no better.

Be cool, Millie. You haven't let your freak fly yet about this. As my dad used to say to his dog, "stay wood, boy."

"HOW MANY BEDROOMS?"

Sterling jumps at the sudden increase in my volume. So much for staying wood. I'm sure the neighbors at the end of the cul-de-sac heard me.

"Does this bother you, Millie?" Sterling's brows knit a bit. He's let go of my hand. I'm too antsy to sit any longer. Not that pacing is a better solution to play aloof, but I need to do something.

"No. Why would it? It's totally a normal thing, right? We're not even a thing. We hang out. That's all. No big whoop. And since I can't sleep with you, you might as well get some somewhere." *What am I saying? More importantly, why did I say it?*

I have no idea where that came from, other than the depths of my incredible insecurity. Or should I say the incredible depths of my insecurity. I imagine it being a well that never seems to have a bottom.

Okay, now I know the look is not a British thing. It's a "holy crap, this chick is cray cray" look.

He would not be wrong.

"Millie, I'm going to say this once, and once only. Candice and I are not sleeping together. There are many other reasons why we go on vacation together, but sex is not one of them."

I can recover from this. I sit back down on the couch and try not to read anything into the fact that he doesn't take my hand. I'll keep going on, like when I'm teaching, and I'm trying to ignore the kid in the back who keeps farting. "So I take it the divorce was amicable? That's good."

Even as I'm saying it, I know it's not right. As parents, they were never together at school events, and we had to have separate conferences for Candice and Sterling. Then there was the whole snack debacle and the scene at the hospital. I got the distinct impression that it was an anything-but-amicable split.

"Not hardly. We do not get along."

"Then why the vacation?"

Sterling puts his hands over his face, dragging them down. His eyes look weary. This is one of the first times I've seen him anything but put together and polished.

"How well did you get to know Piper's mother this year?"

"Not tons, though there *may* have been a joke or two about why she didn't take your last name." The thought of her being Candice Kane still makes me laugh.

"Ahh, yes. Do you know she was so sensitive about it that she'd go ballistic if anyone brought candy canes around her at all during Christmas? It got so bad that she'd go on a tirade if one was brought into the house."

"Oh."

"Yes. Makes for a quite unpleasant holiday season."

Oh no. "We made ornaments."

"Yes, you did."

"They were our parent gifts."

"Yes they were." His eyes begin to twinkle.

"I can't even tell you how long I spent on those."

"I'm sure." Sterling doesn't bother to hide his grin.

Stupid Pinterest. I found these adorable candy cane ornaments made out of red and white puzzle pieces. We glued them together, added bows and some glitter (always glitter), and then personalized them. I bought puzzles at the dollar store and then spent two weekends painting them with high gloss red and white paints. Then all the time cutting out the templates and the ribbon.

We don't talk about what glitter does to a classroom.

Glitter. Every school custodian's worst nightmare. That and lice.

Oh, and for the record, I used the glitter only because I was angry at Johnny for declaring that we weren't at a "gift-giving stage" in our relationship.

I'm pretty sure if I am having sex with you, you can at least get me a Starbucks gift card.

"Perhaps I should put a note in Piper's permanent file to avoid all things candy cane for future teachers." I think about it. "Did she really flip out?"

"Apparently, yes. That's what Piper said. When I picked her up, she was crying because Candice had thrown it out. She said she made it especially for her ma instead of me because it was like her name."

While I'm annoyed all my hard work went unappreciated, I don't understand how a mother could do that to her child. "That's terrible."

"I wish I could say that it was a blip on the radar or unusual behavior."

"I take it it's not then?"

Sterling shakes his head. "I don't want to bad mouth Piper's ma, but I have a feeling, if we continue to see each other, that you'll be witness to something sooner or later. I'd rather you be prepared—not that you can ever really be prepared—beforehand."

"Sounds reasonable."

He sighs. "She had it written into the custody arrangement that we have to approve if either one plans to take Piper across state lines. To her, approval is only granted if she comes with us."

Without meaning to, I wrinkle my nose. That's terrible.

"So you see, it severely limits what I can do with my daughter. Also, it gives Candice a free vacation, as she generally does not contribute."

"You have to pay for everything?" That doesn't seem right. Or possible. Sterling needs a better custody arrangement. And a better lawyer. I make a mental note to ask Lisa who she recommends. He needs a pit bull.

"She's supposed to contribute, but historically speaking, it doesn't happen. Plus, I lose my one-on-one time with Piper. I want to tell her to take a piss."

"Why don't you revisit the arrangement or tell her no?"

Sterling closes his eyes. "This has been going on for a while. She doesn't follow the custody agreement, but calls her lawyer—which I have to pay for—every time she thinks I violate it. It doesn't matter if I take Piper out of state or not. Candice always ends up tagging along. And because I'm trying to bank points with her so I can take Piper to England next year, I'm trying to be nice." Sterling grimaces at the word trying, as if it's painful for him. It probably is.

"Stu is getting married, and I want to bring my daughter. I hope if I go above and beyond, then Candice won't have any grounds to deny me the request."

"Do you think she'll let Piper go?"

He shrugs. "Probably not, but I'm trying to establish a pattern of good faith and good will gestures. For this matter, I'll take it back to court, but I have to show that I've been cooperative."

This is all so complicated. "I've never dated anyone with kids before. Or at least, not anyone who's admitted to having kids." I add, "I was always a bit suspect about Billy Bender. It wouldn't surprise me if there are a few little Billys running around out there."

Sterling chuckles. "Yes, well, it's certainly an important consideration, if you want to date me. Piper comes first. I would have to say that if it's a deal breaker or otherwise unsavory for you, we should probably stop before anything gets started."

I think about that for only a millisecond. "It's not a deal breaker. I willingly spend my days with children, so generally speaking, I do not find them unsavory. I actually like your child very much."

"That's good to know. I'm sorry to say that was not the case with some of the people I've dated in the past, and it was quite apparent the woman was not kosher with the situation."

I have no problem with him having a child. Heck, it's one of the attributes that I find quite attractive. And if there's a kid, there's an ex who will always be in his life. I can even deal with that. But truth be told, I'm totally *not* okay with him going on vacay with his ex, but I'm not admitting to that right now. I'll play dumb. "You know I adore Piper. And I understand that she will always be the primary lady in your life."

As I say that, a pang stabs my heart. I always wanted to be someone's number one. After my mom was gone, I should have been that for my dad. But my mom always stayed number one, with me a distant second, at least on an emotional level.

I'll never stand in the way of a father-daughter relationship.

The ex-wife is a whole other story.

CHAPTER 18

"Vacation?" Claudia asks, repeating the word as if she could not have possibly heard correctly. "With his ex-wife?"

I nod.

"Nope. I don't like it. Not one bit."

"Okay, so I'm not overreacting."

"What does his ex look like?"

I look down at my chest as I try to think of Piper's mother. *Sterling's ex.* Big hair. Big boobs. Low cut shirt.

Now that I'm an expert in all things breast related, I think I can safely say hers are no more real than mine.

Huh.

I wonder if Sterling has a thing for the artificial. Pre-foobs, this would have turned me off. This is one thing in my favor.

I scroll through Facebook and pull up her profile. Yes, I know how to get to it. If a teacher ever tells you they don't stalk their parents on Facebook, they're totally lying. And any teacher who doesn't make their profile so private it's nearly impossible to find is totally stupid.

"Let me see." Erin crowds in. She's one of the most outgoing people I've ever met. She also has the coolest job ever, being a zoologist, and has long legs to boot. If she didn't have the same mutant genes as me, I'd say she's one of the luckiest people in the world.

Even though I didn't know these women two months ago, I can't imagine life now without them. When I'm with them, they fill a void I didn't know existed. I feel a quick pang of guilty that I'm sharing this with Claudia and Erin before Lisa even knows. It's as if my personal tectonic plates have shifted and Claudia with her mellow chill and Erin with her exuberance are slowly replacing Lisa in my life.

I turn the phone around and Erin grabs it. She scrolls up and down for a minute or two. "Drama llama. First, her posts are public. Second, she vaguebooks all the time. Third, she uses all the filters. Totally attention seeking. I wouldn't trust her."

And of course Candice was Rachel in the *Friends* quiz. I was Gunther.

In this safe, supportive space, I know Erin is right. While I don't actually have a tangible reason to distrust Candice, my gut tells me to keep an eye on her. Not to mention that I'm probably super insecure about everything right now.

Sterling's never given me a reason not to trust him.

But every man in my life has always let me down, so trust is not easily granted.

Thoughts—perhaps irrational ones—invade my mind. "What if she gets him drunk? What if there's a hot tub? You know she's going to wear a skimpy little bikini." What if she accidentally jumps on his man business and makes another baby? This idea particularly smarts because if he winds up with me, Piper will be his only biological child.

"Can you tell him you don't want him to go away with her?" Claudia asks. I think she breathes out lavender and chamomile when she talks because I instantly feel more calm.

I totally wish I could. I've thought about it. We're too new in our whatever we are to start getting all weird on him.

Start getting weird.

Ha.

I've not been myself this whole time.

I miss my old self. I keep hoping that every morning I'll wake up feeling like the old me. The old Millie would—hell, the old Millie would freak out about this too. There's nothing good about your hot British man-crush going away with his ex.

"We're not that serious yet. Plus, he has his reasons for agreeing to it."

Not that I know anything about being a mother, because I don't, but I don't understand how parents can use their children as pawns.

"Still, I would be worried. Very worried." While I know Erin's words are not untrue, they are not what I'd call helpful either.

"I don't see as how there's anything I can do about it." Except develop an ulcer. I mentally pencil that in. "Maybe this is a good thing. Maybe it'll help me weed out yet another loser before I get in too deep."

I feel disloyal calling Sterling a loser. I know he's not. But from where I'm standing, he could become one pretty quickly.

"That's one way to put a positive spin on it." Claudia nods.

"Isn't that what this group is for? To put a positive spin on a really negative situation?" My words are grimmer than I mean. The group has been a godsend, and I'm bringing them all down.

"Listen, I get where you're coming from. We all get it. But pull your head out of your behind, Millie. If you want your man, fight for him. If you want to roll over and play dead, then do that. But don't claim to want one thing and do nothing to get it. If this experience teaches you anything, it should be to grab each day by the cajones and go for it. You have a chance at life that your mom never got. Take it and run with it."

This is what I would expect Lisa to tell me. Claudia's always usually so chill and Zen that the strength and intensity of her words surprise me.

Not that she's wrong.

I've been having a super pity party these last few months.

No more.

Like the delicate tendrils of a seed unfurling, my brain—I'll claim addled by anesthesia and hormones— begins to hatch a plan.

And it's either brilliant or the stupidest thing I've ever done.

The jury's still out.

~~~***~~~

"I wish I could, but I can't. I've got a case going to trial next week."

"Aww, come on, Lis. We haven't done anything in ages." I don't know why I'm whining. She can't even get away for lunch. I know she can't take more time off.

"Yeah, why's that?"

I hear her irritation coming through the phone. Sometimes it sucks to have a professional interrogator for a friend. I don't get away with much. Plus, Lisa sees through me like a dollar-store shower curtain.

"I'm finally feeling like a human."

"It's about time you started getting out again." Her tone reads loud and clear that she knows I've not been sitting home alone. I don't need to acknowledge her tone. I can be strong.

"It was only movies and a dinner or two." Okay, I crumble like a cheap box.

"But I had to hear about it from Polly. You didn't even tell me."

She basically hung up on me the last time we talked. Why would I call her?

But she's been my closest friend for years. I should have reached out. I kept meaning to, but with Sterling and UnBRCAble ... I didn't.

Guilt washes over me. It doesn't take a rocket scientist to know that things are different between us. I wish I knew why, other than I get upset with her each time I talk to her. Maybe my cockamamie idea can play double duty and fix whatever is not working between my best friend and me.

"I'm not even sure what's going on. We haven't defined it."

"Are you dating him?"

I shrug, which is useless considering we're on the phone. While I wish I could say yes, the truth is I don't know. It's certainly not like any dating I've done in the past, which was always a lot more physical and a lot less conversational.

Mentally we're totally dating. Physically, we're third cousins at a family reunion passing the time.

"I think we're friends. We hang out, basically. There's really not a lot more to it than that."

"Yeah, so I don't think this is a good idea then. If you can't even be honest with me about this one little thing, then I don't think I can drop everything for you."

"Lisa, what are you talking about?"

"I was there, at the movies. I saw you two. Friends don't hold hands. Friends don't put their heads on each other's shoulders. Friends don't make out in the parking lot. But most importantly, friends don't lie to each other."

And with that, she disconnects.

I stare at the device, trying to make sense of the upside down red phone receiver on my screen.

She hung up on me.

She knows that's my one thing. The deal breaker.

Well, screw her. I don't need her.

In fact, I'm better off without her anyway.

Lisa would probably try to talk me out of this. Tell me it's a bad idea. A horrible idea from which no good can come. She'd tell me I should mind my own business and stay home. She'd remind me that I've been out of work for four months, and I really need to get my classroom in order for the beginning of the school year.

Lisa has proven to be a big, unsupportive disappointment. I'm glad she's not going to try to talk me out of *coincidentally* being at the same beach town as Sterling and Candice.

All I need is a new bathing suit for my new body, and I'm good to go.

CHAPTER 19

I don't expect to hear from Sterling tonight, so I'm delighted when his name flashes across my screen. "I thought you'd be busy packing."

"I'm good to go. Piper's still putting together her car bag, and I'm sure Candice hasn't started yet."

My stomach twists at the mere mention of her name.

"It's got to be difficult, going with her."

Please say yes. Please say yes.

"Not my favorite thing in the world. In fact, I can think of many other people I'd rather go with, but it's neither here nor there. It is what it is."

"I guess that's one way to look at it. "

"My brother rides me about it all the time."

"I take it he's not a fan?"

Sterling's quiet for a minute. "Generally speaking, he's not a fan of the decisions I make. That includes everything about Candice."

There's so much I want to ask him about his family. The idea of siblings fascinates me. It always has, probably because I never had any. I can't imagine what would be so bad that brothers and sisters wouldn't talk. I want to ask, but I don't want to pry. "Yes, well ..." I don't know what else to say.

"Stu thinks I'm stupid for insisting on going out of state. He thinks I should simply go somewhere with Piper in state, but alas we don't have beaches here."

"It's true. Pennsylvania is pretty landlocked. And didn't you say she'd wind up coming anyway?"

"Yes, so I might as well go where I want to then. I grew up on the water. I can't go that long without seeing the ocean. And frankly, I fell in love with this town. Piper loves it too. I don't want to deny her it."

I sigh. "I miss the beach. It's been years since I've been. Last year I ended up teaching summer school because ... well, I can't even remember why. Whatever it was, doesn't seem important now." It was to buy a new hot water heater, but that sounds too desperate. For the record, having hot water is pretty important.

Also, I taught summer school because I was all alone and didn't have anything better to do.

In hindsight, thinking my time here might have been limited, I'd done a piss poor job of living life to the fullest.

"I would bet that this year has put things into perspective for you, no?"

"Yes, quite a bit. Now I need to figure out what to do with the rest of my life." In more than one respect.

"Aren't your plans set? Are you considering something other than teaching? It would be a shame to lose you, but I know you'd be smashing at whatever you decided to do."

I hear rustling and the distinct sound of a zipper.

He's right. I've got the rest of my life ahead of me. The world is my oyster, yet I have no idea what to do with this slimy little mollusk.

"Millie?" He asks quietly.

I think I forgot to keep talking.

"I'm still here. It's just ... I ... well, it's going to sound stupid."

"Try me. You've met my ex-wife. I doubt anything you say can even rate on the stupid meter."

"My grandmother died at forty-three, and my mom at thirty-five. Even though I hoped it would skip me, I sort of always knew it wouldn't. Let's just say, I've never planned a fortieth birthday party. I even adopted an adult cat because I didn't want my pet to outlive me."

I've never said this aloud to anyone before. Not Lisa, not Aunt Polly, and certainly not my father. I didn't want the pity and platitudes and false promises.

"How old are you?"

"Twenty-nine."

"How old was your mom when she was diagnosed? I remember you saying she was sick for a while."

"She was. She was diagnosed at thirty-one." I'll never know one way or another, but after doing my research, there's reason to believe the birth control pills she took after having me caused the cancer to develop early and aggressively. The BRCA gene mutation wasn't identified until 1997, after she was already sick. The birth control link came even later.

I'm lucky Dr. Tremarchi was so thorough. With my family history, he insisted on testing before he'd write a prescription for the pill.

"So you caught this in the nick of time."

"I guess." I shrug, even though he can't see my gesture.

"Why did you decide to do it now?" The rustling and background noise on his end has stopped. I bet he's done packing.

"I was only tested a few months ago. I had to have ... I had to get some other things in order first, and then this. I knew the recovery would be rough. I didn't know how rough."

"Why did you put it off so long? It seems like something they'd have addressed a long time ago, given your history."

I sigh. I hate admitting to this part—my denial. "It hadn't really come up."

"That seems implausible. What sort of quack wouldn't recognize this as a possible issue? This makes me angry. I've seen it at times over the years, first with Samantha's complex medical issues, and certainly with Sarah's numerous health concerns. Though I have no absolute proof, it seems to me like women's issues are often discounted."

He's not wrong, and the passion in his voice moves me.

"Because the only doctor I routinely visited prior to this was Pepper, and that was only if they didn't have Mr. Pibb."

"You can't be talking about a fizzy drink with something so serious. How is that so?"

I twirl my hair around my finger while I formulate an answer. "Because I didn't want to hear what they'd have to say. If there's no one to say it, then it's not real."

"It doesn't make cancer not real. Or not happen."

"It may not, but for me it was an easier way to live than with a death sentence. How do you motivate yourself to work through high school and college and grad school when your career will not last even that long? It's bad enough to know what lies ahead. I wasn't going to acknowledge it and give it power over the short life I had."

"But now they made it so you won't get cancer. So all of that is moot."

I hate when people go and get all rational on me.

"Which is a new perspective to have, after all these years. My mom got sick when I was six. For twenty-three years, this has been my reality."

"How do you live with that?"

"Denial isn't just a river in Egypt, you know."

When he doesn't respond, I clear my throat and 'fess up. "My support group."

I wait for him to dismiss me as some hippy or otherwise flakey individual.

"I found a support group helpful, especially in those early days when Candice and I first split."

"Oh thank God. I thought you were going to think I was some hippy-dippy needy freak for going to a group. But it's the only thing keeping me going some days."

"Jury's still out of the freak thing," he jests. I smile, picturing him winking while he says it. "Just kidding, love. I hope you realize that," he adds hastily.

"It's okay, Sterling. I had my breasts removed. Not my sense of humor."

"Well, someday when we're together, perhaps over a pint, I'll tell you why I stopped going to group."

"I can't imagine not going right now. I don't know that I'll ever be at that point."

"Certainly it was helpful, I don't know that I wouldn't have made it without the group. Several of the members used it more as a dating site than one for single parenting, but my situation was much less serious than yours."

"Yeah, probably. Although if I don't handle things well, it's just me. If you mess up, you're ruining your daughter's life. I think I'd rather not have that responsibility."

"Now you're thoroughly bumming me out. What if I am messing up? I think Piper's mother might be messing up," he says, the concern evident in his tone. "You know, I'd be happier if we were having this conversation in person, if only so I could give you a hug right about now."

I agree. Not only about his ex but the hug part too.

"I don't think you're messing up. I think if you're concerned about it, then it's probably a good indication that you're on the right track." That's always been my philosophy with parents.

"I wish you were here so I could kiss you for saying that."

"Really?" Sterling seems too good to be true.

"Yes, of course. I don't need an excuse to kiss you, but if you want, I'll start a list."

I laugh. "I'd like that very much. It's been a rough few months. I could use all the ego stroking you can give."

"Well then, Millie, my dear, let me count the ways. And for the record, your ego is not the only thing I'd be interested in stroking."

Yowza.

Me too.

"I'll let you know when the stroking can commence." I pause for a moment. "My mind is willing; I just don't know if my body is able."

"In that case, I'll work on ways to seduce your mind."

"Seduce away."

Game on.

CHAPTER 20

It'll be fine. This will go okay. I repeat the phrase over and over until the words have no meaning.

I am not a freak.

I am totally a freak. Who does this?

Freaks. That's who.

If Lisa were with me, it wouldn't be so bad. This is sad and desperate, and I have no idea what possessed me to do this.

I didn't tell Aunt Polly the details. I'm sure she would have tried to talk me out of it. She did, however, think "getting away with some friends" was just what I needed.

My phone tells me to take the second right at the rotary on 109. I'm slightly disappointed that there's not more of a hoopla for Exit 0 on the Garden State Parkway, for all the publicity it has. There aren't even toll booths. It's really a regular road at that point. But still, the ocean is a few blocks ahead. As I drive over the harbor and toward the beach, I roll down my car window and inhale deeply.

There's nothing like the smell of the ocean, and it's been way too long since I've visited.

As the briny air fills my nostrils, I can't for the life of me remember why not.

See? This isn't a bad idea at all. Nope. Coincidentally coming to Cape May at the same time as Sterling—and Candice—is really not a bad idea. This is time for me to reboot and recharge.

I'm only here for three days, since I really do need to get into school and get my stuff—and mind—ready for the year. There are hours of labeling and laminating fun to be had.

Before I can even get to the beach, I'm completely distracted by the adorable Victorian houses in all shades of the rainbow. Bright houses with intricate gingerbread trim and inviting front porches line each street. My little bungalow would fit right in, in color, if not style.

This is the most adorable place I've ever seen, and I never want to leave.

A few minutes later I'm pulling into the Stockton Inn, where I have a room reserved in their Victorian Manor house. Someone else's last minute cancellation turned into my salvation. The woman on the phone was so nice and friendly, and she didn't even laugh at my optimistic last-minute plans. Every other room on this strip has probably been booked for months.

I find my room on the second floor. While wallpaper normally gives me traumatic flashbacks to when I was redoing my dining room, the soft blue, purple, and yellow bunches of flowers are immediately soothing. My favorite colors together. It's like this room was meant for me. Like deciding to come was fated in the stars.

Sterling texted me last night when they got in. The trip, by his accounts, was long and arduous, and delayed not only by Candice's lack of preparedness, but also by tremendous amounts of traffic. I filed that information away for future use, and as a result was on the road by six a.m. An early check in has me ready to hit the beach with plenty of daylight left.

But there's one small issue.

The bathing suit.

I probably should have shopped before I left. I probably should have tried on my suit before I left.

I did neither.

I take my old suit out and lay it on the bed. The black looks dark and ominous on the purple bedspread.

Last year, it did the job. This year, I fear it's woefully unprepared for the workload. The foobs have a significantly greater land mass than my old boobs had. I wouldn't be surprised if these had their own gravitational field.

It's not my bathing suit's fault. It's the same piece of spandex it always was. It was me who went and changed. And since it hasn't miraculously expanded into a turtleneck, it's not going to work.

I guess I'm sort of fortunate to have had my surgery during the summer, as it kept me from hiding behind a closet full of turtlenecks. Some of the women in UnBRCAble talked about not being able to wear anything else for years. My hot flashes wouldn't allow for that either, so that's one less hurdle to overcome.

The bathing suit is another story all together.

"It's not you, it's me," I tell it.

Dear Heavens, I'm losing it. Or maybe I already have. I'm talking to my clothing, trying to let it down gently for not being woman enough to wear it anymore.

Maybe there are some stores here that sell swimwear. There's got to be something that will work for me. And if not, I'll get a wetsuit.

Nothing says, "I'm a stable candidate to be your girlfriend" like crashing a vacation and dressing like Jacques Cousteau.

I strike out at the store on the boardwalk. Though they do actually sell wetsuits, I opt out. I feel if I go that route, I'd be obligated to attempt to surf, and we all know that will end in nothing but disaster.

Although I now have my own built in personal floatation devices, so it might not be so bad.

That's another thing I'm trying not to think about as I'm looking at spending an insane amount of money for this trip.

I cross Beach Avenue to a small boutique on the corner. I won't even look at the prices.

One-hundred and fifty dollars! Is this fabric woven from gold or the locks of hair from albino virgins? Will it clean my bathroom or change my oil?

Breathe, Millie. This is important. You are at the beach. You need a bathing suit. You can do this.

I cannot do this.

I have to do this.

I have lots of summers left in my life now, and I cannot hide during every one of them. I have to put a bathing suit on and show my body as it now is.

Just like I had to undergo having my breasts and womanhood amputated. As I had to endure the painful recovery, I will surely survive the trials of bathing suit shopping.

Surgical recovery may be the preferential activity. At least that came with painkillers and homemade Paula Dean mac and cheese. Shopping entails three-way mirrors and fluorescent lights, which seem to highlight the after-effects of the mac and cheese.

Fantastic.

The first suit I pick is a two-piece. It's got a high, athletic style neckline that ties like a halter, so it should work perfectly.

But it doesn't.

And neither does anything with plunging cleavage, keyhole cut outs, or anything that shows too much armpit cleavage. I never knew side boob was a thing, but since my foobs are still riding high and wide, I have it in full effect, and it will not do.

I finally settle on a suit in a pretty periwinkle that has a wide, flowing ruffle along the neckline. It comes right up to the top of my armpits and covers everything. I have to get a floral wrap to cover the lower half, and while I'm at it, I add a wide-brimmed floppy hat. Two-hundred and fifty bucks down the drain, but it's only money.

I have the rest of my life to work, which will thankfully be much longer now.

By the time I grab an Italian ice from Rita's and head back to my room, the overwhelming need to nap hits me.

I didn't drive all this way to sleep, but my body has other ideas. I put on my new suit and sarong, slather myself in an SPF lead shield, and head across the narrow driveway to the hotel pool. I need to listen when my body says 'stop' and trudging all the way to the beach is too much right now.

It's not like I can haul tons of stuff without hurting myself.

I didn't think this one through.

I carry my towel, book, and water bottle to the pool across the driveway and stretch out on a lounge chair. I want to make it to that hot sand, but I don't have it in me right now.

Another thing I didn't think through. I can't lay on my stomach. Not that I tan well to begin with, but now I'm going to be all lopsided. The knowledge that laying on my back is the only position nags at me, preventing me from being comfortable. I finally manage to doze off a few times, the dull lull from the ocean and the heat of the sun dragging me under until children's voices wake me up. I don't know if I've been asleep for two minutes or two hours.

There are a lot of people here in this quaint beachside town. I don't know how I'm supposed to even find Sterling. I doubt he's the type to post every move on social media, either, to make it easier to casually bump into him.

I really didn't think this one through.

Maybe it's for the best. I do think I need this escape before I head back to work. I know I've been off for months, but it hasn't exactly been a vacation. I take a long sip of cool water and decide to go for a little walk by the water. It's late enough that I don't have to buy a beach pass, but the clear blue skies mean the sand is still packed with chairs and umbrellas. People stretch out on mats and towels, their skin baking to a dangerously crispy tan.

Between the crashing of waves and squawking of gulls, there's a consistent background din that equates to solitude and peace. I mostly watch my feet squish in the wet sand and the water swirl around my ankles, but every so often I stop to look out.

I can't believe I'm here. This is, without a doubt, the stupidest thing I've ever done. I'm not usually the irrational sort. This is not me, and I don't like it.

But that's sort of the problem. I don't know who I am anymore. In the last few months, up has become down and left has become right. I'm no longer preparing myself for an early death. That's a secret reality I held onto for so long. I never even told Lisa about it.

She wouldn't have understood. Maybe Aunt Polly would have, but I didn't want to worry her. She's spent too much time as it is doing someone else's job and trying to boss her older brother around. I never wanted Dad to know. He's already so broken. Having to deal with losing me—I think it would kill him. Dad's certainly not okay. I think he could benefit from a support group too, even now. I think he did his best, but it still wasn't good enough. So I did the best I could not to make anyone worry about me more than they already did.

I was already the kid who lost her mother.

I didn't need to be the kid who was facing an early death too.

I was the happy kid. The girl who adjusted. Who carried on. Who talked about college and career and a husband and family, even though I was positive I'd never have that.

Lisa'd ask me why I dated loser after loser. I wasn't dating for longevity. I was dating for the here and now. He didn't have to be a lifetime companion. I wasn't expecting that out of anyone.

I wasn't going to be selfish like my mom was. After all these years, I'm still mad at her for leaving us.

I'd never make anyone who was really good and really deserving fall in love with me. It wouldn't be fair to him when I left him high and dry, facing a lifetime of broken heartedness.

My brain has yet to catch up with the new reality I'm facing. That's the only reason I can think of for my eccentric behavior.

That and estrogen replacement.

I never believed it when women would say they went crazy during menopause, but it's totally real. I know I'm being irrational; I can't control it.

But standing here on this beach at the very tip of Southern New Jersey, one thing is quite clear.

I'm in no place to get involved with anyone, let alone someone as good as Sterling Kane.

CHAPTER 21

I've dodged a bullet on this one.

Sterling will never have to know how irrational I was. I'll politely break it off when he gets back, claiming that it's too much between work and still recovering.

He'll understand. He's that kind of guy.

The guy who would be perfect if I were in a place to date and commit.

But I'm not, so someone else will have to reap the benefits of his perfection and delectable lips and sexy accent.

I must have been really bad in a former life to deserve this lot.

My surgeries went well, which is more than I can say for some. I have my health. I have my life.

At least I kept my nipples.

Once back in my room, I have a sizable cry. Then I pick up my phone to call Lisa. If all I ever get to be is auntie to her kids, I need to start mending that fence. Of course, I need to convince her to have kids, because she's told me she doesn't think she wants them. I'll come clean with her about my thoughts, she'll tell me I'm irrational, and then we'll be fine. And then she'll tell me, for the hundredth time, that she's never having kids. I can practically hear her saying, *"I've worked too long and too hard to throw it away on some kid. I'll never make D.A. if I do that!"*

My phone blinks with a notification, interrupting my walk down memory lane.

A text from Sterling.

Saw a woman on the beach who reminded me of you. I miss you.
Also, you should wear light blue.

Oh God. I walked by him at some point! I'm so lucky he didn't recognize me!

Glad you're having fun.

I never said I was having fun. It's no fun without you.

I should be coy. I should be cool.

I'm sure you're having a great time without me. You don't need me.

Super.
That doesn't sound passive aggressive at all.
Why isn't there an 'undo' option for texts?
It's a good thing we're not in this for the long haul.
I'm no good at dating with the potential for longevity.

I wish you were here.

I know I should answer, but instead I power my phone down. There's an inviting claw foot tub calling my name. I wasn't allowed to bathe until I was healed up, but I've avoided it for other reasons. The small laparoscopy scars on my lower abdomen don't bother me, even though they represent a bigger loss.

The purple lines arcing on the underside of my breasts are disgusting. Probably because my foobs are disgusting. Large and hard.

There's no way they'll ever pass for natural, no matter how much fluffing I do. I bounce up and down and watch them. They don't move like my breasts used to, and they certainly don't feel like them.

My breasts themselves still don't feel anything, although I have had the weird phenomenon of getting a shooting pain my breast when I eat something cold. Like an ice cream headache except in my case, it's a foob ache.

I can't ever imagine letting someone touch them.

I can't imagine someone wanting to. Sterling might say he wants to, but he doesn't know what he's saying. No one in his right mind would want this.

Soon I can't tell if my face is wet from the bathwater or the tears.

As my hands turn to prunes, I decide it's time to call it a night. If I go to bed now, I can't get into any more trouble.

~~~***~~~

The problem with going to bed so early is I wake up before the sun. I glance at the clock. Five-forty-five.

I power up my phone, and a quick internet search tells me daybreak is around six-fifteen. I could go for a walk on the beach and watch the sunrise.

Watching the sun break the horizon over the Atlantic Ocean is a rare treat I haven't experienced in ages. Hastily I throw on some leggings and a T-shirt. I grab my sweatshirt and sunglasses, throw a few bucks in the small pocket in my waistband to get a coffee after sunrise, and head out.

The water's still today, making it easy to see the dolphins as they break the surface of the water. I'm mesmerized watching the dorsal fins rise and then disappear.

It's a magical moment, and I wish I had someone—anyone—with which to share it.

Not anyone. Sterling.

But still, I had this and it's mine forever. This will be my grounding moment when I meditate and practice mindfulness. As the sun rises, pinks and purples swirling around the red sphere, some of the doubt from last night starts to fade.

I will be okay.

I'm going to be okay. I'm going to live, and I don't have to figure out everything right this instant. I've got time.

Still, I'm sad that it won't be with Sterling, but it's not fair to ask him to wait for me to be ready.

I reach the end of the stretch of beach as the sun breaks free of the clouds swirling about, pinks and purples arcing the sky. I head to the sidewalk, my legs feeling like lead from trudging up the sand for what feels like miles.

I need to start exercising soon, otherwise I'll never make it through the school day.

The walk back on the sidewalk goes quicker, and I admire all the houses that face the ocean. I'm surprised that none of the occupants are sitting on their decks and balconies watching this beautiful splendor. That would be the best part of a house here.

I now officially have a retirement goal.

I think once I get my coffee, I'll sit on the porch of my bed and breakfast in one of those rocking chairs and watch the world go by. There's no rush for more.

I've got all the time in the world.

"Miss Dwyer!"

I hear the voice, breaking my reverie, before I see where it's coming from.

Not that I need to see to identify the owner.

Busted.

CHAPTER 22

I freeze, torn between running away and diving into a hedge. My sense of flight is in full effect.

"Daddy, come quick! It's Miss Dwyer." I hear the voice, knowing exactly who it belongs to. The bushes look prickly. Maybe I can pull up this manhole cover and jump in. All drains lead to the ocean, right? I could be in the Bahamas by lunchtime.

Instead of executing my ninja escape, I stand on the sidewalk, looking at the house. Then, because I'm super suave, I look down at my feet. My braid falls over my shoulder while loose strands of hair whip around my face. I'm dressed in completely frumpy outfit consisting of capri leggings, a baggy T-shirt, and have a sweatshirt, also baggy, tied around my waist.

I probably look like a bum.

Remove the probably.

"Millie!" Sterling calls from the porch. He pretty much skidded to a stop when he saw it was really me.

Ten bucks says he's questioning his judgment ever to get involved with me and is telling himself to get a restraining order.

After a momentary pause, Sterling continues down the steps, stopping just in front of me. He leans in and whispers, "I'm not ready for public displays of affection in front of Piper yet. Is that alright with you?"

This was not what I expected to hear. I nod. "Of course."

I glance up at his face for a minute, and then return my gaze to the ground. At least my toes look cute this morning. Glitter nail polish for the win. Maybe the sparkles will distract Sterling from realizing I'm off my rocker.

"I can't believe you're—" he pauses. "What are you—Millie, are you unwell? You seem off."

"I'm making the most of my time before school starts. Once you mentioned the ocean, I started to long to see it again for myself."

Time to face the music. He's going to know what a big fat liar I am. He'd have to be blind not to see through my lies. He's going to know I followed him. "I'm glad you're here." He flashes a quick grin.

Well, that was unexpected.

Always the unexpected from Sterling.

"Are you upset with me?"

"Not in the least. Knowing that you're not simply on the other side of town has been terrible for me. I know we've only started seeing each other, but I missed you dreadfully the past two days. Millie Dwyer, you consume all my waking thoughts." He pauses and then nods, almost as if to himself. "And several of my sleeping thoughts, for that matter."

His words plow into me, causing me to take a step back as if I was actually hit. "You're not mad that I followed you down here?"

He shakes his head. "I love it. Best possible surprise."

I don't know what to say to that so I do what I do best. Ramble incessantly.

"I don't know what I was thinking." I can no longer hold his gaze and look down at my feet again. "I hated the idea of you here"—I look up and nod toward the house—"with her. I know why you're doing it, so that's why I didn't say anything. But I … I didn't want you to forget about me." My voice drops to a whisper, and I don't know if he actually heard that last part.

"Never."

A smile dances at the corners of my mouth. I try to rein it in, lest he think I'm a fool. "I decided it was a stupid thing, so that's why I didn't tell you I was here."

"I wish you would have."

"I'm sorry I crashed your vacation."

"I'm not."

We stand there, staring at each other. Piper can no longer contain her excitement. "Miss Dwyer! I can't believe you're here and we're here! This is the most awesome thing ever! Isn't it, Dad?"

"It is." The smile on his face tells me he actually means it.

"Can you come to the beach with us later?"

"I, uh … I'm not sure. I don't know what my plans are yet. I haven't had my coffee, so it's hard to think clearly enough to figure out what I'm doing today."

"Daddy doesn't drink coffee."

"But we certainly have some. Why don't you take a seat up on the porch and I'll bring you a cup?"

I nod and then follow him up the stairs. He heads inside while I take a seat on the porch. Staring out at the ocean, I feel a peace wash over me. God, this is the best.

"How do you take it?" He calls through the screen door.

"Milk and sugar, please."

He mumbles something that I can't make out. It sort of sounded like, "I'll make sure to remember that," but I can't be sure.

What am I doing here? Why didn't he freak out? I'm not sure which of us is more messed up in this moment.

Before I know what I'm doing, I call out the next thing that pops into my head. "You know, I just saw something on Facebook that said people who drink black coffee are more likely to be psychotic." Right. Like he's going to believe I'm not a psycho just because I use milk and sugar.

Sterling emerges from within and hands me a steaming mug.

"Thank you. None for you?"

"Daddy only drinks tea, but I told him drinking tea is treasonous." Piper pipes up from the porch swing. Piper's staring at me intently.

I start to ask, "How is tea … oh never mind."

"I honestly don't know where she gets these things from. But she's not incorrect," Sterling supplies.

"Tea is treasonous? Is that like a British-American-colonists-tea-party thing?"

Now Sterling laughs. "No, that I'm not a coffee drinker."

"I'd suspect that more for psychotic behavior than drinking coffee black. Perhaps the great minds of science ought to do some research into that."

"Did you ever wonder how they come up with their topics?"

"I remember hearing someone on the radio talk about some government research group did a study that showed how drinking leads to unplanned pregnancy. I couldn't believe they spent federal money to figure that out, but I have to buy my own glue sticks and tissues for my class."

Piper pops up. "You can have a baby from drinking? I'm never drinking again!" She puts her cup down on the floor.

"Oh, darling, not that kind of drinking." Sterling grins at me.

"Oops" I mouth to Sterling.

"Little ears have big mouths."

He doesn't need to tell me that. "Don't I know it. You wouldn't believe some of the things I've heard from my students. Nothing is sacred."

In this moment, I feel perfection. This perfect setting. Sterling and Piper. And me. Almost like we belong together.

"What the hell is going on out here?" The shriek makes me jump.

Sterling seems nonplussed.

Perfection ruined.

"We're out here," he calls, not bothering to get up.

"Why are you up so early? I'm on vacation and I want to sleep—" Candice locks eyes on me. "What in God's name are you doing here?"

"I was walking on the beach to catch the sunrise and passed by here on the way back to my B and B. Piper saw me and now we're having coffee." Just the facts, ma'am.

"Sterling doesn't drink coffee."

"You have to get up earlier in the morning if you want to deliver that sort of breaking news." I don't even try to keep the sardonic tone from my voice. It's out of character for me to be so snippy. But hell, following the guy I'm dating to his vacation is out of character for me too.

"You know I like to sleep in when I'm on my vacation. I didn't expect you to be entertaining *company* at such an indecent hour."

In my head, badass Millie rips off her earrings and punches her. In my reality, I take a sip of coffee.

Candice and I stare at each other for a minute. Erin was right. She does use *all* the filters. Even so, Sterling loved her once, which at the moment totally baffles the mind.

She even gave him a child.

I put my mug down on the small table next to the chair. "Well, I should be going. Piper, Sterling, it was good to see you both again." I trot down the porch steps, praying I don't wipe out. Once safely at the bottom I turn and nod, channeling my inner bitch. "Ms. Hopkins."

Inside my mind I'm flipping a table so Candice knows not to mess with me. Finally, a tiny piece of rational brain takes over.

Finally.

CHAPTER 23

Will wonders never cease?

Sterling didn't call me a psychopath or weird or tell me to lose his number. He seemed ... pleased ... to see me.

Huh.

I won't think about how I'd made my mind up that I'm not ready for whatever this is. That I can't do a relationship right now.

My body's willing but my mind isn't there yet.

My hand reflexively touches the top of the implant, the feeling still alien under my fingers. I hate it.

But it beats the alternative, I guess.

I have years ahead of me. My story is not entering the final chapters. I'm barely through the prologue. I can finally plan for my retirement, like most of my teacher friends. While most of my coworkers can tell you the year and month, and sometimes even how many days left, I never bothered to count. I assumed I'd be out of the picture long before I'd reach that point.

I guess I should probably start saving more for retirement.

A summer house here overlooking the ocean isn't going to come cheap.

Tomorrow. Today, I'm going to enjoy the beach.

It's too early to start baking in the sun so I head out to the spacious front porch and pull up a roomy wooden rocker and watch the world go by. Runners, sweating in the early morning light. Dads pushing alert babies in strollers, obviously trying to let the rest of the family sleep. Dogs and their owners, stretching their legs. Cars pulling up and parking. Couples with chairs strapped on their backs, heading to the beach to claim the best spots before it fills up.

It's like paradise, where I can pretend to be someone else and that my problems don't mean anything.

I only have one day here, so I'm going to make the most of it. Maybe I'll rent a bicycle. Or perhaps go on a whale watch or fishing boat. In years past, basking on the beach would have been the hands down winner. Knowing that it'll be virtually impossible for me to get comfortable on the sand is making me anxious. Plus, you know, I'm kind of sensitive about the whole cancer thing.

My phone dings, altering me to a text.

What are you doing today?

In a former life, I would have texted back something like 'you' to let Sterling know I was interested. But that was then and this is now, and he's with his daughter and ex-wife, so it's not appropriate anyway.

Still, I'm pleased my mind finally went back to that flirty, risky place. It's good to know that my game is still there, and that it wasn't surgically removed as well.

Not sure yet. Thinking about renting a bicycle and going for a ride.

Sounds fun. I'm afraid I'd hurt myself.

Hmm ... Sterling has a good point. I don't think I've ridden a bicycle since I was about ten or eleven.

How hard can it be? I mean, it's just like riding a bike.

I follow that text with a series of emojis.

The three little dots wave on the screen, indicating he's working on his reply. A minute passes. Then two. Is he writing a paragraph? Finally his text balloon pops up.

Piper isn't interested in going, but I am. Name the time and place.

My heart jumps with joy, but I try to contain my excitement. He wants to be with me today. But then I read his text over again and now my heart sinks.

Are you sure you don't want to spend the time with Piper? This is your vacation with her. I don't want to get in the way.

The three dots dance again.

She wants to shop with her mother. If there's one thing Candice is good at, it's shopping. I consider this a win-win.

Are you sure?

The dots torment me again. Goodness, he's a slow texter. I never noticed this before.

Looks like we can rent them at Cape Island Bike Rentals. Beach and Howard St. In Hotel Macomber.

I probably need to stop doubting Sterling. He is obviously one of the most together people I've ever met. Certainly not like the guys I'm used to dating.

That's right next to where I'm staying. Stockton Manor. Meet you there? What time?

Once we've come up with a plan, I hurry to get ready. I quickly shower off sand and sweat from my morning beach walk, ignoring my foolishness as I'm bound to get even more sweaty and sandy. A baseball hat covers my out of control hair. My somewhat curly hair has revolted in the briny ocean humidity and needs significant containment. Probably military grade.

It's not until the bell tinkles on the door to the bike rental place that my reality hits me.

"I can't ride a bike."

"Sure you can, love. It's like, well, riding a bike." Sterling's voice behind me makes me jump a bit. Also, the realization that I actually said that out loud. That could be bad.

I shake my head, tentatively reaching out for the handlebars of the bike on the rack. The pulling in my chest stops me. "No, I don't know what I was thinking. I can't yet. It ..." I lift my arms up and down a few times. "I'm not recuperated enough."

"Oh, right. I'll go back in and tell them we've had a change of plans."

The bell tinkles again while Sterling goes in and cancels our rentals. I kick the crushed white shells that line the sidewalk. I swing my arms up and down, side to side, testing them. Definitely better than they were but not like before.

Sterling exits, hands casual in his khaki pockets. "What shall we do instead?"

"I'm so sorry. I didn't think about it beforehand. I can't believe for a few minutes I forgot ..." I trail off.

"Isn't that a good thing? That you could forget? I think that it means you're getting better. Before you know it, you'll be right as rain and you'll never think about it again."

I offer a tight smile. That's not something I ever see happening. At least not as long as there are mirrors. "I hope you're right."

Sterling reaches down and takes my hand. "We've got a few hours. How do you want to spend it?"

His hand is warm in mine, and the heat is starting to radiate somewhere else. Holy cow! I didn't know I could still get ... you know ... action in the bullpen. It's not like I'm ready to rip his clothes off. Not yet, but well, I'm happy that some of my bits and pieces still seem to be functioning.

I smile at him. "I don't care, as long as I'm with you."

He grins and leans in, his lips brushing mine. "Same here."

Our mouths mingle, exploring for a moment before he pulls back.

"We're standing on the street," Sterling states as he steps back.

"Yes we are." I don't know what else to say. Great. Another guy who doesn't like PDAs. I can sure pick 'em.

"Piper is somewhere around here."

"Oh, right." At least that makes sense. I think.

"I'm not sure where she and Candice will pop up."

Candice. Again.

Candice's entire being is akin to nails on the chalkboard for me. Yet she'll always be in the picture. She's Piper's mother.

From her reaction this morning, I'd say she's as excited about me as I am about her.

I take a small step back, increasing the distance between us. If there's space, maybe I'll be less likely to want to melt into him.

"How shall we spend this glorious morning together?" Sterling's so kind and conscientious.

I think for a minute. "I'd have to say kayaking, paddle boarding, and fishing are probably also out."

"Fishing? Really?"

I nod. "My dad likes to fish. Only lake or river fishing for him usually, but that was something we used to do a lot. Even after Mom ... it was his way of spending time with me." There was something about sitting out on the water that was so peaceful. We didn't talk a lot but I reveled in just being there with him.

"I grew up in a fishing town. You could tell by the smell alone. For a while, I thought I'd be doomed to a life on the docks."

We'd started walking while talking, weaving down shale sidewalks and even some cobblestone streets.

"Okay, so fishing's out."

"At least for this year. Maybe I'd be willing to give it a go next year. It'd be nice to see why people consider it a sport rather than a livelihood."

Next year.

He couldn't possibly mean ...

Millie, get your head on straight. Don't read into this. Don't make a big deal out of it.

I laugh nervously. "Next year? Are we going on vacation next year?"

I'm a moron, clearly.

Sterling smiles. "I hope so."

A warmth spreads through my belly. And this time, it's not even a hot flash.

"Um, okay."

Wow.

It's like my brain is malfunctioning. I press my lips together before I say something incredibly stupid.

"Millie, I know the timing isn't ideal for you, but give me a chance. Please." The look in his eyes is sincere. I will never deserve this man.

"Give *you* a chance? I'm the walking disaster here! I can't believe you keep giving me chances. Of course I'll give you a chance!"

I want to hug him so hard right now. Instead, I shove my hands in my pockets, lest I throw caution to the wind and throw myself at him.

Perhaps I am ready for this after all.

CHAPTER 24

While I had a brilliant time on my impromptu vacation, I don't know what I was thinking.

I'm *never* going to get my classroom ready in time.

It's Tuesday. Our Superintendent's Conference Day is in one week. That gives me approximately one-hundred and sixty-eight hours to get my room ready. I haven't done a blasted thing since I went on medical leave in early May. I'm not even sure what condition my classroom was left in. Here's hoping my sub followed instructions and packed everything in the bins I left for her.

All I know is, even if I was one-hundred percent healthy, this amount of work would be virtually impossible.

Last October when I decided on my theme, three-ring circus seemed cute and fun. I'd spent the year pinning things on Pinterest. I had so many ideas. I'd even been stockpiling supplies as I found things on clearance. Paper lanterns and tissue paper flowers on large stems. I've pulled out all my bins—book bins, mail bins, bins for bins.

But even if I wasn't going to decorate my room, there's so much prep work to be done.

So. Much. Laminating.

A quick aside about laminating—I have a love-hate relationship with it. I love things that are laminated. I love that they aren't destroyed with the first use. I love that they can be wiped down to stop the germs from totally infesting everything. I love how neat and shiny they keep things. But man, I hate to make them. It's the printing. Then the cutting. Then the gluing (because what good is something if it's not mounted on coordinating colored paper?). Then the laminating. Then the cutting again.

So. Much. Cutting.

Last night when I got home, I should have started. Fatigue won over and I went to bed. Now, from the looks of it, I won't be sleeping until October.

I spent this morning printing out names. Names for cubbies. Names for hallway hooks. Names for desks. Names for mailboxes.

Names. Names. Names.

And they all have to be laminated.

It reminds me of the first day at my first job in a linen store. I spent eight hours folding towels. Bet you didn't know it was possible to fold towels for eight hours.

It's also possible to laminate and cut for eight hours.

The cutting has caused muscles spasms in my pecs that feel like knives stabbing straight through from my chest to my back. I'm tempted to look in the mirror to see if there's a blade sticking out back there. I pop a Valium—or two—and wait a few minutes.

Once I feel the vice grip relax, I start the next project. I'm onto unrolling the large sheets of paper I squirreled away before I left last year. I need to cut out the big top where our spelling words will be housed. A tightrope and trapeze will serve as our number line. I was lucky enough to find an alphabet animal train, but I want to use some of this black paper to make tracks.

My stomach rumbles, reminding me I should probably eat something. I will, I promise myself, as soon as I finish the big top.

I'm almost done with this stupid tent. Dumbass me cut the tent out in white and have now spent an inordinate amount of time cutting out red stripes and contrasting yellow fringe.

I've begun to despise the vision I had for this year's theme.

Another hour later, I think I hear a knock on my door. "Come in," I yell. I hope whoever is coming in is in full combat gear because my house looks like a war zone.

It's a holy mess.

"Millie? Are you in here? Do you need help? Should I call for a rescue squad? I don't know where I can move without ripping or ruining something."

I stand up, peering over a tower of bins. "Oh, Sterling, thank God you're here. I ... oh no, we're supposed to go out, aren't we? What time is it? Crapballs."

The enormity of my task at hand, combined with hunger, fatigue, and overall overwhelmedness, consumes me.

I burst into tears.

"I'd been putting this stuff aside all year. I've been pinning and planning and everything. Even before my surgeries, I thought I was good to go for this year. But ... look." I spread my arms before letting them collapse down, my shoulders pulling forward. If I could curl into a full fetal position, I would. "I'll never be ready."

The chaos in my house has rendered Sterling speechless. His eyes are wide and all he can do is nod.

I continue, trying to justify the internal combustion that has apparently happened inside my house. "I thought this would be easier since I had all the stuff at home. I planned to get it all ready here and then all I have to do is put it out in the classroom."

"You may have thought wrong."

I look around, trying to see it as he must be seeing it.

It's bad.

"I don't know what happened ..." My voice is dazed. "Maybe I shouldn't have taken that extra Valium."

"Perhaps that was where you went astray." He looks around again, his eyes surveying and tallying the situation. "But we need to do something to get this under control. Where to start?"

I look to my right and then my left and then back again. Finally, I lift my gaze to Sterling, processing what he said. "Will you really help?"

"Of course, love. What else would we do tonight?"

I vaguely remember we hand plans to do something, but I can't for the life of me recall what they were.

I give him a watery smile. "I really don't know what happened. I'm not usually like this. I ..." I look around. "I don't know where to even begin."

I've seen houses on Hoarders that didn't look this bad.

"Is there anything that's done that can be moved out to the car? I assume all of this at some point will have to go into school, and if we can make space now ..." he trails off.

I nod, seeing where he's going. "The yellow bins are all labeled. They can go."

"Even this one?" Sterling laughs, pointing to one that is filled with a sleeping overweight gray tiger cat. He hasn't seemed to mind this entropy one bit. Or he's being passive aggressive because he's still mad about being shipped to Dad's and then dumped back here. He's a cat, so it's hard to tell.

"Cornelius, shoo." I dump him out of the bin, earning me a dirty look. I don't think his irritation will last as I watch him promptly lay down on a large sheet of paper and begin grooming himself.

Sterling takes a stack and brings it out to his car. It makes no difference in the clutter. After several repetitions, I finally start to see a small area of clear space.

"I'm loading up your car as well as mine. From the looks of it, we'll be making multiple loads. Taking both cars might cut down on the trips needed."

"Many hands make light work." I say this to my kids all the time when we have to do lots of picking up in the classroom.

"I don't know that I'd consider four many, but it's certainly better than two. My dad would've helped, but we got this done much faster."

Slowly but surely, we tackle the mess. Order is created. Four hours later and I almost have my house back. A few manageable piles remain on my table, held in place by King Cornelius. At least he's good for something.

"You really go through this every year?"

I nod while feeding the plastic through the laminator. Can you believe I *still* have things to laminate? Now that we've moved out all the big items, like the storage bins and stools covered to look like tubs of popcorn, there's much more room to work in the house. I've pressed Sterling into cutting detail, so we should finish up the labeling for my reading bins shortly.

"Yup, although this is one of my more detailed years. Go figure. I didn't know when I started stockpiling the turn my life would take."

"I'm glad I'm here to help. You shouldn't be lugging these things around."

He's not wrong, and I'm so happy he was there to move the packed up ones from my classroom out to the shed in the backyard. They'd sat at school all summer. Silly me had thought maybe Johnny would have brought them over for me. Before he dumped me, obviously.

"Probably not, though I keep forgetting. Still, getting everything to school is the biggest part. Now that it's almost all there, I should be able to set it up in a day or two."

Meaning forty-eight hours straight.

Okay, thirty-six hours straight.

"How much does all of this cost you?"

It impresses me that Sterling thinks about this. Most parents don't consider the time and effort teachers put into making their classrooms bright and vibrant.

"I give myself a budget of three-hundred for the year. I try to re-use as much as I can. The aqua and red bins were from when I did a Dr. Seuss theme, and the yellow were from my barnyard year. The stools were already in my room. My dad brought them over at the end of the school year so I could work on them when I felt better. I thought I'd get to them earlier in the summer."

"How long does it take you to come up with all of this?"

I finally finish my laminating while filling him in on my process. "If I hadn't been stupid and put fish and sea creatures on my reading bin labels last year, I wouldn't have had to re-do these. Lesson learned. For items that don't change, use a generic label."

Now it's Sterling's stomach's turn to growl, which again reminds me that I still have yet to eat. I don't even know the last thing I had.

"Are you hungry?" I ask, saying a mental prayer that he is so we can stop and eat.

"Starving." The look on his face tells me he's famished and could probably eat a horse. It is—holy cow!—how did it get to be nine already?

Suddenly the fact that we had an entire evening planned, including dinner and theater in the park comes flooding back.

"Oh Sterling, we were supposed to go to dinner! And the theater in the park! Why didn't you say something? I can't believe I forgot!"

"Didn't seem important at the time. But now I believe I may want to take a break to grab a bite. Shall I order us something? You must be ravenous too."

"Don't order. I've got tons in the freezer still. Let's heat something up." He follows me back to the kitchen. Cornelius decides to join us, letting me know with a loud meow that he, too, is ravenous. His dish is two-thirds full.

I pull open the freezer to reveal stacked containers, all neatly labeled and dated. "Ziti, meatballs, mac and cheese, chili, chicken and rice casserole ..."

"What are you in the mood for?" Sterling sneaks up behind me and before I know it, threads his arm around my waist. Reflexively I stiffen, but only for a minute before allowing myself to relax into his warm touch.

"It doesn't matter. I'm easy."

Sterling leans in and kisses the base of my neck. "I certainly hope so."

CHAPTER 25

Okay, so this is happening. I'm ready. I can do this.

I cannot do this.

I wriggle out of Sterling's embrace. "Okay, chicken and rice it is. Let me just pop this in the microwave," I say too loudly. Too cheerfully.

Sterling leans casually against the counter. Seductively. He certainly is a yummy looking man, isn't he? "How long 'till they're ready?"

"Oh, you must be starving. Let me see what I can get for you in the meantime."

Sterling steps to me, gently sliding his hands over the sides of my hips and around my rump. I'm not sure if he pulls me to him or if my feet close the distance on their own. "There's only one thing I need right now."

His lips meet mine, and I think I died and went to Heaven. I could eat this man up. He makes me feel like … well, he makes me feel.

I didn't expect it so soon. I didn't think I'd be able to do this. To let someone explore my body and touch me and feel the …

Dammit.

My mind is off and racing and there's nothing I can do to put that horse back in the gate. Doubt, self-consciousness, and shame all swirl, vying for first place in my psyche. "Sterling, can we pause for a moment?"

"Certainly, love." He steps back, adjusting the front of his shorts.

Oh my.

There's a certain something to knowing that, even in my current state, I can have that effect on him.

I close my eyes, taking a deep breath in and then out. I don't even know how to broach this with him. The thoughts are pinging around in my head like bugs dancing on a streetlamp on a hot summer night.

"I ... um ... well ..." Even with spurting and stuttering, I can't seem to find the words. I look down at my feet as if they're the most interesting things on the planet. "I ... crap. This is hard."

It's at this moment that I raise my gaze to meet Sterling's and can't help but notice the wicked look. I also can't keep from glancing down where other things might be hard.

"I'm not sure yet."

His smile falls and I see his shoulders slump. "About me? How can you not be sure about me?" Sterling looks down at his feet. He turns around and starts to walk toward the living room. "I'd best be going then." The edge to his voice is unmistakable.

Crap. Crap. Crappity crap crapola.

This is not what I meant to do. Not at all.

"No, Sterling." I rush to him and put my arms around his broad shoulders. The pressure on my chest is uncomfortable, but I won't let go. "It's not you. It's me."

He shrugs me off. "I'm not falling for that line again."

"No, Sterling. Really. I ... what if ..." I don't even know how to put into words what I'm thinking. How do I say that there's no way he will still find me attractive once he touches me? "My chest ..."

"Oh dear heavens, Millie! Why didn't you say something? I thought you were healed. I had no idea. I'm so sorry. Forgive me, love."

He's turned so he's holding my hands.

"Of course."

"I ... I have no experience with this. Candice had her augmentation after we split. She said it was her present to herself. Her recovery seemed easier, as I seem to remember her preening about within a few weeks."

I turn away and busy myself putting the container in the microwave. I should let it go and not justify why my recovery is longer. But the words of the UnBRCAble women echo in my head. I hit the start button and turn back to face Sterling.

"I didn't have an augmentation. I had a mastectomy first, in which all my b-breast tissue was removed," I stutter a bit, the words coming too fast and rushed. I take a deep breath. I see Sterling wince as I explain my procedure, and how it differs from Candice's experience. "For me, after they scraped everything out, there's nothing left but a very thin layer of skin. Most of the nerves and blood vessels are gone, so early on, there's a really high chance of losing everything. Healing is very important."

"I'm sorry. I didn't know."

I put my hand on his arm. "Let me finish. I need to tell you it all."

Sterling nods and I take another deep breath.

"Some of the implant fits in under my pectoral muscles, like in regular augmentation, but the bottom of the implant hangs out. Since there's no tissue left to hold the implant in place—like a box that's too big needs those packing peanuts—they have to put it in a pocket. A cadaver pocket."

I expect him to grimace. Vomit. Run for the hills.

"Is it like a transplant? How interesting. Do you have to take the anti-rejection medication?"

I startle at his response. "Um, no. They process and treat it so there's no immune cells left, but ... well ... it's sort of gross."

"I disagree. It's amazing science has come far enough to do something like this." He steps back. "My sister had a transplant a few years back."

"So the knowledge that I have part of a dead body in my chest doesn't gross you out? It grosses me out. All of it does."

That's the first time I've ever said it out loud. I haven't even admitted that in group.

"Not at all! I'm glad they had the technology to help you and so many others. I didn't know they used organ donation for this."

"I didn't know either. I wonder when the guy checked the box on his driver's license, he thought he'd spend eternity holding a breast implant up."

Sterling winks. "I'm sure more men would check the box if they knew. I find it fascinating what they can do these days with the transplants. With Samantha, they were looking for a living donor."

I feel my eyebrows knit together. "Um, how do you have a living donor? Isn't death always a part of it?"

"Not for her. She needed a liver transplant. They only need about ten percent of the liver, so you can donate some of yours and still carry on just fine. She wanted to do that, but unfortunately, it didn't work out that way. She ended up with a cadaver donation." His face darkens a bit. If I had to guess, I'd say he was recalling what a difficult time it was for his sister. No wonder he's so compassionate and understanding.

"Why'd she need a transplant? How old was she when it happened? Weren't any of you guys a match for her?" It's my turn with the rapid-fire, overly-invasive medical questions. It's nice not to be the one we're talking about for a change. "You don't have to answer any of those. They're none of my business."

Sterling smiles. God, he's so freakin' sexy when he looks at me like that. "Let's have a drink and then we'll play tit for tat."

I raise my eyebrow.

"Not that kind, love, though I'd be willing. You ask a question, you answer a question. Full disclosure."

"Deal."

"Okay then, you go first."

"Why'd she need the transplant?"

Sterling takes a deep inhale. "That's a bit of a tricky one. Samantha was in a car accident, and she smashed up her leg but good. Bones sticking out. Truly gruesome business."

I seem to have lost all control over my facial muscles and am one-hundred percent certain I'm making the 'eeew' face.

"Exactly. She had to have surgery to fix it. Rods and pins and plates and all. She can't go through a metal detector without the whole thing going off like she robbed a bank. While she was going into surgery, they gave her anesthesia and she had a reaction to it. Caused her liver to totally fail."

"Oh, my God. That's awful!"

"I know. It's about a one in one-hundred-thousand thing, but that doesn't matter when it happens to you. So, her liver was basically shot and if she wanted to live, she needed a new one."

"When did all this happen?"

"Ah, no. It's my turn."

He's right, but it doesn't make me dread his question any less. "Okay, fine. Shoot."

"Are you still having pain?"

I should be prepared for the "Sterling switch" at this point. "Um, not really, but occasionally. It's more that I get muscle spasms in my pec muscles. The implants are wedged under them, so that's what hurts now more than anything else. That happened earlier today." I shrug. "Hence, the Valium. My turn."

The microwave dings, so I stir the now defrosted contents of the casserole. Only a few more minutes and we should be able to eat finally. "When did all this happen?"

"About five or six years ago. It was quite the cluster. First the accident, which on it's own would have been bad enough." He leans against the counter, arms folded over his chest.

"What could be worse than a bone sticking out of your leg?"

"Un uh. My turn. Did you *have* to have your surgery?"

"I felt like I did. Without it, I had over an eighty percent chance of developing breast cancer." I don't know why, but I leave out the ovarian cancer part. I know I should tell him about the hysterectomy as well. It's something he needs to know. I'll answer it with the next question.

"That's bad. Really bad."

"Yeah, so sort of a no brainer. The odd thing is that everyone kept trying to make me feel better that I didn't actually get the cancer first. I mean, I know that's an upside, but it didn't make the whole experience any less traumatic. It was still a lot to undergo."

A tear slips out. Jiminy Crickets. The full-on waterworks are close behind. Other than the physical disfigurement, it's the part of this that I hate the most. The estrogen replacement patch I wear makes me feel like I'm constantly PMSing. Ironic, no?

Sterling moves to me and gently takes me in his arms. "Oh Millie, I cannot even imagine what you're going through, but I know it must suck."

I pull back so I can look directly at his face. He didn't tell me I was lucky. He didn't say it could have been worse. He didn't start a sentence with "at least."

I think I may be falling in love with this man.

"Thank you," I say, my voice husky and quiet through my tears. "Thank you for being you and understanding. And I know I have no right to ask this, but can you please give me a little more time?"

Sterling gives me a quick peck on the nose. "Of course, love. Whatever you need. However long you need. There's only one thing I can't be flexible on."

Oh no. Here it comes. The deal breaker.

"Yes?" My hands begin to tremble.

"Is that blasted food ready? I'm completely famished."

Relief floods my system.

"That, that I can do."

The dish comes out of the microwave, steaming hot. I portion it out onto our plates. A quick glance tells me that for the all progress we've made, both my dining room table and coffee table are still covered with classroom supplies. I nod toward the stools at the counter and slide the plates in that direction.

"This'll have to do until I get more stuff finished. At this rate, maybe by Columbus Day. Halloween at the latest."

"I've seen you work. It'll be done by the time I get here tomorrow."

My stomach does a flip that even after shutting him down, he still wants to be with me. I know this should not be a surprising reaction, but considering my track record, I'm not used to it.

We eat in silence, shoveling the food in at an indecent speed. I hadn't realized how hungry I was. Perhaps all that stomach twisting and flipping was actual hunger, not Sterling's manly prowess. Yeah, right. I don't believe me either.

"I can't tell you the last time I was this famished. I think my appetite might actually be coming back." I glance down at my thighs, thicker than last year, my shorts straining a bit. "Not that you can tell from looking at me."

Sterling follows my gaze down. "I think you look perfect. You're beautiful."

"How can you say that?" Lots of adjectives run through my mind. Deformed. Chubby. Pale. Defective. Broken.

"Because I have eyes and I like what I see. Every inch of you is just the way it should be, Millie Dwyer. And I'll do whatever it takes to convince you of that."

Before I can control myself, before I even know the thought has formed in my brain, I hear myself saying, "Stay here. Tonight. Stay with me, Sterling."

Oh crap.

What did I just do?

CHAPTER 26

"Is this okay?" Sterling asks for perhaps the hundredth time since lying down next to me. This is just as awkward as I feared it would be.

Not because Sterling isn't trying.

I simply cannot relax. Not that he needs to know that though.

I sigh. "Perfect. I'll tell you if you're not. I promise, holding my hand will not hurt me."

"What about this?" He lets go of my hand, slides his arm under my neck, pulling me into him a bit. That does not work so well.

I move, pushing pillows here and there before I can nestle in and rest my head on his chest. Still not great, but I can probably tolerate it for a few minutes. I take a deep breath in and exhale slowly, trying to get the muscles to relax.

And cue hot flash.

"This I like, but I will probably need to move. You're too hot."

He grins a sweet yet sexy smile. "Thank you. You're pretty hot yourself, but I've already told you that."

I shove his leg with mine, and try not to smile back at him. For as terrible timing as this is, Sterling is quite terrific. "Not hot as attractive, though you are that. Hot as in I might catch on fire. I have ... sometimes I can't regulate my temperature. My thermostat must be broken."

"I like holding you for as long as you can stand."

"I like being held. I ... I didn't know that I would." I didn't think I'd be ready for this for years to come.

"Being held by me or just being held?" His voice is expectant. His look, hopeful.

"Being held at all. Frankly, if it were anyone but you, I wouldn't be ready." I'm not sure I'm totally ready now, but he's definitely making the trip easier. I'm quiet for a moment. "Funny to think that at the beginning of all of this, I barely knew you. If you'd have told me when they wheeled me in for the mastectomy that ten weeks later, I'd be here with Hot British Dad, I would have thought you were smoking something."

"Hot British Dad?"

Shoot me now. "Um, yeah. That's what Lisa calls you."

"Who's Lisa?"

His question is a bit of a gut punch. We've been hanging out—dating even—for six or so weeks now, and he doesn't know my best friend. Former best friend. "She's—was—my best friend. We, um, haven't been seeing eye-to-eye lately. Plus, she's super busy at work, so she doesn't have a ton of time for me right now."

Somehow the work excuse seems easier than she's been rude and unsupportive.

"That's too bad," he murmurs supportively. "Let's get back to the Hot British Dad thing though. How long have I had this moniker?"

I laugh and so does he. He continues to try to soothe me. "Life takes funny turns, doesn't it? I try to go with it." He chuckles, but I don't understand what's so funny. "Actually that's not true. Everyone tells me I need to go with it. I know I probably should, but I can't seem to mind my own business. I try to fix things that I should leave well-enough alone. Stu is always telling me," he rolls his eyes, "to stop trying to save the day. Not everyone is a cat who needs rescuing."

Dear God. It's as if someone dumped a bucket of cold water over me. "Is that what you're doing here? Fixing me? Saving me? I don't need saving. My surgeons already did that." I sit up desperate for air.

"No. I want to help you, not fix you. That's why I started the Helping Wagon. It's not why I'm here now though."

"It's not?" I don't know if I believe him. It makes sense, this fixing business. Makes a lot more sense than anything else.

"You intrigue me, Millie. I find you fascinating and beautiful and precious. I don't think you need fixing, not at all."

I slide away, leaving a cold space between us. "Sterling, I … I don't know that I know how to do this."

"I don't know what you mean by that. Do what? All we're doing is talking."

"I'm afraid I'm going to say the wrong thing, and you'll get all mad and leave. I don't want you to leave." I don't, even if he's here for the wrong reasons.

"There are only two things you could say to make me leave. One would be something about Piper and the other would be to ask me to leave. That's about it."

I adjust myself, scooting back so the headboard supports me. "Even if I'm moody and snap at you?"

"What kind of people have you been dating?"

"Losers, but that's neither here nor there. I ... I keep pissing off my best friend. I'm afraid I'll do the same to you. I already told you she's not talking to me."

"Why not?"

I'm quiet. Do I tell him the truth? Do I even know why? I feel like I'm being disloyal to Lisa, but Sterling's been here for me when she wasn't. "She was upsetting me with her comments. So apparently I upset her with mine. We like to keep things equal like that."

"What sort of comments?"

"The same ones everyone else said. You know, the free boob job. That this isn't a big deal because I don't actually have cancer. Mostly about the free boob job. About how she should try having surgery to pick up a guy."

"So why was it different when she said it?"

I sigh again and slide down so I'm lying on my back. "I don't know. I just felt like she should know better. She's got the same parts I do. I thought she'd be more understanding. She should know that this wasn't an elective surgery so I can have a better rack. Death has always been a real possibility for me because of my genes."

"Those seem like valid points."

"I don't know how to plan for the rest of my life."

I didn't mean to actually say the last one out loud.

I continue, "She says stupid things trying to be funny, but I didn't find her comments funny. I mean, maybe someday I will, but I'm not there yet. I didn't tell her when you and I started hanging out more, but she found out and got upset."

"Why didn't you tell her about me? Am I some dirty little secret?" His tone is light, and I appreciate what he's doing, but I need to get this off my chest.

"We'd talked about you in the beginning, but well, I just couldn't handle her reactions."

It's his turn to sit up, eager like a new puppy. "What did she say about me? Other than the Hot British Dad thing, obviously. That I'd undoubtedly be the best shag of your life, and you'd never go back to a lazy American lover after me?"

This makes me laugh. Damn, I need to laugh. "No, but God, it's so embarrassing."

"Aw, come on, love. You can tell me."

Well, this part is no laughing matter. "I told her that even though I thought you were cute, things probably wouldn't go anywhere, because I was closed for business."

"Yes, and I'm sad about that, but more sad that you called me cute. What about hot? Dashing? Sexy? Cute is for puppies."

I sit up again and lean in, planting a delicate kiss on his nose. "You are cute. And dashing. And sexy. All of the above. Lisa's response was that you'd like my new—this is her term, not mine—fun bags better than the chest I used to have." My voice quiets. "I'd sell my soul to have my old chest and still be able to live."

"Pardon me, but this Lisa sounds like a wanker."

This makes me smile.

"I'm sorry I'm not ready yet. That I'm not whole for you. That I can't be who you need me to be."

He reaches up and pushes the hair back off my face. "Millie, I only need you to be you. As you are, right now. I will take whatever you have to give, however it is."

CHAPTER 27

I should have told him about the hysterectomy last night.

The thought races through my head all night and well into the next day as I continue tackling my classroom chaos.

I know why I didn't tell him.

It's because I have a feeling it will be a deal breaker.

Fake boobs? Lots of women have them.

No uterus? Nope, I'm out.

At least I can't trap him with a pregnancy. From some of his comment, I wonder if this is what Candice did to him. If so, maybe he'd find the sterility a good thing.

Can't fall into that trap again.

Something he said still nags at me. About fixing— and saving. It's easy to see that Candice is the type who always needs saving. A "drama llama" as Erin puts it. I'd never been able to make sense of what the attraction was between Sterling and Candice. If he was trying to save her, well that makes sense then. Has he really changed? What if he tries to save her again?

I should probably not draw parallels between myself and his ex-wife. While I'd like to think that perhaps I'm better for Sterling than she was, she did give him the one thing I'll never be able to. And that chaps my ass.

Life is so not fair.

The pity party has to be short lived. I have to get this classroom ready. I don't have time to sit here and wallow. However, I can continue wallowing while I decorate.

I'm good at multitasking like that.

Once again, I consult my Pinterest board to see what I should be doing.

At least most of the supplies are out of my house and at school. Sterling promised he'd help after work this evening, but I hope to be done by that point. I only have two more days before our Superintendent Conference days start. Students will be here in one short week.

I'm starting the year at a very nice twenty students. Chances are my roster will change and rise, but this is good to start off. I'm looking forward to this upcoming year. It'll be good to get back into a routine and have a schedule and not be recovering.

Well, I'll still be recovering, just not to the same degree as right after surgery. Frances said in group last week that it was a good six months before she felt one-hundred percent.

Ain't nobody got time for that.

I need to be back and better and move on. I'm sick of being an invalid. I'm sick of having to move with caution. I'm sick of everyone looking at me as if I have leprosy.

I am back and nothing is going to stop me.

Except pain and extreme fatigue of course.

I hate my body.

It's betrayed me more than anyone ever has, and that's a lot considering my mom, dad, and the losers I normally date.

I quit at about three o'clock. I'm so wiped out, I'm not sure I can even drive home. Calling Aunt Polly crosses my mind. I know she'd come in a heartbeat, but I'm sick of needing people.

I muster up every ounce of strength I have left and drive to the Genevieve T. Wunderlich Women's Health Center. UnBRCAble meets in an hour, so I can doze in my car until then.

When the alarm on my phone begins, its auditory assault jars me upright. I'd always been a power napper. Seven to ten minutes could refresh me. Sixty minutes and I wake up disoriented with drool crusted on my cheek. I feel groggy and fight off the need to go back to sleep. A quick glance in the visor mirror tells me I should avoid all reflective surfaces for the rest of the day.

Working all day in a hot sweaty classroom in the August heat and humidity hasn't done anything for my smell either.

I'm hoping the women in the group will ignore the horror that is my current appearance. And smell. This is the first time I'm coming to group, not as a sense of duty or obligation, but because I need to. I *have* to. I don't know that I can make it without the strength of them.

I make it through the door before I start crying again. Erin and Claudia rush me.

"What's wrong?"

"What happened?"

"Is it your nipple?"

Voices surround me, pounding with questions.

"I don't know. I ... I'm so tired." Fatigue weighs my limbs down. I want to cry. Oh wait, I already am.

At least I can cross that off my list.

I'm nothing if not accomplished.

With a little wiggling, the crowd dissipates, and I sink onto the couch. If I have trouble rising, it most likely will be because I don't have the energy to stand.

"I've spent the last two days getting my classroom ready. It's still not done, and I don't know if it will be. I can't move anymore. I almost couldn't drive over. I had to nap in my car before I came in."

Murmurs of support and shared issues with fatigue.

"Are you sleeping at all? I couldn't after the hysterectomy."

Most—all—of us here know that we don't really mean only hysterectomy. While some doctors are conservative, most of the gynecologists around here seem to favor removal of the uterus too. The hormonal changes are actually brought about by the risk-reducing salpingo-oophorectomy, which is the removal of the ovaries and fallopian tubes. Hysterectomy is so much easier to say. I've never even attempted to say oophorectomy out loud. I'm afraid I'd sound like an idiot.

Some ladies here have their uteruses still. Some have had the mastectomies, but are waiting until later in life to remove their ovaries. Lucky ducks.

I was so afraid of cancer developing quickly and stealthily that I couldn't even consider keeping my ovaries for later.

I didn't know about hormone-replacement therapy until this group either. It seems that new studies are coming in all the time about it. Technically, I don't need HRT. The early menopause puts me at risk for brittle, thin bones as I age. And of course, there's the hot flashes, weight gain, sleep disturbances, and dryness, you know, down *there*. Nothing life threatening, certainly.

Minor inconveniences.

Until you go postal from chronic sleep deprivation and get arrested for public nudity due to rampaging hot flashes.

With information from this group, I did my research and talked to Dr. Tremarchi. I now wear a small patch on my butt that delivers estrogen so some of those things aren't as bad as they were.

But let's face it—horse hormones are no replacement for my own, and I'm still a quasi-psychotic menopausal twenty-something mess.

"Sleep's okay. Well, I didn't get much sleep last night, come to think of it." I see Sterling in my bed, tangled in my sheets. I was so afraid I'd snore or drool or fart all night that I barely slept.

Claudia sits down, her face drawn with worry. "Hot flashes?"

"No, I was worried about Sterling hearing me snore. I mean, I don't know if I snore, but what if I do and he was like, what was that? And then it all ends before stuff ever starts to happen."

Erin leans over Claudia's shoulder to look at me. "Sterling? Snoring? Are you guys? Did you ... you know?"

This is not stuff I normally talk about in a room full of people, let alone *to* a room full of people. It's hard enough to tell my best friend sometimes. But since the ten or so women in the room know all about my breasts and vaginal dryness and all those other personal things, I might as well tell them this too.

"Nothing happened. I told him I'm not ready yet."

"What'd he say?" I think it was Frances who asks.

"He was great. He is great. He said he'd wait until I'm ready."

"What if you're never ready?" That was Kelli. This is only her second meeting or so. She's pre-surgical still, and you can see the terror in her eyes every time she walks through the door. I don't want her to be scared.

I don't want to be scared anymore either.

"I don't know. I mean, there are times where my body is like, 'hells yeah, we got this' but then my brain takes over."

"Stupid brain." I don't know who said that. I nod in agreement anyway.

"Yeah, so how do I stop my stupid brain from taking over?"

Claudia puts her hand on my knee. Calmness exudes from her voice. I wonder if she'd record a meditation session for me. "What is your brain telling you?"

I think about it for a minute. "All the normal stuff. He's not going to like to touch them. He's going to want to touch them. They're going to feel revolting. I'm not going to be able to feel anything there, so I'll get pissed if he wants to play with them. What if he's a boob guy? What if I don't let him touch them and then *he's* not turned on? What if he's disgusted?"

I take a deep breath.

I cannot believe I've said all those things.

Out loud.

To other people.

Because it's UnBRCAble, no one laughs. No one tells me I'm being ridiculous. No one tells me there's nothing to worry about.

There's a lot to worry about.

A lot of partners leave. Mine did, if you could even call Johnny a partner. The divorce rates are high.

It's hard to tell if it's because the significant others can't hack the new body or if it's the self-loathing that drives them away.

"Go all Carrie Bradshaw and keep your bra on." Frances suggests.

I have no idea what she's talking about.

"You know, Sarah Jessica Parker wouldn't do topless scenes for *Sex and the City*, so she always had a bra on. If you get yourself a nice, sexy one, it'll be enough to get you over the hurdle. At least for a while."

"Has anyone done this?" More than half the room nods.

I want to ask if they were ever able to finally take the bra off, but that seems like prying. I know the question would be welcome, but nonetheless I don't ask.

Suddenly, I don't feel quite as overwhelmed anymore. Sure, my classroom is still in disarray, and I'm dog tired, but at least I think I have one problem solved.

Now all I need to do is get some sexy bras.

CHAPTER 28

The support of the group bolsters my confidence and my spirits, and suddenly, I have the energy to tackle the mall even though I should probably go home and rest up. Sterling and I made plans for tonight, but he already texted that he will probably have to cancel.

Wednesday nights are normally his nights with Piper, but Candice had requested this one to go to a concert or something. Sterling's not happy about giving up his time, but he seems to think that this will make a difference. Now, she's cancelling the concert, and Piper's back at Sterling's. He hopes his flexibility will be to his benefit next summer.

I hope he's keeping track of this.

I have every suspicion that it will make zero difference.

I hope Sterling can see that. All that matters is she cancelled Piper's concert and expects Sterling to pick her up after work.

Which of course he will.

As he should.

I could probably use the sleep tonight anyway.

After I purchase some lingerie.

I have a gift card to *Voulez-Vous*, courtesy of Lisa. My heart pangs. She was so happy when I opened the card.

"I can't wait to go bra shopping with you! You'll get fancy new things. They'll be so hot, Johnny will be eternally grateful to me."

I'd put the pink plastic in the back of my wallet where I wouldn't see it all the time.

The idea of bras made of scraps of fabric, wire, and see-through lace has been about the furthest thing from my reality since my surgery. Firstly, I need more support than that. Secondly, I'm not allowed to wear an underwire. Thirdly, the thought of that fabric on my delicate and tender skin—no thank you.

But, if it's the only way to get through this next step with Sterling, I'm willing to give it a try.

And while I'd love to just order something online, truth be told, I have no idea what size I am. My breasts are in a different location (still riding high) and such a different shape than before, that I can't even fathom a guess. I need to be measured.

You think by now I'd be used to having my foobs handled, but I don't know that it's something one should get used to.

The overly perky clerk follows me into the dressing room. "Let's see what you're currently wearing."

I don't know why this makes a difference. I mean, I'm here to buy new bras. It doesn't matter what my old one looks like.

Okay, yes, I'm still wearing the surgical bra. I went back to it after the debacle at the auto parts store.

Seemed safer.

Plus, this one was clean.

"Oh God, what is that thing? Is it your grandma's?" The saleswoman doesn't even bother to hide her disgust. "Thank goodness you're here. You need us." She shakes her head, muttering in disgust as she whips the pink tape measure off of her neck and tells me to hold my arms out. She measures in about three places.

"36-D."

"D?"

I couldn't have heard that right. I was a small B before. I don't understand how I could be that large, but it might explain why none of my bras feel comfortable. I'd actually been thinking that my chest was smaller now that the swelling is *finally* starting to abate.

"Let me go pull some options for you. What style—never mind. I don't think you can be trusted to make good bra decisions."

My mouth opens and closes as she swishes out of the dressing room. I stand there, looking at the ceiling, at the rug, at the white stool. Anywhere but in the mirror. I don't need to see the twin freaks on the front of me.

I chuckle in spite of myself and the torturous surroundings. A good pun can always make me do that.

My smile fades faster than a New Year's Resolution the minute the clerk walks back into the room. I swear, every single scrap of fabric she has is already making me itch. I cross my arms nervously over my frumpy yet functional surgical bra. Not to mention there's more padding than in an overstuffed sofa.

"Um, no."

"No what?" She looks at the black, red, and leopard prints dangling from her arm. I swear, I have pillows with less stuffing.

"No to all of those." I wave my hands at her.

"Why? You haven't even tried them. They are our best sellers."

"Do I look like I need *more* padding? I've got enough in there as it is. I can't believe I'm a D cup!" There's a chance my voice is rising to a pitch where soon only dolphins will understand what I'm saying. "How did I get to be a D?"

Then, the saleswoman from hell, lays it out there. Her gaze is firmly glued to my doughy midsection. "Well, have you gained weight recently? That can do it."

In my head, I scream, "No, you twatwaffle! I just had a mastectomy."

In reality, my face burns with embarrassment, I yank my T-shirt over my head and rush out of the store. It's only once I'm in the mall, panting like I just finished an Ironman, that I realize my shirt is on inside out.

And backwards.

Because, of course, the humiliations can't end, I run smack into Lisa. Like literally.

"Watch where you're go—oh, it's you."

"Hey Lis." I look down at my feet, praying she doesn't comment on my appearance. I mean, I looked disheveled when I got here. I can only imagine what I look like now.

"What are you doing here? I thought you were all sick, except for when you go out with your boyfriend."

"I, um, well, I was trying to go bra shopping."

The defiant look falls from her face. "I thought we were going to do that together. You went without me?" She seems hurt.

Her tune changes so quickly, it could just about give me whiplash. "Well, Erin and Claudia thought I should try it. In case I want to be, you know, a little more intimate with Sterling." At least I'm able to drop my voice into a whisper, instead of the shrieking that was coming out of me back in the store.

"You're going to sleep with him?" Lisa's voice is not so quiet. Yes, people turn to look.

"I don't know. Not yet, but I want to be ready in case."

"Who told you to go bra shopping? I mean other than me, but apparently my opinion doesn't mean squat."

"Erin and Claudia."

"Like I'm supposed to know who they are."

"They're from UnBRCAble. My support group."

"Nice. Real nice."

"What exactly is your problem, Lisa?" I have no idea why she's being so bitchy, so I say that to her. "I'm the one going through this, not you. It wouldn't kill you to be a little nicer to me, would it?"

"I thought getting the surgery would make you better since you wouldn't have to worry anymore, but it's only made you worse."

Worse?

"Worse how?"

"You're moody and irritable, and you jump down my throat every time I say anything."

I reach in my purse and take out the gift card. "Here. Take this back. I don't need this crap from you."

I stuff the card into her hands and turn on my heel. From a reserve I didn't know I had, I run. Actually run. As if a bear is chasing me or a food truck is in front of me. I'm panting like nobody's business by the time I reach my car, and there's a good possibility I may throw up.

On the bright side, at least I know my bra size. Time for some online shopping.

CHAPTER 29

"Don't be mad."

"Let me guess, change of plans?" Keeping the irritation from my voice is a measured effort.

"Some days I hate my ex-wife," Sterling mutters.

You and me both, buddy.

It's like Candice has realized Sterling's dating someone, so she's jerking him around with Piper. Yes, it's your night but I need her. It's my night, but I need you to take her.

"Just think, you get a lot more time with Piper. School starts next week, so get your quality time in now."

See? I can be positive.

"Yes, but you also go back to school next week, and I'm afraid I won't get much QT with you."

Aww, he's so sweet. He's also right. While I've been disappointed that he's had to cancel, I've also been burning the candle at both ends trying to get my classroom in order.

"Plus, I think she's doing this on purpose. She'd never stand for me acting the way she is. I should call my lawyer."

I've never heard him this agitated which is probably a good thing. I'd rather have him upset with her than with me.

"Is it really worth getting that upset over?"

"Hang on."

I wait a minute.

"Sorry. Gotta run. I'll text you later."

This is fine. We don't need to see each other. He has a valid excuse. Like a daughter. And an ex-wife that will probably always wreak this kind of havoc on his life.

Our life.

If we make it that far.

The thought of the long haul makes my heart race and my palms sweat, and my lunch hovers dangerously high in my esophagus.

Let's face it, I'm not the long-haul kind of gal.

The long-haul gal, let's call her LHG for now, has been looking for a relationship since she discovered boys. She hopes dreams, and dresses up, makes wedding veils out of her grandmother's doilies. She's had the names of her children picked since she was twelve. LHG considers every date she has could be *The One*. LHG doesn't waste time on fun. LHG doesn't go out with men with unsuitable last names.

Yes, my friends all got a big laugh when I dated Patrick Vannelli. Lisa offered to pay me to go to Vegas to marry him so I could be Millie Vannelli. Needless to say, I declined.

LHG is looking for a soul mate.

I never considered the possibility that there was one out there for me. And certainly if there was, I didn't want to find him. Or for him to find me.

That wouldn't be fair to either of us.

To love him and leave him.

I'm not that selfish. I wouldn't do that, even if it meant spending my own brief life without that special someone.

My phone dings with a text from Sterling.

Gah. I can't take it anymore. 3rd day in a row she's changed plans last minute.

He doesn't have to tell me twice. I was there when he canceled on our Wednesday and Thursday plans. I shouldn't be too disappointed. He's doing the right thing. I wouldn't want someone who didn't care for his child.

Look on the bright side. More P time.

After I hit send, I worry that my casual use of "P" instead of Piper might be too soon. LHGs have to be concerned about making mistakes like this. I never have before. I quickly add,

Don't know why my phone corrected to P. Obvs meant Piper. :-)

I watch the three dots dance. I really hate those dots.

Obvs. :-)

I hate how she calls, with P in the car, to tell me she's got other/better plans. Worry that P will take it personally.

Oh, poor girl. I was always an afterthought too, but at least it wasn't because my dad got a better offer. More like sometimes he forgot I was still around.

She's lucky to have you.

I mean it.

This is what C does when she starts dating someone new. Dumps P all the time. It's a pattern.

I knew I didn't like Candice. On the other hand, if she's dating someone, then she shouldn't care that Sterling and I are dating.

Oh, is she dating someone?

Haven't heard. Usually, she primes P with too much info. P can't keep a secret.

This, I mull over. Who would use their child as a pawn like that?

Sterling texts again:

My ma was like that too, always flashing the latest "catch" about. Needless to say, they were never a catch.

Poor Sterling.

I used to think any mother would be better than no mother at all. Of course, to me a mother is someone who loves her child above everything and everyone else in the world. It makes me sad that Sterling and his siblings didn't have that.

I send him virtual hugs.

While I'd have liked to see Sterling tonight, especially since he's cancelled the last two, it's not like I don't have plenty to keep me busy. These lessons aren't going to plan themselves. Now that the classroom is almost ready to go, I need to figure out what I'm actually going to teach.

Looks like another fun Friday, just me, my cat, and my work.

It's like nothing's changed.

~~~***~~~

"Please help." The panic in Sterling's voice is real.

"What's wrong?" I'm not used to him asking for help. Now my panic matches his.

There's some rustling and movement on the other end before Sterling finally whispers, "I need you."

I smile, a warm fluttering spreading through my stomach. "Oh really." Yes, I'll play coy and hard to get. The new bra came today (thank you, Amazon Prime!).

Maybe Candice came home early, and Sterling wants to come over. I'll just have a glass of wine or two and—

"Seriously, I can't believe ... oh my God, I can't even process this."

I have a nagging suspicion that our minds are in two very different places right now.

"She's only eight. I don't know what to do." Sterling's voice is barely audible, more rustling crowding the line.

"Sterling, what's wrong?" I think I hear a car door slam.

"I ... dammit. Hang on. Switching you to my ear. Pips is in the car with me."

I wait for further instructions.

"S.O.S. I need your help. We are at a level red emergency."

The change in his demeanor surprises me. A moment ago he seemed flustered. Now, downright jovial. I try to match his tone. "What do you need?"

"We're on the way to the mall. Can you meet us?"

"Us?" Okay, so Piper will still be with him. I didn't know we were ready to go public or tell Piper. Maybe he wants me there only as a friend? I don't know how to clarify without asking directly.

"Yes. Piper is having a, um, wardrobe issue, and I could—we could—use some assistance. Lots of assistance."

I can't imagine what a crisis could be for an eight-year-old. Certainly no wardrobe crisis that needs to be handled with such urgency. Still, I roll with it.

"Sure. Where do you want me to meet you?"

Sterling pauses and I hear the unmistakable click of the turn signal. "How about in front of the pretzel place? When can you be there?"

"Ten minutes?"

"Sounds good."

I pause for a moment before I give him one last out, "You sure?"

"Yes, I'm sure."

He can't really mean he's going to tell his daughter? I'm not even sure I'm ready to tell anyone. Because once we do, that means it's serious, right?

"Are you okay with it too?"

I panic. "I think so. I mean, it's not like we're getting married. We can always start with being friends."

There. That was slick. He won't even know that I'm freaking out a tad.

"Okay. We'll talk about it later. See you in a few."

Deep breathing. That's what I need. Piper's a cool kid. She'll be okay with me.

I've never been a step-mother before.

Not that I'm saying I'm going to be her step-mother. That's putting the cart about a mile ahead of the horse. Still, will she see me as competition? Will she think I'm trying to replace her mother? God knows I strive for bigger things than trying to fit into Candice's shoes.

I drive up a row, then down another. Seriously, is everyone at the mall tonight? It's August, not December, for Pete's sake.

Now I'm late.

Crap on a cracker.

It's only as I'm rushing in that I take stock of how I look. Frazzled ponytail. Old T-shirt. Snug shorts. There's about a ninety-five percent chance I'm sporting a camel toe. Sexy.

Winning again.

"Sorry, I'm late," I pant. Not that I was ever the picture of fitness, but man, am I out of shape.

"Miss Dwyer!" Piper runs up, throwing her arms around my waist. I try—unsuccessfully—not to flinch as her head hits my chest. "What are you doing here?"

"Your dad said he needed my help with something." I smile down at her.

Piper steps back, her eyes growing wide. "Dad told me the lady he's dating was meeting us." She looks from me to Sterling and then back again. "You're dating my dad?"

I swallow and nod.

Piper's gaze swings sharply to her father. "*You're* dating my teacher?"

Yuck. I don't want to be one of *those* teachers.

I correct, "Former teacher. Who do you have this year?"

Classroom assignments. Perhaps the biggest source of drama for the kids—er—parents. Kids think their lives are over if they're not in the same section as their besties. Parents all think their child's needs supersede everyone else's.

I've known who was in my class all summer. We don't send out the letters to the families until the third week in August, simply to cut down on the amount of time people complain about it.

"Mrs. Romer."

"Mrs. Romer is excellent, and you're going to love her."

"But Riley has Mrs. Baker." Piper's face scrunches up into the most adorable little frown. I don't dare admit that I recommended splitting them up. Riley could get a little overbearing and manipulative. Piper often was lured into her schemes. I wanted to put the kibosh on that before it got out of hand.

"Yes, because Mrs. Baker is the best fit for Riley, just like Mrs. Romer is best for you. Now, where are we going?"

Piper looks down at her feet, so I look at Sterling. Is he blushing? "All right then. No use dilly dallying. Um, well, this way." We start walking the all-too-familiar corridor to *Voulez-Vous*.

Oh God. No.

Not twice in one week.

Please keep walking. Please keep walking.

There's about a fifty-fifty chance I'm going to vomit. "What are we doing here?"

"You see, apparently Riley got a bra, which I'm still trying to figure out why an eight-year-old is wearing a bra, but regardless, Piper's life will end if she too does not get a bra." Sterling shrugs. I think his chances of puking rival mine.

I get his concern. Piper's years away from needing a bra, but her BFF is a bit more developed.

"Riley's nine, if that makes you feel better. I think she redshirted kindergarten."

"It does actually make me feel better." He nods, digesting this information. "You know, that might explain why Riley's so tall. I mean, her father is about six-foot-five and played basketball in college. I'd always chalked it up to genetics." Sterling leans in and whispers, "And before she flaked—*again*—Candice told Piper she'd take her shopping. I'm a little out of my league, so I was hoping to tap into some of your expertise."

"Mom always takes me to *Voulez-Vous*. This is where I have to go," Piper announces, trying to make us stop walking and go in.

Sterling looks at me, his eyes wide. "I don't know how to explain that to her."

When explanation won't due, I turn to distraction. I turn to Piper. "You know, honey, this store probably isn't going to have your size. Let's go to Macy's. I bet they have just what you need."

I will not lie. This is odd. I'm taking my maybe-boyfriend's daughter bra shopping.

Also, Piper's flat as a board and has absolutely no business wearing a bra. But I remember being in her predicament. When it was my turn, Lisa's mom took me shopping. Lisa was sporting C-cups in fifth grade, so they were old pros at it.

My heart pangs for a minute, missing Lisa. I didn't need a bra until about seventh grade. My mom was gone, and Dad was hopeless. Aunt Polly was out of her league and depth. Much like I am now.

Okay, we can do this. I take Piper to the lingerie department, only to discover that's not where girls' bras are.

Who knew?

On the other hand, I see a few wireless bras that might be worth checking out.

What's the etiquette here? Can I go bra shopping with my maybe-boyfriend's daughter to get something to wear for her father?

Is that way too high of an ick factor?

Yes.

Piper and I settle on some pull-on camisole-type bras. They seem to make her happy. I leave them behind the sales counter, not that I expect a rush on size seven bras.

I tell Sterling, "They are at the counter in the girls' department."

"Oh, right. Smashing. Piper can show me where that is."

Like the suave creature I am, I try to give a careless wave. Except I kick my leg up too, like when a girl gets kissed in the movies, and the result probably resembles half of my body going into severe muscle spasms.

He shakes his head. At least we're still in the stage where he finds this cute.

For my sake, I hope we never move out of that phase.

Once they leave, I run to the lingerie department.

Thirty minutes later, I emerge, bags in hand. I even tried one on and didn't cry or vomit.

I'll consider that a success.

"Can I see what you purchased?" Sterling looks down at my bag.

"Dad, can I have a milkshake?" Piper asks.

"Certainly." Sterling looks at me. "You'll be joining us, right?"

I nod, switching the bag from one hand to another. I blush slightly, thinking about the contents. Sterling zeros right in on that.

"Did you get anything good?"

I try to swallow the massive lump in my throat. If I didn't know better, I'd say one of my implants was lodged in there. "Um, I'll show you later."

"When we get to Johnny Rockets?"

Good God. Can you imagine?

"No, sometime *later*." Summoning a courage I didn't know I had, I wink at him.

His eyes grow wide, and then a devilish grin spreads across his face. My hormone patch may have just sent me a little extra something.

Oh dear, I think I may be in love.

CHAPTER 30

What are the odds that date night includes bra shopping for an eight-year-old who's flat as a board?

Even still, it was a fantastic night.

While Piper was in the dressing room, she talked about how her mom promised to take her shopping, but never delivered.

Poor kid.

I'm paraphrasing of course. Piper had excuse after excuse when it came to her mom.

I don't blame her. Moms are supposed to be the dependable ones. The go-to's. They're not supposed to flake out. Or get sick. Or die before you know what a period is.

Before this year, I'd never given myself permission to think about having kids. It's not responsible to bring a child into this world, only to leave it. And though I'd avoided going to the doctor for years, deep down, I knew what my destiny would be.

I guess I can't blame my mother. She didn't know about genetics. Heck, I still don't fully understand it all. The science loses me somewhere after Crick and Watson.

I will not admit how long I thought double helix was a skateboarding move.

And this may be a tad irrational, but I feel like my mother *should have known*. Her own mom died young, leaving my eighteen-year-old mother to figure things out. I doubt she thought she'd lose her own life so soon after that.

It's only now after doing tons of research that I realize my mom may have inadvertently done this to herself. She was trying to be responsible. They didn't know that being on birth control when you're BRCA-1 positive increases your chance of developing breast cancer.

Hell, it's why I was tested in the first place. Dr. Tremarchi was being proactive. He wouldn't prescribe it for me, given my history, until I'd been cleared.

But clearance never came.

I follow Sterling and Piper back to his house. Over milkshakes and conversation at Johnny Rockets, Piper and I discover we share a mutual love of the TV show, Love It or List It. It's on tonight, and we're going to watch it together.

"Daddy, can I stay up to watch them all?"

He runs his hand lovingly over her little head. "We'll see, Pips. You need to get back on your school bedtime soon."

"Can't we start that tomorrow? I've never had Miss Dwyer over to play before." Piper looks expectantly at her father.

"Me neither." Now he lifts his eyebrows suggestively at me.

As much as I like Piper, I sort of hope she gets tired quickly.

We settle in on the couch, Piper between the two of us. Sterling reaches around his daughter and casually strokes the back of my neck. I'm finding it hard to concentrate, but Piper's adorable comments keep grounding me in reality.

"Of course there's not enough to do an addition. Do these people have any idea what a header beam costs? How do they not know they can't knock down load bearing walls without putting up the cash?"

I always thought the biological clock thing was due to hormonal surges from your ovaries.

But I feel the tick inside my soul, and suddenly everything shifts. A clarity dawns on me, so pristine and sharp that I nearly gasp.

I'm a childless mother, just as I was a motherless child. The emptiness I feel is palpable.

"Are you alright, love?" Sterling reaches over and touches my hand. "You look upset."

I tease, "I'm just worried that they're going to list it instead of love it. They should stay in this house." I nod toward the TV.

Sterling's lips form a straight line as he purses them together. He's not buying my b.s., but doesn't pursue anything further in front of Piper.

Of all the times for me to date someone who's not only attractive but smart and perceptive.

Sleep is pulling hard on Piper's eyes. She's not going to make it through this episode. I nod toward her and watch as the softest, most loving smile spreads across Sterling's face as he looks at his drowsy angel.

Forget the accent and the eyes. Being a father is without a doubt the most sexy thing about him.

And maybe it's because of this, or because I know nothing can happen tonight, I want him.

Like right here, right now, right on his couch.

Foobs be damned.

"I'm going to give her a few more minutes, then I'll put her to bed," he whispers.

"Do you want me to leave?" Please say no. Please say no.

Sterling shakes his head. "Give me a few to get her settled."

"Take your time. I'm not going anywhere."

"Is that a promise?"

My heart flutters a bit. Or like a flock of seagulls gunning for a toddler with a hotdog. I nod. I could not go anywhere if I tried.

I need him.

What seems like two hours later—but in reality, is about thirty minutes—Sterling puts Piper to bed. She doesn't stir as he picks her up and carries her down the hall. I try to remember if my dad ever used to carry me around like that.

I read somewhere once that the line between being a child and an adult can be determined in this way: if you fall asleep somewhere and wake up in your own bed, you're a child. If you wake up where you fell asleep, you're an adult.

I've been an adult for far too long, still searching for memories of my dad putting me to bed like that.

I do remember him carrying my mom out to the living room couch when she was really sick. Right before ... you know. If memory serves, it was right before they put the hospital bed in the den. She never made it back upstairs.

"Millie! What's wrong?" Sterling's back.

I didn't even realize there were tears running down my face. Hastily, I wipe them away. "It's sweet, you and Piper. My dad never carried me like that, but I remember him carrying my mom. You know, toward the end." I wipe again. "You'd think I'd be all cried out. Sometimes it just hits me though."

Sterling sits down. "I get it. Sometimes I get down about my ma and my sister."

"The one with the liver transplant? Is she ...?" How do you ask if she's still alive?

"No, she's doing well. At least last I heard. Sarah on the other hand ..." he breaks off. "I don't know if she's even still alive. I'm sure someone would have heard if she's not, but ..." he stops again and shrugs.

How awful. To have a sister that might be dead?

"Well, this night certainly got depressing."

He slides his arm around me. "But that's the thing, love. You can bum me out. I can depress you. And it's fine. You're not going to freak because my family's all sorts of buggered. I know you're dealing with stuff. But you're real. We can do this real together."

I have to get closer to him. I try to snuggle in, but my right foob is sort of squashed. Scooting back, I realize what I want. What I *need* him to do. I stand up and face Sterling. He's relaxed back into the couch but leans forward to stand as I get up.

"No, wait." I put my hand on his shoulder and push him back. Slowly, tentatively, I sit down on his lap. I slide my right hand down to his and intertwine our fingers.

My hands shaking, breath stilted, I lift his hand. My eyes lock on his. I hope he doesn't feel me shaking. And then I do it.

Put his hand on my foob. I let go, leaving his hand there.

"Are you sure?" he whispers.

I nod, then drop my gaze to watch what he's doing. I can feel his hand above my chest.

It looks as if his fingers are barely touching my shirt. Like he's afraid he's going to break an egg or me or something. They glide over, tracing the top of the implant. Then he crosses over and does the same on the other side.

My voice breaks as I whisper, "Is it disgusting?"

He doesn't answer, instead pressing his lips to my breastbone. He pulls back and looks at me. "I don't know what to say other than I'm glad you had this done."

He *does* have a thing for grotesque breasts. I knew it! I need to get out of here!

Scrambling to get off his lap, I'm halted when Sterling firmly grips my hips. "Let me finish."

Fine, but I will not look at him. Instead I look over his shoulder at the picture on the wall. It's a seaside photo, and I suspect it's Ipswich.

"I'm glad you had this done so that you may live a long and healthy life. And that I hope I get the chance to be a part of that life."

That gets my attention. My gaze whips down to his so fast I might have pulled a muscle.

"What are you saying?" There is no way he can be talking about a lifetime commitment, right? Heat swarms my head.

This is no time for a hot flash.

So of course, I'll have one.

He pulls my face in his hands so I have no choice but to look at him. "Millie, don't freak out."

"I'm not," I lie.

"You are. I'm not asking you to marry me."

"Of course not," I scoff. "That'd be ridiculous."

Then why is there a tiny part of me that feels like a deflated balloon?

"Maybe someday, but I'd like you to be my girlfriend first."

Eep. Okay. I'll take it.

Gladly.

"Sterling Kane, are you asking me to go steady?"

"Damn straight I am."

Damn straight.

CHAPTER 31

I wish I had a T-shirt to wear to my next UnBRCAble meeting that said, "He got to second base and I'm okay with it."

Probably shouldn't quit my day job for a career as a slogan designer.

It'd have been better if Sterling and I could have spent the night together, but I didn't feel comfortable with Piper in the house. Sterling didn't come right out and say it, but I think he was relieved that I offered to leave. It's one thing to admit that we're dating. Waking up with her there? Not ready for that yet.

The day goes from good to fantastic when I check my phone.

Candice is taking Piper to her mother's for a family party. Won't be back until Monday.

Hmmm ... two whole days.
Quickly, I text back.

Whatever should we do? ;-)

I don't add 'each other' but you know I'm thinking it.

The waving dots torment me.

Stupid dots of anticipation.

Still. Waiting.

I throw my phone down on the bed and walk out of the room, only to dash back a moment later and grab it.

Still nothing.

Do something fun. Do nothing. Lie in bed all day. Your choice.

All that time for twelve words?

Relief floods my system. He wants to spend the weekend with me. I look at the text again.

In bed.

I suck in a breath, suddenly no longer able to find air. I don't know what I expected after second base. The Macy's bag in the corner catches my eye. Dude, I've been buying sexy bras. I know exactly what's coming.

No pun intended, of course.

My heart is pounding at the mere thought. I know I need to do this now. It's not that I don't want to, because of course I do. It's like there's some massive brick wall in front of me that I have to climb.

The brick wall is my brain, and no matter how hard I try, it seems impossible to chip through, like an impenetrable fortress.

I'm doing fine though. Totally handling everything.

I have bras to prove it.

I have a ton of work to do before I can play, so I need to get out of bed if I ever want to be able to get back in it.

As I do laundry, pay bills, make a grocery list, and research some last minute activities for my class this week, I'm finding it hard to keep my mind on task. It wants to wander back to Sterling, like a dog to a bone.

I have a boyfriend.

Let's face it, that thought alone is somewhat mind-boggling. Never mind in my present condition.

I can finally think about the future.

A future I will most certainly—or at least most likely—have.

I pick up my phone to call Lisa to hash this over with before I remember we're not really friends anymore.

It's stupid really.

I mean, why are we even fighting?

I force myself to call her, but I'm sent directly to voicemail.

She declined my call.

She declined my call.

Hell to the no.

The list and anxiety about Sterling take a backseat as I hop in my car. I didn't even stop to brush my teeth. Okay, that's gross.

Lisa and I have been friends for over fifteen years. How dare she end our friendship with a decline?

I think about the last few months. Insensitive comments, hanging up on me. Yelling at me. Declining my call.

She's getting perilously close to being dead to me forever.

I'm sure I haven't been a ball of fun these last few months, but I've had a crappy summer.

Year, really.

Why doesn't she understand that?

How does she not get that this is all been scary and painful and exhausting and terrible for me?

As I pull up in front of her townhouse, I think about all those things.

Seriously, how does she not understand?

Why did she get so mad that I didn't tell her everything about Sterling?

Is she pissed that I have other people in my support group to talk to?

Why can't she see how hard this has been for me?

Without even getting out of the car, I put it into reverse and drive home.

Suddenly, my enthusiasm for the day and weekend has petered out, and I want to curl up in my house and hide under a blanket while binge-watching mindless television.

That wouldn't be the worst idea, considering that the first week back to school is exhausting, even when I'm in top form, which for me means being able to be out of my house all day without needing a nap. It's not like I'm pushing myself to run a marathon or anything.

Once home, I force myself to take care of the items on my list, in record time. I even put a grocery order in online and schedule delivery for Monday morning. In order to make the minimum dollar amount to get the free delivery, I end up stocking up on things like toilet paper and paper towels. Since the groceries will be brought right to my front door, I include some extra containers of kitty litter and cat food. Cornelius, who is currently sunning himself on the rug, will be good to go. Hopefully by the time his supplies run out, I'll be able to lift the kitty litter containers again.

Groceries, check.

Bills, check.

Laundry to the dryer, woops. Gotta go do that.

I decide to change my sheets, creating another load of laundry. Then I notice that my nightstand is getting a little dusty.

I forgot to schedule my cleaner, Tina. Aunt Polly bought several sessions for me before the first surgery. "I don't want you to have to worry about cleaning, sugar. But mostly I don't want to have to do it."

Tina's last session was about two weeks ago. With everything going on with Sterling and the beach and getting my classroom ready, I totally forgot. A quick text message can get me back on track, but I'll have to dust a little.

And then vacuum.

I should not have vacuumed. As I push the Dyson out, I feel the pulling in my right foob. Great. I try to breathe through the spasm.

At least I got one room done. The rest of the house will have to wait.

I have to stop pushing so hard. It's not like a few tumbleweeds of cat fur will make a difference.

Just as this profound knowledge dawns on me, I hear the knock.

A quick glance at the clock confirms my worst suspicion. It's two o'clock, and that's Sterling at the door.

"Come on in!" I holler.

I haven't showered.

Or brushed my teeth.

My hair—oh Lord.

This weekend is not off to a good start.

~~~***~~~

I want a do-over.

For the entire year really, but I'll settle for the weekend.

I make Sterling sit in my living room while I race around, showering and getting somewhat decent. There are some tasks that probably should not be done at breakneck speed, but that thought only occurs to me as the blood starts flowing.

I should have thought of that before I started ladyscaping.

I'm sure he's going to find a wound on my bikini line super sexy.

Maybe I should have kept up with the Brazilians.

Maybe I need to take it as a sign that I'm not ready.

But I can't wait any longer. Mostly because I'm scared that if I don't do it now, I'll never be able to get back on the proverbial horse.

Then I get a mental image of what that might look like and part of me is excited while part of my is scared that I will be in motion while my foobs will stay perfectly still.

Yuck.

A braid will have to suffice for my wet hair, though I dread the thought of what it'll look like having dried in the plait. I may not be able to fit through a standard doorway. It'll have to stay in until Sterling leaves.

Once I am *finally* able to join him in the living room, two things become quite apparent.

Cornelius may love Sterling more than me.

Sterling is allergic to Cornelius.

"Are you okay?" His watering eyes and red nose indicate otherwise.

"Super."

"Sterling, you are not. Are you allergic to cats?"

He shrugs. "Perhaps?"

It's not like this is the first time he's been here. I don't remember this being a problem before. "Is this new? How come it never bothered you before?"

"I'm not quite sure. He is quite the fluffy thing."

Cornelius gives Sterling a dirty look as he stands up and then flops onto Sterling's leg. He stretches a paw upward and pokes my boyfriend.

It's cat speak for "pet me now, dammit."

"And what's wrong with his feet? They look like tennis rackets."

"He has thumbs." I reach out and shake Cornelius's hand. It's one of my favorite things to do.

"Don't be ridiculous. Cats don't have thumbs." *Achoo.*

"Of course they do. Not all, naturally. Only the cool ones. Like Cornelius."

Sterling sneezes again, forcing Cornelius to get up and relocate. He hides his displeasure by aggressively licking himself.

His privates, that is.

Sterling reaches for a tissue and blows his nose. "I don't seem to remember him bothering me so much before. I wonder what's changed."

The answer hits me like a lightning bolt.

"Tina!"

"What does that have to do with—*achoo*—your cat?"

"She's been cleaning for me. I forgot to schedule some more times, so the vacuuming is a bit behind. I bet if we keep on top of it, you'll be better."

"Right. Maybe. Possibly." Sterling looks—okay, glares—at Cornelius. "Are you attached to him?"

This sort of ignorant phrase can only come from a non-cat person. "Yes, of course! Why would you say such a thing?"

I stand up and huff over to Cornelius where I pick him up and start kissing him.

"Don't get mad. I've not been around many cats." He blows his nose again. "Obviously. He wasn't here for most of the summer. I don't think I even realized you had a cat until the other day."

Cornelius struggles to get down, so I let him. I secretly harbor a fear he might pop one of my foobs. His claws are pretty big with the extra toe.

"Do you want me to vacuum?" Subconsciously, I rub the right side of my chest where the spasm had been earlier.

"Why don't we go to my place?"

I don't want to go there. It's not somewhere where I'm comfortable yet, and I think I'm going to need every single bit of comfort to get through this weekend.

How do I tell him that without seeming weird?

Since there doesn't seem to be a way, I begrudgingly head to my room to pack an overnight bag.

This is so unfair! How can he be allergic to my cat?

I can't get rid of Cornelius. He's like my emotional support cat. People claim that you can train cats to do that, but I think they're full of hooey. It doesn't matter. Just the act of petting Cornelius makes me feel better. It calms me and relaxes me. I wish I'd been able to have him here post-surgery. His absence is probably part of the reason I've been so blue.

"Are you alright in there?" Sterling calls. I glance at the clock and realize I've been in here for over twenty minutes.

My bag is still mostly empty.

Sterling wanders down the hall. "Love, do you need help?"

I look from my bag to Sterling, then back again.

"I'm not going. I can't do this."

CHAPTER 32

When someone asks you, "what's wrong?," it's probably best to answer them truthfully.

Obviously, I don't do this.

"Millie, what's wrong?" Sterling's eyes are red-rimmed, and it doesn't take a medical degree to figure out he's miserable.

"I can't be with someone who doesn't respect my cat."

Did I really say that out loud?

"I do respect your cat. It's simply my immune system that has a problem. Perhaps you have some antihistamine that I can try?"

And with that, my heart melts a little.

"No, you should go. You need to get out of here. Shower to get all the cat dander off you. It's not healthy for you to be here."

Why am I pushing him away?

Sterling's face pinches as if he's been kicked.

Because of me. I kicked him, metaphorically speaking.

"All right then. If you want me to go, I'll go."

And with that, he's gone.

First Lisa, now Sterling.

Add my dysfunctional—make that non-existent—relationship with my dad and I'm seeing a common denominator here. Perhaps I can't people.

Great.

I am determined to prove that I can people. Sterling is worth it.

I throw some things in a bag, bras included, and drive over to Sterling's house.

At least I can admit when I'm being a jerk.

I ring his doorbell, and he seems surprised to see me. "I'm being a jerk. I don't know why. I never thought I was a jerk. I don't mean to be, but here it is, me being jerky."

Sterling stays in the doorway, his eyes narrowing. "I will let you in on one condition."

I should respond with an enthusiastic "anything" but I'm not capable of that yet.

"I'll have to hear the condition."

He grins. "I get to pick the movie."

"No graphic violence."

His face falls. "There is this one scene," he pauses. "It might be a little difficult to watch but I'm sure you can get through it. I'll be here to hold your hand."

He presses play.

A little over two hours later, I turn to Sterling. "What was the scene I couldn't handle." So much of the movie was painful to watch.

"Cat juggling."

I laugh. "I can't believe you made me watch The Jerk."

"Oh, come on. Steve Martin is comedic genius."

"That movie is terrible."

"It's funny." Sterling folds his arms over his chest and pretends to pout.

"I would have pictured you more as a Monty Python kind of guy." I snuggle into him, and then quickly reposition my squished foob.

Sterling reaches across and takes my hand. His pout disappears.

"Why did you freak out earlier?"

"I didn't freak out," I say, staring straight ahead.

"Millie, I need to put this out there, so you know where I'm coming from. I know we've only just started seeing each other, but we've been getting to know one another all summer."

"True."

"I'm going to say a lot, so let me get it all out, okay?"

I nod.

"Candice was always waiting for me to swoop in and save her, which is probably part of what drew me to her initially. It took me way too long to realize that she would always need saving because she was always creating one drama after another. It wasn't until about two years ago—two full years after our divorce—that I finally realized she was one of those people who always need to be at the center of the chaos. And if there's no chaos, she'd create some."

I want to tell him that I can see that, but I know he doesn't want me to interrupt.

He continues, holding my gaze. I wish I could be as straightforward. "My single parent support group helped me see that I couldn't fix or save Candice if she didn't want to change. They also led me to the connection that I was trying to rescue Candice like I'd tried to do for my youngest sister, Sarah."

Sterling pauses, which I take as a time to speak. "Uh, o-okay," I sputter. "I'm—thank you for telling me." I go quiet for a moment. "I'm not really sure what that had to do with me."

"I can't save you."

What?

"I don't need saving." I stand up and put my hands on my hips. "I don't want saving. I'm fine how I am."

Which is totally a lie because, well, I'm a hot mess.

But only because of my health and my mom and my dad and stuff, and all the formative aspects of my childhood. Other than that, I'm perfectly fine.

Sterling cocks his head, watching me. "I need to do what's best for Piper and me."

"I know that."

"I need stability. Piper needs stability. She's not going to get it from her ma, so it's up to me to provide the structure and rules."

"Yes, I know." I sit down and stretch out so my feet are in his lap. This way I can look right at Sterling without craning my neck.

I love watching his face when he talks like this.

"I grew up in a very tumultuous environment. I can't even say home because it never was. None of the locations were. They were houses, if even that. I hated having a Ma's house and a Da's house, but that didn't matter because Da stopped inviting us over eventually. Then, we moved across the ocean, so it was a non-issue."

"It's one thing to have a parent leave when they have no choice about it. I don't understand how someone can ignore the fact that they have kids out there," I add, thinking of my own mother. It's something I've run into a fair amount with my students, but will never be able to comprehend.

"Da hated Ma more than he loved us. Simple as that." His face is blank.

I shake my head, wanting to cry. I sniffle, willing the liquid to stay confined in my face.

"Neither one had much compunction about bringing their lovers around us. Ma paraded man after man through our lives. Da, when he came around, always had a new chippy with him." Sterling looks disgusted. He has every right to be.

"How do you do that? I mean, isn't it weird?" I try to picture Dad dating. Frankly, I wish he would.

"It was awful," Sterling nods. "After a while Stuart and I stopped learning their names. There was no point. We'd nickname them, of course. There was Horseteeth and Stankbreath. Then there was the insult about that one chap's teeth that's not fit to be said in public, but let's leave it as quite unkind."

Part of me wants to press him for details. I can't even imagine what it might be.

"No wonder Stuart went on to become a dentist," Sterling offers with a smile, straight and white.

"And how did the rest of your siblings make out?" He's mentioned that Sarah'd had difficulties, but I don't know what they are.

"Samantha is okay. I mean, she's got to be careful that the liver still works, and her leg's a bit on the wonky side, but other than that she's all right." Sterling looks down at his hands before continuing. "Sarah's another story. She's an addict. She drinks and does pills and Lord knows what else. She's always shacking up with one loser or another, pretty much like Ma did."

"You said that Stuart and Samantha don't talk to her anymore. Why's that?" I know it's none of my business, but it's probably something I should know so I don't say the wrong thing.

"When it came time for us to be tested to see if we could donate for Samantha, Sarah refused. We all thought it was because of the paternity issue, even though it was old news at the time."

"So she didn't want her sister to live?" This makes no sense.

"No, she was using, and that was more important to her than her family."

Ouch.

"So, Stu and Samantha wrote her off for good. I tried to get her into rehab. Again."

266

"Because you were trying to save her," I say, pieces clicking into place. Sterling's a saver. "I don't need to be saved. I only want ..." this is where I stop.

I don't know what I want.

I want my genes not to be defective. I want Sterling's parents to be better people. I want Sarah to be clean. I want Piper to know she's loved.

I want my mom.

There's no holding back the tears this time.

Sterling places my feet on the ground and stands. He pulls me, ever so gently, up, and wraps his arms around me. "We don't have to figure it all out tonight, love."

I nod, trying not to snot all over his shirt.

I am not successful.

When we finally pull apart, Sterling looks down at his wet shirt. "I guess I should take this off."

Now he turns his gaze to me, hopeful.

It's now or never.

CHAPTER 33

If my life were a rom-com (because let's face it, I'd never be able to pull off a dramatic romance), the sex would have been amazing and earth shattering. Truth be told, it was fine. Nice even. But my world remained unrocked.

It would have been better if I could have relaxed a bit more. Wearing the bra helped. Sterling understood. Of course he did.

Lying there after, I decide to take the honest approach.

"Sterling, you need to tell me something." I pinch my eyes shut, as if not seeing him will make this any less mortifying. "How ... how were ... you know ... the girls?"

He coughs nervously. "I know I should say the right thing here, but I don't know what that is. What's the proper answer? Nice. Adequate. More than a handful. Aesthetically pleasing."

"Aesthetically pleasing?" I laugh.

"From what I could see, they look nice. Your surgeon did a good job."

Part of me wants to be insulted that he's not telling me they look natural. A larger part of me respects him for being frank and honest. And yes, the surgeon did a great job. Especially considering some of the stories I've heard, both in UnBRCAble and online. My surgery and recovery was easy compared to most.

"Yes, she did. I'm lucky. Lots of women have to have multiple revisions, and even then remain disfigured. More disfigured." I add.

"Do you see yourself as disfigured?" Sterling props up on his elbow, concern knitted in his brows.

I look down. All I see are the ridges at the top of my implants. I can't see them, but I can feel the scars running on the underside of my breasts. I know my lower abdomen is empty.

"Aww, Millie, love, you're beautiful. You're a warrior who valiantly sacrificed to win your battle. I wish you could see you the way I see you."

I wish I could too. "If people had that superpower, there'd be a lot less depression in the world, wouldn't there?"

"If I could patent those glasses, I'd be super rich." Sterling lets out a content sigh.

The conversation turns toward what we'd do with the sudden fortune from curing depression. Top of our list is an entire summer rental in Cape May. I contribute sensible, yet boring, items like paying off my student loans and medical bills.

Side note—the health insurance system sucks and there's a special place in hell for the companies that make someone jump through hoops to avoid financial ruin at the lowest point of their lives.

"Oh, I know!" Sterling jumps up. He begins pulling clothes on, which I take as a sign that I should do likewise. "I'd fly you on my private jet to England to meet my brother."

"Does that mean I have to get my passport?" I had one in high school, but it expired. Renewing it was never a priority.

"Yes."

"As soon as you make your first million, I'll get right on that." I pull on my leggings and then my shirt, this time without even wincing.

Sterling stops dead. "No."

His tone freezes me. I guess he's not ready for the meet the family. Maybe he's just as commitment phobic as all the losers I'm used to dating. I wouldn't have thought so but ...

"Millie, not when I make my first million."

I shrug, pretending it doesn't sting. "I was trying to take it easy on you. I can wait until your first billion."

"No."

Dear Jesus, what is the deal with this man? Is he trying to kill me? Oh, no. Maybe I shouldn't be talking about money like that. Candice would be all over the money thing. I hope he doesn't think I'm like that. I couldn't care less about the money. I have a good job and good benefits. I can take care of me. I can buy my own plane ticket. All he's done is make me want a future with him and he—

"I want you to meet Stu. You have to come to the wedding with me."

He wants me to ... meet ... his ... family.

Suddenly, I'm finding it a bit difficult to take a deep breath. He can't mean that, can he?

Why is there no air in here?

Seriously, is there something wrong with the atmosphere?

"That's like next summer. You don't want to tie yourself down yet." I don't know why I say this. Maybe because I'm gulping for breath and trying to slow my heart from racing.

And why did I give him an out? Do I want him to have an out? Do I want to lock him in? Why am I doing this?

Oh, right. It's because I'm an idiot. And perhaps the walls have moved in about two feet closer together.

Sterling looks at me. "Millie, we just slept together. We've been dating, whether you want to admit it or not, for a few months now."

"It has not been a few months."

"I've certainly been trying for a few months. Have you not noticed my courting?"

I open my mouth then close it. It honestly takes him saying that for me to realize it's true. I don't know how I didn't see it before.

Duh.

"Um, yeah. I was playing hard to get."

I'm a moron is what I am.

Sterling walks over to me and takes me in his arms. "Why do you doubt me?"

Because I've never been loved. Because I never allowed myself to love.

I don't know how to trust this.

I shrug. "I didn't want to put expectations out there if we aren't on the same page. No biggie."

I can't look at his face. I don't want to see his pity or repulsion or whatever he might be feeling. I can't handle my own feelings. No way I can handle his too. I stare out the window, watching a bright red cardinal hop on the fence in the backyard.

Someone once told me that when you see a red cardinal, it's the spirit of a loved one visiting. Is that my mom? Is she telling me something?

She's probably telling me, "Come on, Millie. Tell him. Do this. Love him."

Sterling looks out the window to see what's holding my attention. "Oh, that's Ray."

"Ray?" Does he see someone out there I don't? There's certainly no one in his yard.

Maybe I'm not the unstable one here? That would be sort of refreshing.

"Yeah, the cardinal. There's a pair of them. See the female on the branch?"

I squint, looking for another red bird. "I don't see her."

"She's just off to the left. Green with a red beak, just like his."

I finally see her. I don't know that I've ever seen a female cardinal before. Makes sense that they're not red. The female birds are never pretty like the males.

Sort of like Sterling and me.

"That's Dawn. They live in that lilac bush."

272

How adorable is it that he named the birds in his yard?

On the other hand, if they're always here, it means that the—Ray—is not my mother, reincarnate, telling ... anything.

It's not a sign.

It's not a message.

It's just a bird.

"It's just a bird," I mumble, my shoulders practically collapsing under the weight of dejection.

Suddenly, I have to get out. I need to breathe, and I don't think I can do it here. Not with Sterling.

Not with anyone.

Why did I think I was ready?

I may throw up.

"Um, I'm not feeling that great. My stomach's a bit off right now. I think I'm going to go home and lay down for a while." I look around and grab my phone, yanking the charger right out of the wall. I have a bag somewhere ...

"Millie, what's wrong?"

Me. That's what.

Why can't he see that I'm *wrong*?

"Nothing. I mean, maybe it's something I ate or something. Anyway, I'll call you in a ... well, sometime."

I don't look back. I don't stop. I get out of there as fast as I can. I'm so not cut out for this. What could Sterling possibly be thinking? Making plans with me for ten months down the road? Who in their right mind plans that far ahead?

I mean, I do. For my classroom. I start in October for the following August.

That's ten months.

So I know I can make a plan and stick to it.

Why does this freak me out?

And why have I yet to tell him about the other surgery and its implication?

I should.

I should have.

A long time ago.

Driving home, I turn it over and over. Why haven't I? Am I afraid it's going to scare him away?

Isn't that what I want?

It must be, otherwise, why would I be acting so irrational?

So what, my entire life and existence has been turned upside down. That doesn't mean that I can change who I am overnight.

Or over the entire summer.

I need to focus on healing and teaching, and I don't need to be distracted by handsome British guys who are super nice and supportive and maybe even love me a little.

Love.

My skin prickles as goosebumps form.

Does Sterling love me?

He's never said he has, but I sort of think he does. He must. Why else would he put up with so much?

I wouldn't put up with me.

I wouldn't love me.

I don't deserve him. He's too good for me.

Aimlessly driving around, I realize I have no idea where I'm going. I don't want to go back to an empty house.

I don't want to be alone.

If I don't want to be alone, why do I do such a stellar job at pushing everyone away?

A bird flies in front of the car, making me recall that stupid cardinal.

This is all my mother's fault, really. Who needs Freud anyway? I know where the blame goes. If only she hadn't left me alone. If only she'd fought harder. Wasn't I worth fighting for?

Hell, the last thing she said to me was, "But I'm tired, baby girl. I need to sleep."

Why wasn't I enough for her?

And if I wasn't enough for her, how can I be enough for anyone else?

CHAPTER 34

"Maybe you should just ghost him," Frances offers. "It's got to be easy enough to do."

Erin nods. "From the amount of times I've been ghosted, it must be. I mean I'd ask one of the guys who did it but ... ghosted."

We all laugh at this.

"I can't. Sterling's been too nice and kind. I could never do that to him. It's a dick move."

A tiny little irrational part of me wishes I could do it, since it'd be the easy way out. None of this is easy, and I'd never be able to live with myself if I did that.

After the meeting today, I'll go over and tell him that I'm no good for him. That he deserves better than me. And then I'll be on my merry way.

It's been a long three days, trying to ignore his texts and calls. I told him I needed time to think.

This is for the best, really. The past two days have been a whirl of professional development and staff meetings. The kids start tomorrow. Once that happens, I'll be too busy and too tired to even think about him.

Or how he held me when I cried.

Or how his eyes would sparkle when he was telling a joke.

Or how his lips tasted ...

"Guys, what do I do?" I wail.

Claudia sits down next to me and pats my back. "What do you want to do?" If anyone can wave a magic crystal to make this better, it's Claudia.

"Get in a Delorean and go back in time before I messed this up."

That would be so easy. 1.21 gigawatts and I'd go back to Sunday morning when I freaked out over a stupid bird and left. Or maybe I'd go back to the freak out over the cat. Or even crashing his vacation. No, I'd go back to the auto parts store!

Of course we all know I can *never* go back to the auto parts store.

It seems I've been screwing this one up right from the get go.

Our first real conversation did involve a vaginal rejuvenation, so I should have known then.

"Do you ever think we're cursed?" I look around the group. Claudia, Erin, Tracey, Kelli, Frances, and some of the other ladies whose names escape me. Strangers who are like sisters, all with the same faulty genetic makeup.

Claudia sits down in her chair, leaning back so effortlessly. Tonight, her shirt says, "I dismantled my ticking time bombs." Every single one of us is or was a ticking time bomb. How hard it is to live like that. And the cost of dismantling those bombs.

My mom was blown to smithereens, and the shrapnel irreparably wounded my dad and me.

I'm intact—most of me, that is—but I still have wounds. Deep wounds that will take years to heal. Long after the scars on my breasts and abdomen have faded into faint lines, I fear that the ones on my heart will still be jagged and angry and red.

Thinking about my mom, and my long-held belief that she didn't love me enough to stay, I know I was wrong. It's a childish thought, almost like my emotional development was frozen at that point in time. She would have stayed if she could have.

And she wouldn't approve of what I'm doing now.

Blowing off Sterling is wrong. He deserves more. He deserves better. He deserves someone who can actually love him the way he should be loved. Someone who can give him kids and loves herself enough to love him.

I wish I could be that girl.

I want to be that girl.

"I have to go see him now. " I pop up out of my chair. Suddenly, it's the only thing I need to do. He needs to know that I'm the broken one.

I pull open the door and head out into the main lobby. Behind me, the elevator dings. Without thinking, I turn around.

"Lisa!"

Her blond hair is scattered all over her head in a very un-Lisa like manner. She looks pale and tired and—

Please God, don't let me be seeing what I think I'm seeing.

I cannot move.

Her hand tenses and slides behind her back attempting to conceal the evidence, but it's too late.

Slowly, like moving through quicksand, my mind finally clicks all the pieces together.

She's holding ultrasound photos.

"How? Why? How could you?" I sputter. I look from her face to her midsection, as if answers will be written there.

"Do you think I'm really happy about this?"

My feet are lead, slowly melting into the floor. I try to pull air into my lungs but it doesn't work. I suck harder, leaning forward and propping my hands on my knees, as if I've just finished a sprint.

"This isn't about you, you know," Lisa hisses. "It's not your life that's going to be turned upside down. I don't have time for this. You know I never wanted this. Don't go putting your issues on me."

The venom in her voice surprises me as I watch her stomp past without even making eye contact.

My legs threaten to collapse, but I will not melt here on the floor of the Genevieve T. Wunderlich Women's Health Center.

Somehow, I make it to my car before the tears start. At one point, I turn on my windshield wipers trying to clear my view before I realize the liquid is coming from my own eyeballs.

I pull over, not wanting to be a hazard to myself or anyone else for that matter.

Before I know it, I'm in front of Sterling's house.

The pain is too great—too intense—to let me think about what I'm doing, let alone why. I make it to the front door before I double over.

"Millie! Are you ill?" Sterling's in the doorway. I feel his arms supporting me. Guiding me into his house.

The sobs are wracking my body, my lungs gasping for breath.

"Miss Dwyer! Are you dying?"

I feel like it.

"Hush, Pips. Please go upstairs. Miss Dwyer will be fine. I've got her."

Sterling pulls away for a minute. I try to slow my breathing, dampen the sobs. I stare at a black diamond shape in the geometric carpet, willing my lungs to fill and empty slower. Picturing the oxygen traveling through my blood.

"Millie, what's wrong?"

One last deep breath. "Lisa's pregnant."

"O ... kay," he drawls. "I take it it's not a good thing? Because if this is your good thing reaction, I'd hate to see bad."

"How could she do this to me?"

Even when Billy Thompson cheated on me, the betrayal felt nothing like this. Nowhere as deep.

"I'm almost positive her being in the family way has nothing to do with you."

"She doesn't want kids."

"Then I think this is her problem, not yours. Right?"

I feel the floodgates straining under the weight of another deluge. "She doesn't even *want* a baby! This is so unfair." I pause to look at Sterling. Behind him on the wall, a toddler version of Piper smiles back at me. "And *you* didn't want a baby either!"

Sterling's brow furrows. "I assure you, your friend's situation has nothing to do with me."

"No, of course not. But Piper. You didn't want Piper."

"Sssshhh, lower your voice. What's wrong with you? Are you deranged or something? What gives you the right to come in here and say such things? I think you need to leave."

He stands and folds his arms across his chest.

Fine.

I march across the room to the door. I pull it open, prepared to storm out without saying another word. But he has to know.

I turn to face him. "It's not fair. I never thought I should have kids because it wouldn't be fair to leave them when I died young, like my mom and grandma."

"Yes, Millie. You were destined to die. I get it. *Were*. You're fine now and you need to get on with living."

"Yes, I'm fine, but I certainly paid a big price. My breasts are gone."

"I understand, and you know that didn't matter to me. The only person it mattered to is you."

Didn't matter. Not doesn't matter.

He's already written me off.

"Yes, but the mastectomy and reconstruction was the second round of surgery for me. First, I had a complete hysterectomy, to prevent me from getting

281

ovarian cancer. So now I have a long life, but I can't have kids. So pardon me if the fact that my best friend getting knocked up is devastating for me. Especially since I know she doesn't want it."

I turn and leave for the last time.

It's good to know that my ability to suck at dating was not at all related to my uterus or breasts.

Maybe I should become a nun.

CHAPTER 35

Piper sneaks in the next day and leaves a card on my desk.

"*I love you, Miss Dwyer.*"

It's all I can do not to cry.

Again.

Seriously, I need to stop crying. I swear, once I get through all this, I'm never crying again.

I've read about people getting Botox in their armpits to stop sweating. I wonder if I can have that done in my eyeballs. But the thought of my eye and a needle makes me a little nauseous.

It's enough to get me focused on day two of school. The kids are at library.

I've had two bathroom accidents so far today. Not me personally, but my students. I think it's a new world record.

If I could add lice or a puker, this day would win for the worst ever.

I really need to get my head in the game. It's not fair to my new class. I'm supposed to be the master of ceremonies here.

I feel like the master of meh instead.

Amy pokes her head into my room. "I brought you an iced coffee." She waves the cup.

"Thanks. How did you know I'd need that?"

She sets the cup down on my desk and steps back. "Have you looked in a mirror recently?"

It can't be that bad. I pull out my phone and swipe open the camera.

Dear Jesus, it is that bad.

"Do you have a bag I can put over my head?"

Amy laughs. "Get some ice from the nurse's freezer and put it on your eyes. Maybe pull back your hair. And for the love of God, get some sleep tonight."

Fatigue and grief have fogged my brain to such an extent that I follow Amy's advice to the T without question.

Thank goodness there's only one more day of school to get through before the weekend. My plan is to sleep from four p.m. on Friday through seven a.m. Monday.

It might make a dent in the bags under my eyes.

But then again, it might not.

As I trudge through the afternoon and evening, I'm struck by the irony of my situation. My whole life, I've been afraid to make people love me because I'd leave them.

Now here I am, alone.

Thank goodness for Cornelius. At least he won't desert me.

Piper leaves me another note on Friday. Two days in a row.

"*Can U come over 2nite to watch Love It or List it?*"

Great, she's already writing how people text.

And she's breaking my heart.

I can't believe I'm going to have to crush her by telling her that I'm not dating her father.

Exactly what he didn't want to do. And it makes it so much worse that Piper knows me and sees me.

I didn't think I could feel worse than I did after surgery.

No best friend.

No boyfriend.

Nobody.

Maybe I'm a lot more like my dad than I ever wanted to admit. Not able to navigate the emotional minefield of relationships. Even though I probably hate hospitals as much as he does, I'd go if someone needed me to. I'd be Lisa's labor coach, unless the father is.

Wait, who is the father? When did she get pregnant? When is she due? Is the baby okay? Is she going to be okay?

I can't believe she's going to be a mother.

Suddenly I hope she's going to be a mother and doesn't make other plans. Dread fills me. There's only one thing worse than her being pregnant, and that would be her being not pregnant anymore.

I don't know if I could live with that.

Not that it's my choice.

My choices were taken away by my mutant genes.

At least the school day is done and I can hide all weekend. Licking my wounds sounds like a great idea.

But when I pull into my driveway, my dad's car is waiting for me. Go figure, he comes over the week I return to work. It's like he knows I'm all better and back to normal—whatever *that* is—and now he can be around me again.

"Hey, Dad." I should summon some energy so he doesn't figure out how poorly I'm really doing, but I can't. My voice is low and flat.

"Millie. How was the first week?" He gets out of his car and then leans back in, grabbing a bag of donuts.

Just what I need—a bag of fat and sugar to drown my sorrows in.

"I meant to stop by last week, but well …"

"You didn't." I'm only telling the truth.

I unlock the door and Cornelius runs to my dad. Great. Even the cat doesn't want to be near me.

"Hey, buddy. I missed you too." My dad sets the bag on the console table and scoops up all eighteen pounds of fur and attitude. I stare as I watch my dad bury his face in Cornelius's side and give him a kiss. The cat squirms for a minute in my dad's arms until his belly is exposed. Massive paws in the air, he starts purring.

Apparently, this is a thing they do.

"Maybe you should get a cat, Dad. It's obvious you're a cat guy."

"I am not," he protests, nuzzling the cat's nose with his own.

"Okay, right."

I flop down on the couch. Dad takes Gertrude. The plan was when I no longer needed it, we'd move her to Dad's house. I want it out now. I want as little reminders of this summer as possible around.

Frankly, I never want to sit in that chair again.

"No, really, I think you should get a cat. You and Cornelius really seemed to hit it off. I think you like him."

"I put up with him."

His answer would be more believable if he weren't patting his lap for the cat to jump up into. Which he does.

Traitor.

And suddenly, before I can think or control myself, I explode.

"Why don't you just take the Goddamn cat! It's obvious he loves you more than he loves me. Like everyone else in my life. I wish I could matter. I wish I could be that important. But I'm not. I've been through hell. I can't even say hell and back because I'm still there, and no one cares. Do you hear me? *No one cares!*"

There's no way he can't hear me, because I'm really yelling. There's a possibility the astronauts on the International Space Station hear me. But I'm just getting started.

"You're my freakin' father, and you barely came to see me. I was in the hospital *twice*, getting carved up, and you couldn't even man up to come by. Once the Helping Wagon got going, I never even saw you."

He's staring at my cat on his lap. "Polly was here. You had all those people. You didn't need me to come," he mumbles.

"But *you* should have been here. Not just to do things around the house, but to keep me company. But you didn't. Just like my whole life. It was sucky enough that I had to grow up with one parent, but in reality, I had none. It was like you died when Mom did. But you were too busy thinking about your loss to even realize that I lost too."

"Millie, it wasn't like that. It ..." he breaks off. He still can't look at me.

"How was it? Tell me, Dad. I get it. You lost your soul mate. The love of your life. At least you knew what love was. At least you had it. Did I?"

"Of course, Millie. I love you. Your mother loved you so much."

Tears fill my eyes. "Not enough. Not enough to fight harder and stay." I don't know why I keep coming back to this line of thought. I know it's not true.

"Oh, baby girl." His tears brim over, using her name for me. I haven't heard it in nineteen years. "She fought so hard for you. The doctors told her that the last round of chemo wouldn't help, but she did it so she'd have more time with you."

"It wasn't enough."

"No, it wasn't. But she didn't want to go. She didn't want to leave you."

"Don't you mean you?"

"No, she'd made her peace. She knew I'd be fine and move on."

A bitter laugh slips out. "Boy, was she ever wrong on that one."

"She wanted me to get married again. She wanted you to have a mother and siblings, but I couldn't. I let her down. I let you down."

"Do you know what I've been thinking about in the nineteen years since she died, Dad? Do you?"

He shakes his head.

"I've been thinking that I'm going to die young too, so it's best not to get attached. Not to fall in love. Not to have kids. Why do you think I spend my days with kids? It's to make up for all the chances I'll never get with my own. All because I saw what it did to you, and I never wanted anyone to go through that. I never wanted my child to feel like she wasn't enough."

I might as well have hit him.

I'm tired of considering his feelings when he doesn't consider mine.

"So now, here I am. Parts of me ripped out. Hollow on the inside. And I could fall in love. I tried. I think maybe I did even." I pause for a minute before saying quietly, "I know I did. But I ruined it because I don't know how to be a partner. I don't know how to give my love without worrying that I'm going to irreparably damage someone the way you were irreparably damaged."

His eyes are hollow. "Millie, I know I wasn't the father you needed me to be. I wanted to be, but I couldn't. I didn't know how. Not when I was going to lose you too."

"What?"

"We knew you had the gene. You were tested when they first discovered it. Your mom was in a study, and they tested you too. I knew I was going to bury you too, and I didn't know what to do with that. I didn't know how to handle that. So I didn't."

"You've known all this time?"

He looks at his hands.

"Why didn't you tell me?"

"What was I supposed to do? Tell you you were going to die?"

"Dad, I've lived my whole life thinking that anyway. Didn't you know there were options? If I'd known, I could have planned better."

As I'm saying it, I know it's true. From the moment Dr. Tremarchi told me the news, I was full-steam ahead at getting everything taken out. There was never a thought of leaving something behind that would later on kill me. If I was doing this, I was going all in. Maybe that was a mistake. I could have—probably should have—waited. Erin from UnBRCAble did. She's waiting on surgeries until she gets a chance to have kids. I could have looked at freezing eggs or something. Perhaps I should have been a little less hasty.

"Oh, Dad, I really messed this up. I rushed into the treatment."

He shrugs. "Maybe. Maybe not. Was your pathology clear?"

The medical speak from him surprises me. I didn't think he knew about any of this. How narrow sighted of me. Of course, he knows. He's been through it. He watched his wife die and has spent the last twenty years preparing to watch his daughter die too.

If I weren't the daughter in this scenario, I might even feel a little sympathy for him.

I glance toward my desk in the corner. Among the stacks of surgery-related paperwork is my pathology report. I never opened it.

I didn't want to read about all my healthy tissue being destroyed. I wonder what they do with it all? Burn it? Bury it? Put it in the landfill?

"It's over there," I nod toward the desk.

Dad gets up and rifles through. "Are you double-checking your bills against the explanation of benefits? Making sure they're matching up? Sometimes they try to slip things in."

His questions are like nails on a chalkboard. Why now?

"Dad, stop. Stop pretending like you care. Does it matter what the pathology says? Does it matter what my bills are? I've got the rest of my life to pay them off."

Dad's hand lowers, dropping the paper on the desk. "I care, Millie. I always have."

"You think you care, but you don't."

"You can't tell me what I think. I know that I love you. I also know that I wasn't enough for you. I was too broken. Am too broken. Too scared."

He picks up the papers and begins shuffling through.

His words actually make me feel slightly better. At least he was aware of it. I always wondered if he knew that he wasn't enough of a father.

"I tried. I say I failed, but look at you. You've done so well. You're so strong. So happy. And now so health—" his voice drops as he looks at the paper in his hand.

"Yeah, I'm great. I'm so great that I can't figure out how to have a relationship. I've gone after losers and rejects my whole life. And I finally get a good, decent man, and I manage to drive him away by being a complete and total freak all the time. And for what? Probably nothing. I was probably impulsive and—"

"Millie, did you really not look at this? Didn't you talk to the doctor?" Dad turns around, holding a piece of paper in his hand. He's looking pretty pale.

"What? Is it a bill? I'll take care of it later."

He reaches out and hands it to me, his hand trembling.

I scan down the paper, not really able to understand much of what's on there. It might as well be written in another language. I flip the paper over.

Final Pathologic Diagnosis: Right breast, negative for malignancy.

Left Breast: Ductal Carcinoma, In Situ. 0.5 cm x 0.5 cm x 0.5 cm

There's a lot more words but they swim on the page.

"Dad, what does this mean?"

"Cancer, Millie."

"But ..." except I can't think of anything else to say.

Dad sits down next to me and puts an awkward hand on my knee. "I don't understand how the doctor didn't tell you."

I cover my eyes with my hands, thinking back to that visit with Dr. Tremarchi.

Millicent, the results of your pathology are back.

Does it change anything? My breasts are gone. Do I need chemo?

Well, no.

Do I need Tamoxifen?

I don't think so, since there's no breast tissue left.

Then I'm done here. Don't take this the wrong way, but I don't want to come back anytime soon. I need to stop seeing you. You're not good for my health.

"He tried to tell me, but I didn't want to hear it. I didn't want to know that I'd thrown out healthy tissue. It was enough hearing that about my ovaries."

"I guess the good news is that you made the right decision, at the right time."

I had cancer and I didn't even know it.

At least all of this suffering was worth it.

And at least no one can tell me to look on the bright side anymore.

CHAPTER 36

I survive one minute to the next. One foot in front of the other. I make it a week. Then two.

I'm on a roll.

L-I-V-I-N.

Not really. The only way I'm making it through is coffee, witty co-worker banter at lunch, and being so exhausted that I practically fall into bed the moment I get home.

Claudia tells me I won't always be this tired. I'm not sure I believe her though.

Wednesdays are the toughest days to get through. I stay after school until it's time to go to UnBRCAble. Tonight, I've got to leave the meeting early to get back to school for open house.

I'm dreading this, because there's a real chance I could see Sterling. He has to walk by my classroom to get to Piper's class. Piper's stopped leaving notes. She doesn't even smile at me in the hallway anymore. I let her down and we both know it.

Her teacher, Mrs. Romer, is two doors down from me. I've already planned to strategically place myself in the back of the classroom so I don't see Sterling casually stroll by tonight on his way to or from the classroom.

For as good as I'm doing—which to be clear, isn't really that good—I don't think I can keep it together if I see him.

Emergency plan in place, I head out to group. The girls will pump me full of good energy and sugar, not to mention false confidence.

There was part of me that worried the results of my pathology report would get me kicked out of this group. Am I still a Previvor?

"Did you talk to the doctor?" Claudia doesn't even let me sit down before holding me accountable.

"Yes, I spoke to him last week, the day after the meeting." I plop down, which may have been a mistake. If I sit for too long, I'm never going to want to get up again.

"And?" she taps her foot impatiently. I didn't know people really still did that.

I let out a sigh. Dr. Tremarchi was none-too-pleased with me that I'd stormed out without listening to the pathology report. He didn't seem to appreciate it either when I told him mood swings were his fault for removing my ovaries, so he'd have to deal.

It wouldn't surprise me if he calls security the next time I come in the office.

Which is why I talked to him on the phone for this issue.

"He scolded me for not looking at it sooner."

"And?" This time, it's Kelli, leaning forward. "Don't keep us hanging."

"They found a very small tumor. Most likely, due to the density of my breast tissue, it wouldn't have shown up on a mammogram. And, because of my age, they probably wouldn't have started doing mammograms for a few years, or until it was large enough to feel."

A hush falls over the group.

"In essence, the prophylactic mastectomy saved my life. Cancer was already there."

"Damn, girl."

"And, because I was so lackadaisical about going to the doctor in the first place, most likely they wouldn't have caught it before stage three. Dr. Tremarchi said that the only reason they did catch it is because I was having the prophylactic surgery. There's no other way they would have been looking for or found it until ... later."

I see the poster on the wall across the room and make a mental note to get it made into a T-shirt.

"Save the woman, not the tatas."

The sign—and it's message—has been here all along. Yet somehow, I didn't see it.

Couldn't see it.

It's right obviously.

They couldn't print it if it weren't true, right?

I'm alive. Now it's time to live.

Time to focus on what was saved, rather than what was lost.

Full of courage, I stand up to head back to school. Maybe, if Sterling crosses my path, I can mend that fence.

I don't expect him to take me back, but if he'd let me apologize, I'd feel better.

I knew I wasn't ready for a relationship, or whatever we had, and I should have respected that.

I should have respected him enough to be honest.

Of course, it's not easy to be honest to someone else when you can't even be honest with yourself.

Look at me, facing reality like a big girl.

~~~***~~~

Being a grown up sucks.

Paying taxes. Going to work on Mondays. Having to be polite to the last *two* men who dumped you in public.

I'm so tempted to glitter *and* slime my classroom.

But there's a distinct possibility that Johnny wouldn't clean it up, and I'd be stuck with glitter trailing after me all year.

As it is, I find the sparkly flecks invading my house like termites.

Johnny is currently hitting on Amy, one of the other second grade teachers. Like, right in front of me.

She doesn't know we dated. Truth be told, I think he's doing it to get back at me for the Sterling episode.

Sterling … sigh.

I didn't see him tonight, though I know he had to have been here. He's the type of man that doesn't miss out on anything with his kid.

Because he's a great father.

And I insulted that.

He'd been up front that insulting his daughter was pretty much the only deal breaker for him.

I have been pretty self-centered this summer. His girlfriend getting pregnant has nothing to do with me, especially considering it was nine years ago.

Just like Lisa getting pregnant has nothing to do with me now.

It's simply a coincidence. A terrible, gut-wrenching coincidence. A bitter pill to swallow, certainly.

But at least it's not cancer, right?

Nope. Too soon.

I grab my bag and water bottle and flip off the lights in my classroom. I've got to be back in about twelve hours, so there's little time to sleep. I want to get home to my cat and my solitude and start figuring out how to be a better human being.

I'll start with this.

"Hey, Amy. I'm heading out. You leaving? We can walk out together." From her vantage point, Amy can't see the dirty look Johnny shoots me. I'm guessing his plan is to keep this hook up on the down low too.

"Um, I guess," she stammers, looking from me to Johnny and back again.

"Oh, you weren't waiting on Johnny, were you?" I smile sweetly. This is sort of fun.

"Well, I don't know. Am I?" She looks at him expectantly. His face reddens.

"Johnny's so nice, isn't he?" I gush. "He came to visit me in the hospital when I had my mastectomy." It's the first time I've dropped this in casual conversation. "I mean, we'd been sleeping together all year, so it was the least he could do." I look at Johnny who's now shooting death rays out of his eyes and then turn my attention to Amy. Her eyes are wide and her mouth's hanging open a bit.

"Actually, the least he could do was show up in my hospital room before the anesthesia had even worn off and dump me, which is what he did. Isn't that nice? He said it was," I tilt my head back toward him. "I don't want to misquote you, with you standing right here and all. I mean, I'd just come out of a six hour surgery. I remember something about it being 'too intense' and then I think something about how I was a 'downer' and 'no fun' anymore. Did I get it right?"

Amy looks from me to him and back. "Right. And then, when he realized I had nice fake boobs, he came sniffing back around to play. Isn't that nice of him?"

"Jesus, Millie, you don't have to be such a bi—"

Amy cuts him off. "I'm leaving now. Millie?" She picks up her tote and links her elbow through mine. As we get ready to round the corner, she calls over her shoulder. "And Johnny, if you stop cleaning our rooms or do anything to sabotage us, we'll tell the District. They'll never promote you to head custodian if you don't do your job."

Once out of earshot, I whisper, "Can you be my new best friend?"

Amy tilts her head back in laughter. "I should say the same to you. He really ...?"

"Yup. I was barely conscious. I don't know how I even remember it. But yeah."

We get to the parking lot and are two of the last cars there.

"Was the surgery terrible?"

I nod. "It's messed with my head a lot. Turned my life—and personality—upside down, really. The recovery was long and hard. And not finished yet."

"Oh, Millie. I'm sorry. I didn't know. My best friend got her boobs done, and it wasn't that bad."

Her tone is kind and compassionate. "Someday, when we don't have to be right back to school in the morning, I'll tell you why it's so much harder. In the meantime, go to the doctor and have your routine screenings done. The district gives you a half-day to get a mammogram done. Use it."

"I'll get right on that." She opens her car door and tosses her bag in. I envy the effortlessness of her moves. I still have to think about every move I make. "You guys really dated?"

"I don't know that I'd call it dating, but yeah." I wrinkle my nose at the memories. "And I've decided that since I'm going to be around for a while, I deserve someone better. And you do too."

"Thanks for saving me. Have a good night!" She waves as she slides into her car.

I think about it all the way home.

I had someone better, and I messed it up.

It's time to figure out a way to convince him to give me another chance.

CHAPTER 37

The thing is, after a lifetime of avoiding deep, meaningful relationships with men worth dating, I realize I have absolutely no idea how to get Sterling back.

If I even deserve him.

Which, we all know, I don't.

I consider all the grand romantic gestures from the movies, including blasting music outside his window, riding a lawnmower, and showing up at prom. I don't have a boombox, I don't have a riding lawnmower, and it's not really prom season, so I'm outta luck.

Maybe, if we're meant to be together, the universe will reach out its cosmic hands and bring us together, like it did at the hospital.

Or maybe, I need to put on my big girl panties, apologize, and hope he gives me another chance.

Finding a working boombox would be easier.

I can even lift my arms above my head now, so I'm totally ready.

Like any difficult task, not dissimilar to my experience with getting tested for the BRCA gene, I decide to put this off for a while. I mean, it worked out so well the last time.

I want to ask the ladies of UnBRCAble but it seems weird to ask about this sort of thing. I mean, we're fine talking about nipples and vaginal dryness. How to unmess up a relationship seems oddly more personal.

Plus, it's only Saturday and my next meeting is on Wednesday. We should probably consider meeting more often—at least until I get my life straightened out. Daily should do it.

The current condition of my house and lawn scream to me, but I'm not motivated to listen.

Also ranking low on the list of things to do is to finish going through my medical bills and go grocery shopping. I don't want to do those either.

Then some little drill sergeant shows up in my head and yells at me to stop putting off things and face them head on. If I did that, I wouldn't be in half of my current mess. No more Scarlett O'Hara for me. I'm going to start with mowing my lawn.

It's a push mower so don't get any ideas about me riding up to fetch Sterling like in *Can't Buy Me Love*. Sigh. Patrick Dempsey was hot, even before he was McDreamy.

Once outside, I tackle the weeding first, popping in my headset so I can listen to an audiobook. It makes the time go by faster. I started listening to them when I was recovering, and it's my new go-to for books.

Naturally, I'm reading a nice, juicy romance. His hands are inching down, about to reach inside her—

Dammit. The ringing in my ear makes me jump.

Hastily, I press the button on my headset to accept the call.

"Hello?"

"Millie?"

I hear a loud sob.

"Lisa?" It can't be her. Lisa is not a crier. That's my job in the friendship.

Assuming we're still friends.

"Millie, can you help me?" It's definitely Lisa and she's definitely crying.

I'm tearing off my gardening gloves and running into the house before I respond, "I'm on my way. Where?"

"The hospital. I'm heading into the ER."

Crap. Crap. Crap.

It's got to be the baby.

Double, triple crap.

Running to my car, then pausing to catch my breath—I really need to start doing some cardio— memories of Lisa flash through my brain. That first day of middle school, my first big first without Mom. Lisa plopped down next to me in homeroom and said, "Okay, this is our year. Let's do this."

She was the take charge, no nonsense voice I needed that morning when I was overwhelmed and self-conscious. But Lisa seemed so confident, and she had boobs, so she *must* know things.

I guess it's a good thing wisdom isn't contained in the mammary glands. Or maybe it is. It'd explain why I've been so stupid the last few months.

Either way, she needs me. No matter how hard this is for me, it's not about me. It's getting her through this.

And if she's asking for help, it must be bad. She doesn't reach out.

My mind whirs continuously on the way over. Things she might need. Calls to make. Gifts to get her.

But first things first, I need to go to her.

Walking through the front revolving door of the hospital, I wait for the wave of anxiety to hit. The PTSD from my surgeries. The triggers of the sights and smells.

But I'm fine.

A quick cataloguing of my emotions tells me I'm nervous about why Lisa is here. I'm not in the best place about the baby, but the thought of her losing it is crushing to me.

She's the only one who can have one, so it's doubly disappointing if she can't carry to term.

That thought stops me in my tracks.

I want her to have this baby. Sure, I'm jealous, but if I can't have one, she should.

If it's not too late, that's what I'm going to tell her.

Finally making my way to the ER, a tired looking clerk buzzes me through the doors. I try not to look at the people on the gurneys, especially that one guy puking his guts out. Gross.

Left, right, down the hall. One more left and I find a scared-looking Lisa rocking back and forth on the bed. Her hands are cradling her barely-there belly the way expectant mothers do.

"Lis, what's wrong? What happened? What are they going to do about it?"

That should about cover it.

"I might have appendicitis."

"Okay." I sink down into the chair, relief flooding me. "I thought it was the baby."

Tears fill her eyes. "No. My stupid appendix."

"Yeah, but that's good. If the baby's fine, the appendix is no big deal. One of my students had it last year. Sick on Monday, surgery Tuesday morning. He was home the same evening and was fine in a day or two. Easy-peasy."

"No, you don't understand. It's different. My chance of miscarriage goes up to thirty-six percent if they have to operate. It's not the same because of the pregnancy." She wipes a tear. "It's a lot worse."

The irony of this situation is not lost on me, but I also know that now is not the moment to point it out.

"When will they know?"

"I'm waiting for an ultrasound now. If they can't tell on that, I might need an MRI."

I nod, not knowing what else to say. Tons of questions run through my head. How far along are you? Are you happy about this? Did you want this? Who is the father? Would losing it be the worst thing for you?

I don't ask any of these questions because I should know all the answers already. The disintegration of our relationship is still confounding to me, but I'm sure I'm to blame.

At least for some of it, right?

Lisa looks at me. "I'm scared, Mil. Not for me, but for the baby."

That tells me all I need to know. Whatever her feelings about this pregnancy and impending parenthood were, this is all that matters to her now.

"Okay, but maybe it's not your appendix. Maybe it's … gas or something."

"If you tell me that this is all because I have to fart, I'm—" she breaks off and starts laughing.

"Let's hope that's it." It'd be embarrassing for sure, but certainly the best option. "Of course, it's probably going to be the most expensive fart on record, especially if you get the MRI."

"I don't even want to think about that, though maybe I'll finally hit my deductible. You know, you don't even think about these things."

"I know. I'm happy I had money in my flex spending account. My union president is always harping on us about putting money in. I only did because my dental work isn't usually covered. I'm glad I had money in it this year. I really needed it."

Lisa looks at me. "Are you doing okay still? Any complications?"

I'm touched at her concern. This is why we're friends. We can fight and make up and move on, no hard feelings.

"Ship shape."

I nod toward her hands, still rubbing her belly. "I think I missed some important details here, you know."

She looks down. "I didn't know how to tell you. You were already so touchy. I didn't know what was going to upset you half the time. Then, when I found this out ... considering your situation, I didn't think it'd go over well."

She was not wrong.

"You still could have told me." I look down at my own hands. "I didn't handle it well, and I can't really imagine a situation when I would have. The timing just sucks."

"I know," she agrees.

"Speaking of timing, when? Who?"

"On the cruise. One of the groomsmen. Melina's brother. We bonded over how terrible she is."

There's no love lost between Lisa and her new sister-in-law. This development is sure to complicate that relationship even further.

"How's it going over?"

"Like a fart in church."

I laugh. "You should be so lucky."

Before we can continue laughing like ten-year-old boys, we're interrupted by the doctor.

Not just any doctor, but *my* doctor.

"I'm reviewing your labs, but it's not uncommon for leukocytes to be elevated during pregnancy. After the ultrasound, they're going to take you right to MRI, and we'll have a plan after that." Dr. Tremarchi finally looks up from his tablet. He glances at me for a nanosecond and then back at Lisa. "Okay then? I'll be back after your results come back."

He's gone as quickly as he came.

"That's Dr. Tremarchi."

Lisa shrugs. "I don't remember what he said his name was before. Maybe?"

"No, that's him. He's my O.B. I mean gynecologist I guess, since I won't ever need an obstetrician. I guess I don't really need a gynecologist either, but he's my doctor."

"Okay. You like him, right? You think he knows what he's doing?"

"I'd say yes, because he did run the test on me, which I needed. He hit the nail on the head. But I'm a little, well, upset, that he didn't recognize me."

I'd think with the hysterics on diagnosis and the way I wouldn't accept the pathology report that he'd remember me. My behavior in his office hasn't exactly been stellar.

Or unforgettable.

Lisa looks at me. "Maybe he isn't good at faces. You should have taken off your pants to see if he recognized your hoo ha."

This is why we're friends.

CHAPTER 38

Seven hours later—*seven*—I drop Lisa off at home and make sure she's comfortable for the night. Her appendix is possibly inflamed, but not enough to warrant surgery yet. Her pain has totally gone away and her white blood cells are normal. She's got a little bit of fluid that could mean irritation or it could mean nothing.

Apparently, there are some people who have low level irritation and swelling in their appendices without it really getting infected. They think she falls into this category. So they're going to watch her like a hawk.

The risk to her baby is too high to operate right now. She's only fourteen weeks, so surgery would probably mean a miscarriage.

They're not convinced it's her appendix, but not convinced it's not. Close watch and plenty of rest.

For some reason, I can't sleep.

Okay, it was probably the vat of coffee I drank while pacing the halls.

Patience is not a virtue I was blessed with. I like to get things done. To make decisions and act on them.

Hence my decision to have my uterus and ovaries removed first.

It could have waited.

All I knew is that I wanted them gone.

I wanted that peace of mind more than I wanted kids.

I probably would not have been a good mother, putting my own needs first like that. Maybe this is for the best.

I flop on my bed and wish for sleep. My mind is whizzing and whirring and every thought is coming back to Sterling.

I wish I could talk to him again.

I'd tell him I'm sorry.

I'd apologize for being such a wanker.

I don't think I've ever said wanker before, and I'm not totally sure what it means, but it sounds like me in this case.

Before I can stop myself, I've selected his name and the green button that initiates the call.

Crap.

What am I doing?

I should hang up.

I can't hang up. He'll know it's me. Gah. What do I—

"Hello?"

Fudge.

"Um, hey. It's me. Millie. I don't know if you still have my number in your phone or not, or if you remember my voice. So yeah, it's me. Millie."

Shoot me now.

"It's nice to see your phone skills haven't improved. Everything else about you is so unpredictable. Can I always count on this stellar communication from you?"

Yikes. He's still pissed.

He deserves to be but still.

"What's a wanker? Am I a wanker? I feel like maybe that's a good way to describe my behavior."

There's silence on the line.

"Millie, I can't do this like this."

Must save face. Must save face.

"Sure. Okay, it's only that I know wanker is a British term and you're the only person I know who's from British. Britain. Great Britain. England. The United Kingdom."

Apparently, I do not know how to quit while I'm ahead.

"Piper's asleep."

I look at the clock. It's after ten. When did that happen?

"Oh, sorry. I didn't mean to disturb you. Sorry. Bye."

I hang up and look at the phone.

I'm too stupid to be trusted with this thing. There should be a competency test or something before they allow you to buy one.

But a moment later, my phone tings.

Piper's asleep. Can you come over so we can talk?

Wait, what?

I didn't totally repulse and repel him?

How on earth not?

Sure. Be over in a few.

A quick brush of the hair, a thorough brushing of the teeth, and a liberal application of deodorant, and I'm ready to go. I don't know why he wants to see me. Maybe it's so he can break up with me to my face, though it's pretty clear we're through.

Whatever his reason, this will let me apologize properly and hopefully move on from here. I wish the outcome could be different, but I'll take what I can get.

Maybe one day, someday, I'll be able to handle a long-term committed relationship. He won't care about the foobs or the fact that I can't have kids. He'll love me for me.

I pull in a mere thirty minutes after the text. It's going on eleven, which is way past my bedtime. Surely this could have waited until morning.

Why am I so damn impulsive?

Too late to back out now.

Sterling opens the door and cautiously steps aside. He doesn't say anything as I walk in and stand there. Sitting seems presumptuous.

Truth be told, I've no idea what he wants or expects from me. Honestly, I don't know what to expect from me either.

So I stand there, looking at him. I imagine my facial expression is what my father used to refer to as my "constipated owl" look. Quite attractive, if you like birds who need more fiber.

Carnivore problems.

Anyway, Sterling finally puts me out of my misery and gestures for me to sit. Propping gingerly on the edge of the sofa, I knit my fingers together. Am I supposed to talk? Is he going first? How is this working?

"You were asking about wankers?"

Oh phew. He started.

"Yes. What exactly is a wanker?"

His face pinkens slightly and he nervously flails his hands about.

Is he going to say something? What's he doing?

Then I notice what his hand's doing.

Oh.

"I thought a wanker was like a jerk or an idiot or something like that. I didn't know it meant ..." I nod toward his hand, "that."

"Americans often use it as jerk, not understanding the 'off' part." His hand is still making that obscene gesture.

I nod toward it. "You can probably stop now."

His face pinks further. "Oh right. Sorry." He slides his hand under his leg. "What's all this about wankers?"

"I thought I was being one, but I was not masturb—does that apply to women too? Women don't jerk-off per se." I cannot believe the words coming out of my mouth right now. I'm tempted to stick my fist in my mouth, but I fear that wouldn't be enough to slow the tide of verbal diarrhea that is currently occurring.

"You called me after all this time to talk about self-pleasure?" Sterling's clearly as confused as I am.

"No, I wanted to apologize for being a wanker, but I'm guessing that's not the right word. Am I a tosser?" I'm trying to pull everything I know about British slang.

He laughs. "I don't know, are you?"

"Am I?" I'm getting equal parts frustrated and panicked. There's no doubt in my mind that I am presenting like a complete and total moron.

"Both wanker and tosser can be used to call someone a jerk or idiot, but both technically refer to someone who lays about all day whacking off." He looks me up and down. "I can possibly support the idiot part, but I doubt the other part is true."

"I'm an idiot. I was just trying to say it in your language."

Which is about the most idiotic thing I can say.

"You know what I mean," I quickly correct. "I swear, I'm really not stupid. My IQ is in the high average range. I'm going to plead temporary stupidity based on high levels of stress, early menopause, and overall turmoil in my life."

Sterling laughs. "Millie, relax. I do understand that you're having a hard time right now."

The tension seeps out of my shoulders, and I stop clenching my teeth. I wasn't even aware I was doing that until I feel my face relax. I lean back.

Sterling continues, looking at his hands instead of me. "I know you're going through a rough patch, but I can't do that again."

He's right, of course, but it doesn't stop me from feeling like I got kicked in the gut.

"I know, and I don't expect you to. You gave me clear hard limits, and I pushed them. I didn't mean to, but I did. It's not really an excuse, but I was upset and my thoughts weren't coming out clearly."

"I gathered."

"I didn't mean that you weren't a good father. You are. The best. Piper's so lucky to have you. I can't imagine you not being a father. That's part of the problem. You should have more kids. Lots of kids. Like a dozen of them."

He puts up his hands. "Let's not get carried away there. That's an awful lot of University to pay for."

"You know what I mean, and I knew I couldn't give that to you."

"Millie, don't you know me better than that?"

I look at my hands. I know he's right. A good man wouldn't mind. He'd tell me we'd adopt or buy them, just Dylan McDermott in *Steel Magnolias*. Why was I so afraid to tell Sterling in the first place? There's never been any doubt that he's a good man.

"Obviously I knew all along that it most likely wouldn't be a deal breaker for you. Somewhere deep down, I knew it. I just didn't want to admit it to myself. This summer has been, well, not my finest to say the least. I don't even want a do over because you couldn't pay me enough to go through it all again. It's been horrible."

Sterling reaches over and places his hand on mine. I stare at it. It's big and strong, and I wish he'd never let go.

"I know, which is why you're here. Why I invited you over to talk." He looks at his hand and pulls it back. "But I can't keep making the same stupid mistake over and over again."

His words hurt, but are more kind than I deserve.

"I make stupid mistakes all the time. Obviously. I'm trying to learn. I'm trying to be better." I need him to know that I know my actions were wrong. I was terrible, and I don't deserve another chance.

But I want one nonetheless.

Sterling clears his throat. "I need to grow too. Repeating my mistakes is foolish. Right now, taking you back would be foolish."

My head snaps up. Not gonna lie, his words are like a spike through my heart.

He's not wrong though.

"I know. I don't even know me anymore. I can't expect you to take me back, even though I want you to. So I need to tell you I was wrong for what I said and apologize. I didn't—it wasn't about you. It was about me and my feelings of inadequacy and frankly, jealousy."

He sighs. "I know."

I put a finger up to silence him. "Please, Sterling. Let me say this. Things have—had—been bad with Lisa all summer, and I didn't know why. Then I found out she was pregnant."

"I recall."

"That's why she'd been acting so weird. She wasn't happy about it and knew it would crush me all at the same time. Plus, we're both a bit irrationally hormonal, just on opposite ends of the spectrum."

Sterling stands up, pulling me with him. "Millie" is all he says as he envelopes me in his arms. My foobs are squished against his chest, but for once it doesn't bother me.

"Sterling, I'm so sorry I'm a hot mess. I'm trying to get better. To be better. For you."

He leans in and kisses the top of my head. "You can't be better for me."

This man seriously confuses me.

I pull back and look up at him. "So it's too late?"

"I wouldn't say too late, but not the right time."

I look at my watch. "I can wait a half-hour."

Sterling gives me a small smile. "You're not ready."

"I want to be ready."

"I know you do, love. Trust me, I wish you were ready too. But you're not. As you are, right here and right now, you're not good enough."

That is the worst, and possibly most honest thing I've ever heard.

"Sterling, I'll do anything to prove it to you that I can be good enough for you. I can do better. I will do better."

He looks at me, a sad expression in his gaze. "You can't be better for me. You have to be better for you. If you can love yourself, you'll be able to love me too."

Damn if he's not right.

I'm ready to start.

EPILOGUE

Nine Months Later

"Come on, Mil. We're going to be late."

"Be right down!" I pull my T-shirt down and yank my hair back into a ponytail. I'd intended on straightening my hair and carefully applying makeup, but I'm running late as usual.

"Millie, can you *please* tell me where we're going?" Piper whines.

"Alas, I cannot. I've been sworn to secrecy in a vow of blood. Your dad says I don't get to go to England if I blab this, and I really want to meet Kate and Meghan so ..." I shrug. "A girl's gotta do what a girl's gotta do. You'll find out soon enough."

"You know that there's more to England than the royal family and the odds of you meeting them are about—" Sterling sighs. It's not the first time we've had this discussion.

"About as great as me meeting a sloth." Piper interrupts, flopping down on the couch. She's wearing a sloth T-shirt and has her stuffed animal sloth clipped to a belt loop.

She's in a sloth phase.

Sterling looks at me and cocks his eyebrow. "Still, don't get your hopes up."

We pile into the car, and I shoot a quick text to Erin before pulling up the directions. Little does Piper know but Erin works at the zoo and recently got moved to the sloth encounter.

The wait list for the experience was over a year, but Erin pulled some strings.

She's good people.

"Is Candice meeting us there?" I'd been waiting all along for her to want to ride with us.

That'd be a hard 'no' on my part.

"I didn't tell her. She'd have spoiled the surprise, just to get back at me." Sterling's voice is low so Piper can't hear.

Candice has been on the warpath recently. It started with Sterling's Christmas declaration that he could no longer stay away from me.

To my credit, I'd been trying hard to woo him. This included some counseling, sharing a weekly meal with my father, and finding a better hormone patch that didn't give me such mood swings. Also, I realized I could no longer stand in the way of the bromance, so Cornelius went back to live with my dad. They were both happy, and Sterling could breathe. It was a win-win.

Oh, did I mention counseling?

In terms of Candice, she didn't take our relationship well, and throughout the year, things have gone from bad to worse. Especially since she found out

I'm going to England for the wedding next month, and she will not be going.

Sterling's lawyer had compiled quite the case and the family court judge easily granted a change to the custody agreement. In fact, Sterling now has primary custody, which means he doesn't pay child support anymore.

Thank you, Lisa, for hooking Sterling up with a fantastic attorney.

Needless to say, Candice is not happy. Obviously, she blames me for all of this, rather than looking at her own conduct. It's pretty sad that she's more upset about losing the money than seeing her daughter less.

Still, Candice's loss is my gain, and Piper is fantastic. I hope I'm being the mother figure she needs and am setting a good example.

"Where are we going again?" Piper whines. "Is it going to be boring?"

"Yes, so dreadfully boring. You may cry with boredom," Sterling says dryly.

"Why couldn't I stay home? I'm old enough." A quick glance in the back seat confirms my suspicion that Piper has her arms folded in defiance across her chest.

"You turned nine last week. You are not old enough to stay home alone all day."

"But I wanted to have my birthday party today, and you said no."

Sterling rolls his eyes. "Yes, I know. I'm the worst parent in the world."

I smile at him and pat his hand that's resting comfortably on the gear shift. He drives an automatic, so I often wonder why he does this.

I wanted to blindfold Piper until we get her back to where Erin told us to go, but Sterling nixed that idea.

"OMG, we're at the zoo! The zoo! Did you know they have a sloth now? OMG, I love sloths!"

"Really? I had no idea," Sterling comments as he gets out of the car.

"Dad, they're so derpy! How can you not love them?" Piper's practically bouncing now.

"Derpy? What is derpy? Did you make up that word?"

Piper stops and puts her hands on her hips. If she didn't resemble Candice while doing this, it'd be super funny. "Uh, no Dad. Derpy is something that's so funny looking, it's cute. Sloths are derpy. Pac-man frogs are derpy. Axolotls are derpy."

We start walking toward the entrance. "I only know one of those animals. The other is a video game and the last isn't even a word," Sterling defends.

"Axolotls are a rare fish that looks sort of like a lion and has legs and walks. They only live in one lake in Mexico, and they are, indeed, derpy," I supply.

Sterling stops in his tracks. "A fish that walks? What?"

I pull out my phone and quickly Google a picture. "See, legs. And that's a derpy face."

Sterling shakes his head. "How do you know this?"

"I spend my day with seven and eight-year-olds. I know things." As I've said before, seven-year-olds are my jam.

He takes my hand and we make it to the line at the will-call window. I nod at Sterling and then toward Piper, in a silent communication for him to get her away so she doesn't overhear the plans.

Passes in hand, we start milling around. Everyone and their brother seems to be here on this beautiful early summer day. It seemed like it rained all May and now that June is here, people can't get enough outside time. I see more than one family from school. Man, they're going to be so jealous on Monday when Piper tells them that she got to pet and feed a sloth.

So much better than a sleepover and pizza.

"Can we go to the sloths?" Piper asks for perhaps the hundredth time. She's been less than impressed with the sleeping cougars, the sleeping otters, the sleeping bears, and a moose that didn't move. The only active animals we've actually encountered are grumpy Canada geese, harassing tourists for food. A quick glance at my watch confirms we're in the zone. I text Lisa. She and little Dexter will be joining us for ice cream after the encounter. My godson and honorary nephew naps midday and Lisa is terrified of ruining a good thing.

I've heard that kid cry, and I don't blame her.

"Lead the way, m'lady."

Piper starts running but we have to keep pulling her back with us. I can't keep up. While one of these days I plan on running a 5K for breast cancer awareness, today is not that day.

We finally make it to the sloth habitat where Erin is waiting outside for us.

"Nice shirt," she says, giving me a quick hug.

I don't remember what I'm wearing, so I have to look. Right. The large teal and pink ribbon sets the background for the words: "Previvor: By choice, My choice."

"Gotta represent, yo." The one-year anniversary of my mastectomy is in two weeks. What a freakin' rollercoaster of a year.

Piper nudges me. "Don't do that. You're not cool."

Sterling laughs. "Yeah, yo."

"Daaaaad," Piper groans. "You're embarrassing me."

I smile. "Totally."

It's moments like this, when I know she's about to explode with excitement, that stop me. I almost missed out on all this. I almost blew it. Good thing Sterling finally came to his senses.

Or I started going to therapy in addition to UnBRCAble to deal with my losses and have almost stopped acting like a nutter.

Almost.

And because I've finally straightened myself out, I'm able to relish in the rewards. This is what I've always wanted—needed.

A family.

I'm not going to leave them, and they're not going to leave me.

We're in this together.

And not that I really need to share this, but I'm more comfortable in my own skin, foobs and all. This means I'm *much* more comfortable in the bedroom, if you know what I mean.

Erin punches our passes and starts to bring us inside. As predicted, Piper's enthusiasm hits a new high and her voice is so high pitched that only dogs can hear her.

"Calm down, you don't want to scare the animals," Sterling whispers.

I think she's so excited, she might not sleep for a week, but she manages to pull it together as we step inside the building. It's hot and humid, mimicking the Costa Rican rain forest where most sloths live.

I'm now relieved I didn't take the time to straighten my hair. I can feel my ponytail puffing up.

Sloths are really cute, by the way.

Totally derpy.

Over the course of an hour, we feed them, pet them, and Piper even gets to hold one. Well, she gets to hold a pillow that the sloth is perched on. I take picture after picture and video after video. She's going to remember this forever, and I'm so lucky to be a part of it.

I want a picture to remember it too.

"Erin, can you take a picture of us with the sloth?"

Erin grins and nods at Sterling. "Why don't you get in there too?"

A family picture, plus sloth.

It's perfect.

Piper's in between her father and I, holding the pillow with Barry the sloth. I tilt my head slightly and try not to stick my foobs out too far while sucking in my stomach.

Erin takes one picture then another. My face is getting a little stiff from smiling when Sterling moving catches my eye. I turn to see what he's doing, but it looks like he's going to tie his shoe.

"Sterling, stand up so we can get a good—"

Oh. My. God.

Sterling's not tying his shoe. He's holding a ring in a box.

A diamond ring, in case you didn't get that.

My brain struggles to process what's happening.

"Millie, Piper and I would like to know if you'd be willing to join us in marriage."

"Dad, she's not marrying me. Get it right," Piper interjects.

"Right. Will you marry me and join *our* family?"

I'm crying again, but for once they're happy tears.

"I know this year has been crazy, and how we got together almost seems unbelievable, but from my ex-mother-in-law's vaginal rejuvenation, to you exposing yourself in public on our first real date, to helping deliver your friend's baby, to sloths, it seems we are suited to be with each other. I don't need to save you, but I think you saved me."

"You definitely saved me."

"Then it's mutual at least."

"Are you saying yes or what?" Piper yells and Barry the sloth turns his head in slow motion to look at me.

"Of course. I'm the luckiest woman on the planet."

"You can't be luckier than me. I'm the one holding the sloth," Piper pipes in. Her name is fitting, I've come to realize.

Sterling stands and puts a beautiful solitaire on my finger. He pulls me in and I kiss him, not caring that we have an audience.

I glance over and realize that Erin's been videoing and taking pictures this whole time.

"Did you get that all?" I wipe the tears with my left hand, not wanting to let go of Sterling with my other hand.

"I did, but I think we may need to edit out the part about the mother-in-law's you know, *surgery*." She points down toward her own crotch.

Sterling's face turns bright pink. "Um, right. Not the smoothest bit, I suppose. I've been looking up sloth jokes but couldn't find any good ones. I panicked because I didn't know what to say."

"Usually, that's my role. This is why we're perfect for each other."

I hug him again. I'll hug Piper as soon as she gives up the sloth, which may be never.

You know, this is one hell of a bright side after all.

THE END

ACKNOWLEDGMENTS

The whole concept for this book (and series) was born out of the drug-induced haze of the lovely and talented Erin Huss. I'm not sure why anyone let her text when she was barely conscious from anesthesia, but I'm really glad they did. Your feedback and input along the way has been invaluable.

To my editors, Bria Quinlan and Tami Lund: Thank you for pushing me for more. To show without telling and to give the reader what they want. My books are infinitely better than when I sent them to you.

To Whitney Dineen, Michele Vagianelis, and Erin Huss for beta reading. Sorry it was not good. I promise, it's a lot better now.

To my accountability team: Becky, Melissa, and Wendy, thank you for encouraging me and not letting me give up.

Thank you to Laurel Cremant for the interesting discussion about genetics and pointing me in the right direction.

Thank you to Kristan Higgins for your help and insight with the all important cover and blurb.

To my writing sounding board, Ginny Frost. All those nights at Denny's really do pay off. And not just because of the horchata ice cream.

To the members of Capital Region RWA: thank you for being an environment where I can learn and grow. We are great!

To Michele: I think this is the first book you didn't make it into. Whoops. But you know you're still my person.

To my parents, my husband, and my children: Thank you for your support and for leaving me alone when I had to do massive edits in a very short amount of time.

Sophia, while you may think I "stole" the name Millie from you, I didn't. It was my great-aunt's name 100 years before you named your stuffed sloth Millie. I did, however, use the term 'derpy' and stole your love of all things sloth.

ABOUT THE AUTHOR

Telling stories of resilient women, Kathryn R. Biel hails from Upstate New York where her most important role is being mom and wife to an incredibly understanding family who don't mind fetching coffee and living in a dusty house. In addition to being Chief Home Officer and Director of Child Development of the Biel household, she works as a school-based physical therapist. She attended Boston University and received her Doctorate in Physical Therapy from The Sage Colleges. After years of writing countless letters of medical necessity for wheelchairs, finding increasingly creative ways to encourage insurance companies to fund her client's needs, and writing entertaining annual Christmas letters, she decided to take a shot at writing the kind of novel that she likes to read. Kathryn is the author of twelve women's fiction, romantic comedy, contemporary romance, and chick lit works, including the award-winning books, *Live for This* and *Made for Me*. Please follow Kathryn on her website, https://www.kathrynrbiel.com and sign up for her newsletter.

Stand Alone Books:
Good Intentions
Hold Her Down
I'm Still Here
Jump, Jive, and Wail
Killing Me Softly
Live for This
Once in a Lifetime
Paradise by the Dashboard Light

A New Beginnings Series:
Completions and Connections: A New Beginnings Novella
Made for Me
New Attitude
Queen of Hearts

The UnBRCAble Women Series:
Ready for Whatever

If you've enjoyed this book, please help the author out by leaving a review on your favorite vendor website and **Goodreads**. A few minutes of your time makes a huge difference to an indie author!

63265542R00196

Made in the USA
Middletown, DE
25 August 2019